DYING FOR PARADISE

DYING FOR PARADISE

BILL GREEN

A Coronet book

This edition published in Australia and New Zealand in 1995 by
Hodder Headline Australia Pty Limited
(A member of the Hodder Headline Group)
10–16 South Street, Rydalmere NSW 2116

Copyright © Bill Green, 1995

This book is copyright. Apart from any fair dealing for
the purposes of private study, research, criticism or
review permitted under the Copyright Act 1968,
no part may be stored or reproduced by any process without
prior written permission. Enquiries should be made to the publisher.

National Library of Australia Cataloguing-in-Publication data

Green, Bill, 1940– .

Dying for Paradise.

ISBN 0 340 62184 2.

1. Title.

A 823.3

Printed in Australia by Griffin Paperbacks

Cover concept by Button Design

For Helen

Chapter 1

All fingers had been worn from each hand as the corpse floated over the reef and into quieter waters. The legs were gone below the knees where a predator had decided on a tasting, but left the meal. The various orifices of the face were filled with tiny, grey-backed fleas of the sea, reluctant to leave their various food parlours despite being out of the water. Perhaps they thought another wave would come to save them.

Certainly Charlie Manchester had imagined there would always be another wave. He rode life like that, astride only because he had confidence in his own cunning, and the nerve to employ it.

I knew it was Charlie because of the size of him. He was still close to my height despite the missing perambulatory equipment. His hair had gone, along with much of anything else that swayed in the elements. He would have avoided this death if he had imagined he'd be seen in such a condition. And he certainly would have hated the ignominy of being brought to the beach behind a small dinghy rowed with caution.

The beach was the classic curve of white sand, a saucer under the glimmering clear water of the bay. We were north of Cape Tribulation in North Queensland where the Daintree rainforest ran down to the Great Barrier Reef. Four hundred metres away a tidal river exchanged thousands of reef species with thousands of rainforest species, usually as food or fertiliser. Life mingled. If you looked closely you might think, horrible.

Before Charlie was brought in I had stood looking into the sea studying my feet, magnified at least three times, along with the seaweed and rocks, and a quick small shoal of bright blue fish. It was sobering being half a giant. No wonder Charlie had thought it was his responsibility to have a good life. People had treated him differently, with deference, because of his size, and so he had lived his life for the others, the smaller people—hard and fast.

The bloke who had driven me here and was now floating him in through the shallows was a typical lurkman of this tropical north country. Stevo. Creased leather face from too much solitary drinking and smoking in the bush. Expert hunter, skilful with explosives and firearms, and nearly always taking things that weren't his. Knew it all. Could live, and usually did, for long stretches, on the coastal animals and sea life. It was abundant on the coast. A few nights ago in Cairns I had watched as a woman with the red rubber from a party condom attached to her hook had taken seven fish, each half a metre, from the waters at the end of the jetty.

Her catch had taken five minutes, and the condom had been unused, straight from the pack. And that was in the city boundaries. That might make Cairns seem exotic. But it was still pretty much a country town, with elements of glamour for the tourists.

Stevo stood knee deep in the water looking down at Charlie. He grinned. 'Looks like he used his own body as bait,' he said, his face grave, although he expected a laugh. He didn't know how well I knew Charlie. Didn't know I could have killed him for that comment.

'Always did,' I said finally. 'Caught some beautiful creatures.' I liked visiting this north country. You could let the traditional borderline sexism loose without fear of being taken into a corner and roasted. I was also told women up here didn't tell jokes about men between themselves, but I didn't believe it. I would have enjoyed being in this neck of the country if it hadn't been for the presence of a dead friend.

'Looks like he hit the turps, too,' Stevo said.

'Why? No way he was a pisspot.'

'Yeah, didn't see him pissed me'self. Only way he coulda got into the water though. Been flat calm for weeks, hey.'

Stevo was probing.

'How long's he been in the water, do you reckon?' I asked.

'Four or five days. Hard to tell though; depends what worms got to him first. There's some real suckers out there.'

This was unique coastline. The reef was only a hundred metres out. It stretched hundreds of kilometres north and south of where we stood, but only here did it touch the coast. The heat allowed you to enter the environment and bake yourself to a stupor. No wonder Charlie had loved it. He had been the doyen of a Victorian western district family way to the south, where cold winds could blow for most of the year, and had gambled away his property before he was thirty-five. His style had kept him going until he had been well into his . . . hell, I had no idea how old he was.

I walked up the beach and lay on the sand under a casuarina tree with long, thin, drooping leaves that dappled the white sand with shadow. I pulled the hat over my eyes.

'What are you doin'?' Stevo asked.

'Thinking,' I called, looking at the straw inside the crown of the hat. It rose slightly as I called back. 'Need to remove myself from the stench.'

'Just keep up wind,' Stevo called.

'Where can we keep him safe?' I asked, watching the curved straw interior as I lowered and raised the hat to test the strength of the sun through it.

'Dunno,' Stevo replied.

'The dingoes won't eat him,' I said. 'They only eat stuff they kill.'

'Bullshit,' Stevo said. 'There's no dingoes left. Not real ones. The dogs now, they'll eat anything. Be more like a salty will take him.'

'Crocs? On the beach?' I looked up.

Stevo had reminded himself of danger and was looking around the glossy surface. 'They're made so they don't make a ripple on the surface,' he said. 'I can feel them though.'

Shit, I thought, his own legend maker.

We were a couple of days' drive from Cairns, on a Murray tribe's territory. Land they had been deeded because there was nothing on it a white man wanted—yet. There was no way we were going to load Manchester—see how he changed in my affections as soon as I realised he was going to be inconvenient—onto the four-wheel drive. Call him Charlie, I told myself.

Charlie's death hurt me, but because of his deteriorating cadaver close by, I wasn't feeling too much grief. It didn't remind me of Charlie. The Charlie I knew was whip quick with humour, and always working at living.

Stevo lit a roll-your-own and the smoke went straight up from him. No wind. Beyond him the water glistened invitingly. Peaceful. Hot. Out near the horizon an island wavered in the heat tremors.

Stevo was getting ready to speak again, say something important even. He signalled it with his gestures. He flicked his cigarette butt over the surface. His movement became faster and faster, in the way of a neurotic fussing. He rolled another fag in a couple of seconds, drew deeply. 'Heard ya name before,' Stevo announced. 'Jack Speerman,' he added, trying it out on his memory.

'Doubt it, mate. I'm from the south.'

'Nah, heard it years ago. Not from the big bloke, hey,' he said, nodding towards the remains of Charlie.

'He only mentioned his friends to other friends. He was like that. You got a mobile phone?' I asked him, so he could forget his memory search.

'Nah,' Stevo said. I suspected he did.

'How are we going to get Charlie out?'

'No idea, mate.'

'Well, fuck it,' I said. 'You're the bloody bushman. Think of something.'

Stevo laughed. 'You're not bad for a know-all,' he said.

Quaint, I thought. Old-fashioned. Out of touch with current speech. Bushmen didn't go for expletives much, suspecting the rare company might flee instantly. Now he knew I could curse the way he cursed to the forest or the sea, he was easier. The only way that would change again was if he remembered where he had heard my name. I'd been named as the organiser of a gambling coup, a suspected ring-in, substituting a brilliant galloper for a slow hack on the Warrnambool track—down south. After cleaning up on the TAB and with the bookies, I had driven the ring-in to a remote coastal cliff area, shot him close to the edge, and dropped him into the ocean.

A suspicious steward had followed me out, taken a wrong bush track and when he attempted to block me on my way out I had driven over some low foliage in the four-wheel drive with the float jerking behind, and headed away. He hadn't been able to follow. He traced my earlier tracks to the cliff where he thought he saw a horse way down in the surge of massive waves. In the ensuing court battle he could never prove I had driven past him with an empty float. I had lost him, taking a timber track off a sealed road.

Stevo's voice brought me back. 'We could roll him up in a tarpaulin and hang him from a tree. That'd keep the salties and the dogs off.'

'Okay, do it,' I said.

He laughed. 'You can get the tarpaulin off of the roof. You can fix me up for it later. We can mark the beach so the coppers know where to come.'

'Coppers?' I asked.

Had he seen what I'd seen? No sign of burning. Of course Manchester had been in the water for a while, but you expected a blackened corpse.

We had found signs of the rig all along the beach, small black bits, rocking gently in the wavelets. The explosion had been profound. Had he gone over the side before it happened?

If he had known there was something up he would have fixed it. Manchester was, had been, like that. Could do anything. One of those bastards who could listen to your car and say, tighten the rocker cover, if that means anything. Or, the alternator has lost a bolt and that's why all the rattling. He would have been one who was careful of a gas build up. Always started the exhaust fan before doing anything else.

And then it struck me. His boat was a diesel. Diesels don't usually blow. And dickhead here would know that, too.

An ever so slight tick of paranoia began its fluttering. We were a couple of days from Cairns by four-wheel drive, but how many by foot. Eight? But then there were rivers and streams to cross, with their ever present salties, and mangrove swamps with their delightfully toxic inhabitants.

No, I was okay, his high-powered rifles were slung behind the front seat, with full magazines loose in the net there, more accessible to me than him. And he didn't have a hand gun anywhere on him. And the knife? Well, I had a knife, a small one that locked the blade—a Gerber, with a lightweight synthetic handle that was tougher than steel, I had been told. I liked knives. They were silent, inspired more fear than a gun, and were completely innocuous in a pocket or a sheath.

There is no exhilaration in wrapping a body, carrying it to a tree, carefully avoiding its juices, and hauling it some 6 metres off the ground.

'Course a really big one could get it,' Stevo said. 'But they stay around the rivers. They love the big barra close up in the shade.'

'Another bloody nature poet,' I laughed. 'Don't try it on me. I can't get you a documentary series on the ABC.'

We stood looking at our handiwork while a stream of reddish yellow water came from the tarpaulin. The sun dazzled from behind the crown of the tree.

'That's the tarpaulin and the rope and the pulley you owe me.'

'Maybe a croc got him anyway,' I said.

'Nah, shark mate; clean bite like that.'

I remembered a story about a retarded crocodile who had dragged an academic into shallow water and tried its death turn on her. Spinning like mad a few times and then resting, waiting for her to drown, except because it was shallow water she could always breathe. She escaped when the silly bastard exhausted itself with its death spins and opened its mouth. She ran for it, held her own guts in, and crawled 3 kilometres to a tourist camp, the croc still looking for her in the bush. She kept hearing it thrashing around, chasing away the wild pigs that may have become a definite nuisance if she hadn't made it by nightfall. But she did, and she was flown out; kept alive to mark her literature papers at the end of the semester.

Stevo began the drive back on what looked to me like a non-existent track.

I had been searching for Charlie Manchester for a fortnight because I needed his spirit coming to me over the phone. I had told everyone he owed me money but I had been alarmed I hadn't heard from him. We kept in touch almost on a weekly basis, sharing racing information and gossip. The last time I had spoken to him there had been a hint of darker things troubling him.

It wasn't until I read in the city papers of the bird and animal smuggling in the area that I remembered that he had been in the game before. Not birds exactly, but eggs, the fertilised eggs of the native brolga or native companion. He had flown them to Japan himself. On order they had sold for $10 000 each, and that was back in the seventies. He kept the farm mortgage payments up that way for years. He had refused to let duck shooters onto his property and the local conservationists had thought him something of a hero. But the brolgas could take fright at the gunfire on weekends. According to some nervous Vietnam vets the sound burst across the country with more amps than a firefight.

Once Charlie had panicked when he counted thirty of the huge birds in a thermal, spiralling away to the heavens, but they hadn't been his mob. He had laughed when he told me about it. 'I wanted to get in my plane and try and talk them down,' he said. 'Failing that, I saw myself flying through the flock grabbing them in through the cockpit window.' That was really how far he was prepared to go to win, and if he lost after that he could laugh. No bitterness, no self-pity over loss. It was all: Okay! Now, how can we get the most out of the next scheme?

We had been bound to each other by knowing we could go all the way. And he had laughed, as I had later, over the split second on the edge of the cliff with the horse, when the halter lead had wrapped around my arm, and I had thought I was going over too.

That was why I was expecting grief. I had no-one now who could laugh with me at some of the horrors I created for myself. Wait till Charlie hears this one, I would say to myself. He'll kill himself over this. And that was it—the gallows humour. We laughed about escaping from death or discovery. He once had to land on the coast of the South China Sea, one engine overheating, and the notorious pirates of the area had swarmed around the plane and he knew he was about to lose not only the brolga eggs, but also his life. He saw they were hard men. Vietnamese boats had often lost crew and paying customers plus children along the coast.

As he descended amongst the forest of gun barrels levelled at him, the leader whacked him to the ground with a blow to the side of the neck. Instantly rising, Charlie became an arms pedlar. He pointed to himself, held an imaginary weapon, and fired it seaward. He pointed to their guns, shaking his head, and then to himself, smiling: my gun's better. Pointing to the cabin. He was carrying a lightweight automatic .223 with a Ruger action, a Chinese barrel, and a South African skeleton folding stock. It had a scope sight with a red dot that bounced around the lens. The cheapjack piece of shit looked total quality, and it could be held at arms-length and fired like a pistol. He knew he had to invite the leader into the cabin, otherwise his cargo of eggs would be destroyed. With gestures he coaxed him in. As they were both sitting in the seats he leaned back and uncovered the weapon, inviting the chief to look at it. As the bloke reached for it he drove a knife into his chest, undetected, because the fuselage was high to small windows. He knew he was certainly dead now if the motors refused to start. He knew also they wouldn't shoot while they thought the chief was approving. Starting the motors with one hand he used his other to hold the neck of the chief, and nodded and shook it like the puppet in sunglasses it was.

The engines kicked over and he looked out his side and smiled. He headed the plane down the beach of firm damp sand, and took off over a rocky point. He flew back along the beach, dropped the chief out, and wheeled to the north again. The engine gauge had been faulty, giving an overheat reading on a normal temperature. The thing that had kept him cool and alive was the thought of his brolga eggs being wasted on a beach by some ignorant bloody thugs.

So, remembering that story, and realising that birds were often his interest, I'd talked to some Aboriginal activists working as strappers in a local stable, put the word out I was looking for Charlie. Often in the bush they noticed nefarious activities they never officially reported. These blokes were straight, knew the shady dealings in most areas, but kept their mouths shut to whitey. They were never believed anyway. The old Bourke and Wills racism was still alive and well in the north, and the way things were going the whites up there would end up the same way as those dumb explorers. The rainforests would be gone and the poor soil they cleared for planting would be denuded.

Lecko Sterling, a former jockey who had taken to Land Rights activism, told me it was often former bureaucrats from the Fisheries and Wilderness Department who spotted the rare birds and animals, and brought in the smugglers. 'See, it's mobile phones, mate. No time waste. See the birds, right, and next day they smuggled out, like.'

It was my bet Stevo would be in the game. Australia was one of the few countries with rare birds these days. Mining, farming, and industry were despoiling their habitat and their air—placing them on endangered species lists. Seed smuggling of rare plants had also become a murderous game, as multinational companies fought for base materials for their genetic programs before the plants disappeared forever.

It had been Mick with the dreadlocks who had stopped me in the street in Cairns, outside the newsagents, where the huge tree in the street was often burdened with parrots that could have sold for thousands of dollars each and, above the screeching, had told me of the explosion on the reef. The boat had burned quickly, within a minute or two. 'If it was your mate,' Mick said, 'he was blown into the dreamtime, hey.'

It rained on Stevo and me as night came on. It seemed to rain every night in the forest, and in the morning the sun would be bright columns against the cathedral gloom of the huge packed trees, steam rising off the forest floor. We each had our own tent, but that night I had opened up the back seam on the tent with a knife and crept out of it to squat in the protective roots of a huge old gum, the slicker buttoned, my legs drawn up into it and the hood pulled over and the strings drawn. Only my eyes were visible.

The forest at night has its waves of sound pulsing through the stillness. Not a breath of wind, but a blind man would have sworn the place was in constant turmoil. The frogs were a carpet of sound, and piercing that thickness were the shrieks of night birds and the snufflings of the giant bats, flying foxes with their metre or more wing spans, soft membranes using the night air.

It was probably paranoia, but while I had been taking the tarp off the four-wheel drive, as a heavenly giftwrapping for Charlie, the movement had opened up a stowed bag in the back and I was sure I had seen a mobile phone. I wasn't sure it would have reached Cairns but Stevo could have said something about it: we might be able to ring when we're a day out of Cairns, something like that. Instead there was only that negative bushman's whine in his voice. And he was so slow he was suspicious. I knew northern bushmen only tell you anything on a need-to-know basis. This is because if they tell you their bush secrets you might use it to their disadvantage. If they have more knowledge they're in control. Leave you if you're a burden.

'Good night?' Stevo asked in the morning.

'Nah,' I said. 'I tried out something Mick told me to do in the bush, become part of it.'

'Hey, that's bullshit. Those fucking boongs'll tell you anything.'

I rushed in then, taking the advice of an old bush writer, Xavier Herbert: 'When you're in the bush,' he'd said, 'whoever you're with is your mate, and you don't take them up on any issue they feel strongly about, because by the end of the day you're going to need their help.'

Xavier knew what he was about. He'd been crew on the pearling luggers in the early days when they raped and murdered the Aborigines whenever they felt like it. He wrote about it, too, which I guess took away some of the guilt.

I looked at Stevo. 'You know this has been a bloody waste of time. I'm sick of this place. The sooner I get to the Cairns airport the better. My chance of getting the money from his estate is about zilch.' I held up my finger and thumb close together, almost touching. I was looking through my fingers at him, seeing if there was any relief there.

His eyes tightened just that fraction and I knew whatever I had said had hit something in him. You can always tell by the eyes. If you watch a person's eyes they'll tell you a fraction of a second before they move against you. You never watch the hands, let them be outside your field of vision. There is the slightest trigger in the pupil. I was glad Stevo didn't wear sunglasses the way I did. He thought I was soft wearing glasses, but I had learnt, while being confronted a number of times by the police forces of Asia on suspicion of trying to corrupt their local media with stories of press freedom, that sunglasses will get you past them, when staring them in the eye won't.

Half a day out of Cairns the track became clear. Any mug could follow it. I thought I'd seen the coast road through the trees, high up on the hills. The problem was getting to it. Stevo was becoming strange too. There was no conversation. He was just riding the motor as he negotiated the climbs. There was no way in hell I could have driven out of there.

I controlled the quaver in my voice. Newcomers to four-wheel driving in rugged country tend not to breathe properly and don't use the diaphragm solidly enough to stop the quaver. You sort of breathe out and hold it. I knew from some deep and dark reasoning that I shouldn't show any weakness to this bloke. Keep the voice level, tough.

We stopped beside the river. The muscles in my legs were jumping from the ride and I was glad to get balanced. 'Tea, mate?' Stevo said. A change in his voice: let's be friendly.

It could have been that we were out of the rough stuff, but I didn't think so.

Whenever he went to the vehicle I began talking, having an excuse to follow him. It would take at least three seconds for him to grab a magazine, whack it home in the rifle, and pull a shell into the breech. I'd be on him before then. It would be total madness in the rough country that we'd been going through, especially as the barrels of the weapons ended behind Stevo's back.

When he came for me it was with a breadknife. He was using it on the damper, across the fire, probably 2 metres away. The smoke had drifted upwards, lit by the fire. It was a beautiful scene. No-one would have expected an attack to come over the fire. Most would have thought, I'm safe here. Not me. I had been force fed on *Livy's War With Hannibal*. I had even worked out how he had taken his elephants over the Alps. So I saw it coming. I jumped back and let him roll through the fire. He thought he would have the knife in me by then, and so the quick flip from the fire would have been nothing, but I kicked his face and the fire got to him for a second before he came at me again, his shirt a puff of flame that went out, and by then I had locked my knife open and caught him across the throat. A kick again to the head and he dropped the knife. I kicked the knife away. I had missed the carotid artery and only cut his windpipe. He was whistling like a pig stuck by a novice.

What did you do with a prick like that?

If I took him to the Queensland cops it would be me who was charged with attempted murder. They were probably all in the rare-creature racket, getting pay-offs. Sure I was speculating, but with Australian police you could never be certain. Again with my foot I rolled him away from the fire where his face had bloomed, a hot coal stuck to the flesh. I scraped the coal from his face with the toe of my boot. The ash had been sucked into the windpipe but he didn't seem to mind. He just stared at me expecting the *coup de grâce*.

'Fuck you,' I screamed at him, my nerves coming back on me like the wash behind a boat with its engines cut. 'You're going to die, bastard. Jesus Christ.' I even kicked out wildly at the dirt in front of me. I went to the vehicle, grabbed one of his rifles, a 30-06 for the long shot through foliage, snapped home the magazine, worked a shot into the breech with the bolt and went back to him. He was dead. He was slumped down, on the arms that had been trying to push him up. No he wasn't, grass fluttered red where his wind was coming and going. Gently though. The bastard had passed out.

I couldn't kill him. I should have done. What held me back? If I had taken the knife and lightly cut the carotid while he was out to it he wouldn't even know. He'd just pass away in his sleep. He was helpless though and I was an absolute sucker. I hurled the gun into the river, kicked the vehicle and slammed my fists down on the bonnet, all to burn up the coursing adrenalin.

Rummaging through the back I found the first-aid kit, threw it down beside him, left him with a flask of water. If I was lucky he wouldn't need it, he would be carried down into the depths of the river by a Neanderthal monster, and tucked away under some overhanging ledge to decompose. I spun the wheel of the vehicle to make it back on the track and headed for the main road to Cairns. If he made it back I couldn't care less. I'd be out of the city by nightfall.

A serious person would have waited until he woke, interrogated him and killed him. I was driving away without knowing where he fitted into the picture, or whether there was even a picture at all. At the coast road I left his vehicle and hitchhiked into town.

Chapter 2

Before setting off with Stevo to find Charlie I had booked into a scungy motel north of the city on one of the beaches where you can't see your hand 5 centimetres under the water. The dirt is from land-clearing upriver. No-one cares about the state of the sea because no-one swims much in salt water. Backyard pools are the thing. For the hottest part of the year the sea wasps invade the lukewarm ocean. They'll kill you with their stings, dragging their metres-long lacy tentacles across your body, turning your organs into a playground of toxic chemicals, and paralysing you forever. The only way to beat them is to wear a bodysuit of panty hose, but unless you're a crossdresser of some extreme tastes—the head would be reshaped in the style of your average bandit—this doesn't jell with the image of the far north.

Along the beach from the motel I walked into the sea and washed myself. I spread my clothes on the sand and lay beside them. In fifteen minutes they were dry. I was presentable when I walked into the foyer of the motel. Not that anybody would have noticed. The reception area was empty. I touched the bell a few times and the clerk emerged from the back room. She

was a smart woman and when I asked for the
bill she smiled and told me I should read my
messages before I made such a rash decision.
She leaned back to the pigeon holes, a movement of which she had made an art form, for
her shorts of soft linen fell against her hip and
thigh in a way that made up for the general
shabbiness of the establishment.

The main message was from Charlie
Manchester's common-law wife. She said she
had heard that Verveine Zwigger had been
spending time with Charlie and that I should
see her. She would certainly know where Charlie was. Jean was insistent on this point. Jean
was chasing money as well.

The other was from a detective inspector of
the Queensland police. Updine. It could wait.
The evening was close and police stations are
bad places to be interrogated in at night. Only
police staff them in those hours. Not only do
Aborigines die but white drifters as well.

The door to my unit was slightly open. I
pushed it with my foot and stood back. It had
been thoroughly trashed. Even the motel drawers had been pulled apart. The stuffing had
been slit from the pillows, the mattress springs
were sticking jauntily from the ticking, my suit-
case had been razored, and the motel prints
examined with a rough hand. As I eased in I
saw the small fridge with its permanent rime
of green mould had its door hanging and the
ice blocks melting on the floor. Without

moving I saw the tube of toothpaste slit over the bathroom floor.

I didn't move for a minute or two, just leaned against the door jam casually as if I saw this stuff all the time. I was trying to sense if there was anyone still in the room.

The aura of the room drifted over me. It was a sad place. Barren. The bed ends had been covered with a sort of varnished ply that had either dried or grown damp enough to curl away from the wooden frame. The curtains were yellow, inadequate for preventing light. The table was laminated plastic. A room people travelled through fast. The ones that went through here had thought, hey, let's go to Queensland tomorrow, so they drove over a thousand kilometres in a couple of days, turned up dog tired, confused, no idea where to find the real Queensland, and left the next day. The best parts were the dozen ibis on the roof of the two-storeyed house next door. One flapped his wings the way a man might yawn a little.

I stepped inside the room, saw a flick of light and found myself on my knees.

The kick in the chest felt like being hit with a pillow there. I had been kicked by a horse once and this had the same feeling. Tossed aside all right, but no initial pain. The filly had been playful. I had taken her from her box the morning after she won a race, and been cow kicked affectionately; no real power there or my chest would have been crushed. But now I rolled with the kick, despite sucking air with a shrieking sound, and placed my head under the bed. Always protect the head first. Most other things can be fixed up. From my vantage point I saw a pair of white-soled Kodiak boots run from the room. I lay there winded, unable to do anything but concentrate on getting some real air into my lungs. Slowly the breathing function returned.

I backed out from under the bed and sat down on it. There was a feeling of life catching up with me, of knowing I was never going to find the answers.

If you walk away when you're still adrift like this, not knowing where the trouble has come from, you don't feel quite the person you've always thought you were. Having to stay to find out is where depression comes in.

If most of your acquaintances are still alive at the end of the trip your spirit cleans itself, picks itself up, and is helped by remembering how badly you felt at the beginning of it all.

I picked up the phone and dialled reception, picturing her. 'Lips,' I said, when she answered. 'Sorry,' I said, shaking my head at my idiocy. Realising there was no way out I had to plunge straight to the truth of my attraction to her. 'I just had a mental picture of your lips close to the receiver,' I said.

'Do me a favour,' she said.

'No,' I said. 'Your smile is marvellous.'

'What do you want?'

'I need the room cleaned and tidied,' I said, feeling along my ribs for the source of the sudden pain there.

'It's been done,' she said.

'I'm a bit of a stickler for detail,' I said.

'It'll be done again in the morning.'

'Need it done now. You know how it is with perfectionists. You just hate fluff on the carpet, that dribble of toothpaste on the basin.'

'I'll see what I can do,' she said.

I changed into clean jeans, a khaki shirt, and some black German runners made of leather. I somehow felt better, although my ribs would be stiff in an hour.

The evening was cooler than I thought it would be. The nightly rainstorm was already building up overhead. The dark purple changing shades like a bruise. I reversed the VW convertible I had rented from Mucked Up Autos and headed off for Coronation Drive and Verveine Zwigger.

Verveine's apartment was of dark red brick but of the style of cream brick apartments in the southern cities. No flair, no facade, no cost, and no fucking good. The lawn around the structure hadn't been able to grow in the clay that had been dug up to put in the foundations.

Her flatmate had patchy sort of blonde hair grown to a good length, but then the nutrition had run out. The body was lean though, used to working outdoors, dancing through the night into the warm mornings, but her mouth had a petulant pout, and her eyes were suspicious of anybody she didn't know. Her disposition meant that she would go through life with that look on her dial because people she would know would be few and far between.

'Verve is not in,' she said.

'That's too bad,' I said. 'Will she be back this evening?'

'No,' she said.

'I have a message for her from down south.'

'You can give it to me.'

'No, it has to be delivered personally.'

I wished I had a Rolex on my arm or something. The expensive watch works wonders on models and air hostesses in this country. Elsewhere women of that style expect some extra clues. I looked at my wrist. 'God, I've lost my Rolex.'

I looked at her. 'Swimming,' I added.

Immediately she was all attention.

'Aaaah, it was insured,' I said. Perhaps I was too enthusiastically dismissive, for suspicion was added to her unfortunate expression.

'The problem is,' I said. 'I'm flying further up the reef tomorrow and I really need to see her before I go. It's urgent and personal.'

'She could ring you.'

'I'm at the Hilton,' I said.

It was too much for her. 'If you really want to see her, she's down at the wharf. She's one of the hostesses travelling out to Fitzroy Island on the hydrofoil.' She was pretty when she smiled. Too many people had taken advantage of her since she was a child. Her suspicions were unhealthy and negative: only the wealthy had rewarded her.

The hydrofoil was enormous, perched at the wharf like a wounded bird without the strength to fold its wings completely. I had travelled on a smaller one from Hong Kong to Macao for an attempt to pull off a betting coup. It had been exhilarating standing in the stern, occasionally sprayed with sea water. We had loaded up a Hong Kong racing tipster at the Foreign Correspondents Club and he had begun to leak real tips. Hong Kong racing was totally controlled by the bookies. Charlie and I had cleaned up on that little effort. We had been sensible. We hadn't bet enough to alter the odds more than a few points, so no-one took too much notice of us. It kept me comfortable for six months of Australian living.

There was no way to get on to the hydrofoil without a ticket to Fitzroy Island. I joined the queue, boarded, and descended into the cavernous bar, the feature of the craft. Seats of the style in movie houses were fixed to the floor, and waitresses were already serving drinks.

The woman overseeing the operation was vital, smiling and capable of being the centre of attention without effort. This was Verveine. She wore a sari of light purple that allowed her tan legs some dominance, and the neat jacket showed strong and capable arms. Her hair was dark and lush.

She smiled as I approached her. It was nice, welcoming and totally sincere. 'Verveine?' I asked.

'Yes,' she said, focusing down a few stops. The smile was now only friendly.

'I'm looking for Charlie Manchester,' I said.

I wasn't prepared for the physical blackness of her response. Her shoulders slumped, her eyes lost lustre, and I thought she might sob from the effect of total devastation. I felt such a drag of sorrow my eyes brimmed in sympathy. She touched my arm. I thought she would fall against me.

'I'm sorry,' I said.

She caught her bottom lip with her teeth and quickly pressed the heel of her hand against the bridge of her nose. 'I'll meet you on the deck,' she said. 'Once we're under way the drinking slows a bit.'

I walked up on deck to find the scents of the evening. The craft made its way to the open sea past some harmless grey US navy frigates, their missiles tucked away from the sea and the heat. They were in town to test new jungle landing equipment or something. That would all be bullshit. If they told you about it it certainly wasn't true. Security forbade it.

The bridge of the hydrofoil was glassed in from front to back and green screens shone dimly through the darkened tint. The instruments looked as impressive as those of a small jet.

In open water she began to open up, standing up on her slicing foils. I was the only one gawking into the dim light of the bridge. Looking over the stern it was as though the boat had created its own highway across the night sea. The feel was as if we were on rails.

After I had become used to the speed—around 30 knots—I sat with my back to the bridge and watched the golden lights of Cairns growing smaller.

Ten minutes into the trip Verveine walked through the concealed entry from the interior stairs. She had a neat way of walking, everything totally controlled, throwing her feet gently to the side like a horse that has slowed from a gallop and is relaxing. The wind blew the sari tight against her. I could see she had forgotten how I had empathised with her and she was very wary.

I began apologising immediately. 'I'm sorry about this. I thought you would be living at Charlie's place.'

'You knew him?' she asked. 'You're not the police?'

'No,' I said. 'Charlie and I were sort of educated together in a way, although we were grown when we met.'

'Why are you looking for him?'

I told her I was here to acquaint Charlie with the facts surrounding a large gambling debt. It was a debt he could cope with, but he had vanished, hadn't been in contact with his creditors.

Verveine was cool now. She wasn't going to leave until she discovered exactly how I fitted into the piece of life that Charlie had given her.

I realised she was a real trier. One of those women whose parents had stopped them thinking as kids because they were so beautiful thoughts would only spoil it for them. She knew she had to reason all the time, calculate how it all worked, because that was how she had begun to break away from mum and dad.

I wasn't going to tell her about Charlie's resting place. That was what the cops were paid for. Besides it might just stop her from saying anything. If she had been one of those women who were wide open to everything so they could discover exactly how it all was, I may have told her. But she only had her first foot on the rung of that ladder. Women like her were Charlie's forte, the type of woman wealthy men go for. And then one day all those collected thoughts and facts coalesce into some very perceptive chemistry, and the suppressed rage emerges. Assets are split down the middle, or the company that is under her name, because she would never threaten the running of it, is suddenly very much hers.

'I need Charlie's address,' I said.

She looked at me, her gaze level, although without a challenge.

'It would help me,' I added.

'You know he's gone,' she said. Her voice was definite about that. I wondered if she was.

'Yes,' I said. 'His ex-wife has been looking for him for a while.'

'She's after the cheque account,' she said.

From the edge of my vision I saw a movement at the door leading from the stairs. I didn't see the face, but I knew who it was from the presence. Earlier I had wondered why an American with his sort of style was on this fast trip to what amounted to a singles bar on an island. I sensed his face motionless there for a few moments, and then it was gone. Something like Orson Welles in *The Third Man*.

'Someone was watching us,' I said.

'Truman,' she said, quietly. 'He's looking for Charlie.'

'Why?'

'He's worried about him. That's why you're here, too—because you're worried about him. He usually pays on time, right?' She was fluctuating between hard and soft.

'Yes,' I said. 'Does he owe Truman a great deal?'

'No,' she answered. 'Truman's loaded. It's more a friendly thing.'

She turned to the rail to watch the water swirls from the foils, occasionally they left a quick breath of cool fog across the high deck. 'I don't think I'll see him again,' she said. She left the rail and I watched her walk back to the stairway, placing one foot in front of the other. It gave her a sway her legs emphasised. Charlie had chased beauty as if his welfare depended on it. Hadn't been enough though.

I stayed on deck. I didn't want to get into any eye contact or covert observation with Truman. I wanted this to be clean cut from now on, and watching someone of Truman's obvious wealth—gold Rolex, linen suit and yachting loafers—would tend to have me imagining large-scale crime. I didn't want him to have to regard me as a nuisance. Whatever the problem, the Gulf War, drug wars, Pacific expansion, Americans were eager on the trigger.

The change in engine tone alerted me to the approaching island. I stared into the blackness, hoping to catch sight of the shape silhouetted against the sea and the night sky.

Then we shifted course, rounded a small point, and were in a bay lit by lights from the wharf. Lighted windows seemed to be in small bungalows. A two-masted schooner was anchored 50 metres off the beach. And then I saw the high ground in the centre of the island. This was no overblown sand dune of an island. This had its own steep cliffs and staggering deeps. A schooner with a huge keel that close to the shore was unusual. Different country here, I thought. Anything can happen in Queensland. To steal a Bernard Shaw line: the rules are there are no rules. It wasn't as if I didn't know that. But it had just caught me with the strength of a physical truth.

The hydrofoil was allowed a slow glide into the small wharf. As we were made secure I stayed on the upper deck watching the passengers assemble prior to disembarking.

Truman walked to one side of the gang plank, leaning casually on the rail. His hair was white and even under a bright light he was tanned. His nose was sharp and his jaw hadn't begun to sag. He could see me watching but he didn't give me a direct glance. His physical attitude was tough and independent. The stance was a challenge, it bunched the shoulders as it relaxed them. Most men his age had been knocked around by life. They shrank a little as though they were avoiding bad luck. This bloke was open to challenge. Occasionally you see this in sportsmen, but rarely in people who know how the world works. He wasn't the sort of person Charlie would let get away.

If Charlie had followed his usual pattern he would have moved in the exclusive, wealthy circles in Cairns. He knew he belonged to them. But he would have kept himself in check. If he won at the races he would have mingled, picking up any worthwhile information, but when down on his luck he would have moved away, until he pulled off enough in his next coup to impress with his generosity for a few weeks. He made it a rule never to chance being off side by requests for small loans. If he hit them it would be with a scheme for large investment. His disappearing acts in his times of low finances only made his schemes more alluring. He fascinated women like Verve. He was the mystery man who could, given the right lighting, solve all their anxieties. He was certainly the mystery man now, hanging off a tree on a Robinson Crusoe beach. It would be unlikely anyone would find Stevo by the river, let alone Charlie's last swaying place.

Chapter 3

The merrymakers wound their way along a white path of crushed and crunchy coral to the disco. I walked behind them, watching how responsible people behave on holiday. They were looking for diversion. Grog already consumed had livened their spontaneity, and they were squeezing the buttocks of their companions, whispering sweet vulgarities, or looking for wayward relationships. The hostesses, I could see, could often be in for difficult times. It was interesting to see how they casually removed themselves from circumstances that could be embarrassing.

Above us gulls wheeled overhead taking fat jungle insects attracted by the lights of the Entertainment Centre. I picked up a handful of coral because it was unusual to walk on such a textured carpet. It was crisp with salt. Rubbing it with a thumb it came up shiny. A new path.

The restaurant was attached to the disco and with the ticket purchase came a meal. The decor was Pacific island, the windows no more than lattice shutters, now raised to allow in the warm ocean night. The schooner was framed in most of the windows.

Nicely directed by the hostesses, I found myself near a window table, looking at Truman who was seating himself. His handsome face was pleasant and not at all threatening, until you noticed his eyes, which appeared not to be part of his face. They were the eyes of a successful politician, guarded, with flashes of eagerness any time he spotted a voter.

'You seem to have the best table,' I said.

He gestured. 'Join me. We need to talk.'

His accent was a stylish drawl. A hint of a clipped English accent stopped the drawl from being outrageously southern. More a fey sort of Boston.

'You're Jack Speerman,' he said. He offered his hand. Firm, with a hard bulk of muscle around the thumb. A martial arts grip.

I sat down, my arm along the window sill. I removed it when I realised it gave the impression I would like to crawl through the window and into the night.

'And you're Truman,' I said.

'Truman Severin.'

'Why do we need to talk?' I asked.

'We're looking for the same person.'

'He could be anywhere,' I dismissed.

'Wherever he is, he's in my boat.'

'Really. You should be able to find him.'

'No, he could be anywhere in the thousands of uninhabited river mouths, inlets and estuary waters between here and the Cape. It's a cigarette boat.'

'What sort of boat?' I could only think it must have a hot end and be incredibly fast. An exploding smoke.

'A cigarette boat is the type that smugglers used to bring cigarettes into the States. They called them that in the late thirties, early forties. Very fast machines.'

'Okay,' I said. 'Hold it there. I want to tell you something. I have no interest in anything else but Charlie's whereabouts. I'll find him, tell him what I have to say . . . some old business he and I were involved in . . . and then I'm flying out again.'

'And you were going to leave without seeing him. What stopped you?'

The bastard was obviously responsible for my aching neck and my trashed room. Only the receptionist and I had known I was about to leave Cairns.

'His ex-wife gave me a lead.'

'To what.'

'His whereabouts.'

He looked at me. I recognised his stare. He had the look which strains to tell you in every look, every gesture, that he is right, and he's going to lay down the rules.

Now my look is different. My optics say, I know what you are and I don't give a fuck. So, after that exchange we knew each other.

'You know,' he said, smiling. 'I've had you looked at, but I don't know what you do. There is nothing about earning a living. You don't appear to be earning money.' The statement was a question.

'I'm a gambler,' I said. He sat back. He was amused. He pushed himself back from the table. His wrists were thick and capable. The chuckle that came from him had a sinister edge, although it didn't show on his regular features. The features worried me. They were undamaged. Nothing physically bad had happened to this man. If this bloke killed you it wouldn't be because he held you any ill will. It would be for expediency, efficiency, and because it was the best for everyone. Why hold it against him? Even Charlie might have met his match. I relaxed. I heard the strangest sound from the beach. The wavelets as they ran into the shore produced a tinkling sound that started up one end of the beach, ran loud past the restaurant windows, and ran off into the distance. I looked out into the night. The beach was also coral. They struck with the sounds of small bells.

'Marvellous sound,' I said, wondering at how concentration can lock out the best of the world. I had been going to tell him I was a journalist, but it was ten years since the papers had been prepared to allow me a living. I had a press card that still got me parking at airport carparks reserved for the press, and occasionally got me into the test viewing of movies, if I claimed I had lost my invitation. Being a journalist here would have placed me into another category. No more information would be forthcoming. No more good table beside the window listening to dead coral sounds.

'That's the only thing that's free on the island,' he said.

'You look too rich to have to pay for anything. Only the poor have to pay for luxury.'

He laughed. The tone was genuine. 'Can you give me Charlie's address?' I asked.

'Verve didn't?' he asked.

'She's very close,' I said. 'Didn't trust me. Can you believe that?'

'What form does your gambling take?

'You mean what do I gamble on?'

He nodded. 'Horses,' I said. 'Gee gees. Chaff bandits. Whatever.'

'And you make a living?'

'Sure. There's half-a-dozen of us in the country who make a living at it.'

'And the secret is?'

I didn't answer him as Verve came up and sat down with us.

Truman looked at her. I could see he had a deep appreciation. And then I saw the weirdest thing. He was embarrassed knowing I was watching him watching her, knowing I was calculating whether he was in love with her. The bastard had a soft centre; where she was concerned anyway.

'I think,' he said to her, 'that none of us are very good trackers. We should probably hire some of the Aborigines to instruct us in the art.

It seems Charlie Manchester has run out on the three of us.'

It sounded very cosy—the three of us—like a pop song lyric.

'Can you eat with us?' I asked Verve as the waiter handed us a menu each.

'I have to keep an eye on the customers,' she said. 'Stop any rowdiness.'

'She doesn't eat,' Truman said as she rose and walked away. I wished our windows had glass so I could catch her reflection without being drawn into any male bonding conspiracy with Truman. He watched her go, making it perfunctory, as if he was preoccupied with something else and there he was watching this beautiful woman walk away, and how silly, what were we talking about?

'A person of your resources,' I said, 'always knows more about the things that interest him than anyone else. Where do you think Charlie has gone with your boat?'

'He gave me no clue,' he said.

'What's a boat like that worth?' I asked.

'Three hundred thousand.'

'A plaything?' I asked. 'Or do you use it in your work.'

'Depends how you define play,' he said. 'Or work.' But he was getting irritable. Who the hell was I to question him, a rich man?

'I think play in this sense is when you buy it when you don't need it.'

'But then you might buy something, and *then* find a use for it.'

'If you make up a use for it, it's still play.'

I saw his dislike. He didn't like the treatment. This was banter and second guessing. He had indulged me enough. 'You know, you'd be no help to anyone,' he said.

'Not used to it are you?' I asked.

'What?'

'Someone following you into areas you think about.'

'I like to use what I've got. I don't like sitting around thinking about it.' He leaned forward and whacked my arm. The blow could have been interpreted as Aussie affection, but it had muscle. 'You know what I mean, don't you? It takes a lot to stop me.'

I looked at him. He was sincere in trying to impress me with something, but what? He wasn't a thug. That type wouldn't be bothered about the niceties of trying to impress me, someone whose weights he already had.

'I'm going to take a leak,' I said. 'If the waiter comes I'll have a dozen oysters, natural, and barramundi.'

I stood up and began to thread my way through the tables. I stopped mid-stride when I heard it. The slightest ppppft. But if the last time you heard it was when it was used to put down a champion racehorse on which you had laid a bundle, you don't forget it.

I was slow in turning around, not really wanting to see. Truman had been shot in the side of the brain. The couple at the next table each had a mouthful of prawn cocktail close to their open mouths. They were stunned in the way they might be if a waiter upturned the soup over them. And in a way that was what had happened. A fan of blood and pink tissue had sprayed them just as thoroughly.

Slowly Truman slid sideways, a deep pulsing of his blood drenching his side before he hit the floor. The lady with the prawn cocktail screamed then. It was a piercing cry of dark horror. It contained all the elements that had troubled her for most of her life. She had worked hard for this holiday, worked hard to get where she was in this life, and now it had all been spoiled by brain sauce on her prawns.

Truman's head had collapsed in the way of a balloon that has leaked air after prolonged inflation. It was a parody of anything human. I looked around to prevent Verve from seeing this brutality. I saw her walk through from the kitchen door and sink to her knees. She had sensed this assault on her friend, the way she had sensed Charlie's death. She didn't even look towards the window table. One of her friends knelt beside her. I saw her chest heaving. She hit the floor with a clenched fist. She hadn't been flattened by hopelessness but by the shock of her rage.

I wanted to see the shooter, but knew it was dangerous for me to run now while the room was stunned. I would be found outside and blamed for the mess. People would swear they had seen me do it. Once I had stopped to help a woman hit on a pedestrian crossing on a busy street. I'd been grabbed when I tried to leave after the ambulance arrived. 'You're not hitting the road now, Jack,' I was told. It had taken me half an hour to extricate myself.

I grabbed the nearest waiter, waited until his eyes focused through his shock. 'Ring the mainland for the cops,' I said.

'Yes,' he said vaguely.

I shook him gently. 'Hey, hey,' I said to him. 'Come back to earth.'

He was pale now, his lips drooping with a bad taste in his mouth. 'I'll do it,' I said. 'Just point to where the office is.'

He raised his arm to point through the entrance hall. 'Come with me,' I said. He saw he was being offered a chance to get away from the death scene, and dashed between the tables with me following.

In the foyer I told him to phone while I checked outside. I ran to the corner of the building by the water and cautiously glanced around it to the beach. Barely a minute would have passed since the shot, but the scene didn't look as if it would tolerate disturbance. A sailing craft at anchor, barely moving on a gleaming sea. The moon on the water was lighting the front of the restaurant. It was an ordinary scene. A tropical shack on a warm summer night. It could have been any time in the last two centuries. The small slop of waves were still giving the beach coral some tone. One wave ran the length of the beach before the next started. The sound was so unique it was hard to drive your listening through it. I listened for the sound of movement through the rainforest? Nothing. The beach would be avoided because the sound of running on coral would be like a magnified gravel drive. I looked at the schooner. It had to contain secrets, but there was no light and no movement.

The weapon had been a hand gun. A high-powered rifle shot from the schooner would have exploded the head and I wouldn't have heard the distinctive sound of the silencer.

The shot had been made no more than 2 metres from Truman's skull, and triggered upwards. The bullet would be found in the ceiling. The water looked so peaceful I doubted whether a rubber-suited assassin was flippering his way to a boat offshore. To the east the big hydrofoil was dark and sinister at the small jetty. The lounge lights had been turned off.

Several people ran up behind me. One was apparently the manager of the place because he ordered an underling to cross the island to check the boats at anchor. He had a record of all boats on the island. They were paying anchorage fees. We heard the sound of a small motor start up beyond the headland. It had the scream of an outboard at full throttle.

'No-one could have swum around the point in the time,' I said.

'Probably a fisherman then,' the manager said. He was a man of fifty, deeply experienced in the sleaze practices of the world, and we looked at each other with some recognition. I could never feel easy with that. He might feed off sleaze, but I was attempting to pick my way through it to find solid ground. I had made it a few times, but when the ground moves you're abandoned again.

'This is something best left to the police,' the manager said. He began shepherding the few of us away. I stood still, looking at him. He looked at me and dropped me from his gestures. His face had authority. His hair had come loose from its net of hairspray and hung down his forehead. He brushed it back. His eyebrows were thick and should have met in the middle. His jaw was carrying extra weight.

'Who owns the schooner?' I asked.

'He did. Pulled in here a few weeks ago.'

I walked back with him to the foyer. 'You would have got to know him pretty well then?'

'What's your interest?'

'I was sitting next to him the second before it happened.'

He didn't comment but walked into the foyer where the merrymakers were emerging from the restaurant in small shocked groups. 'Drinks are free at the bar for half an hour,' he announced. People turned pleading looks to him. They weren't going back to the dining room. 'The drink orders will be served out here.' He disappeared into the restaurant.

I went up to the receptionist who was now juggling calls, begging people not to ring the mainland while he was dealing with calls to the manager. One woman said, 'But it might be a serial killer, still on the island. We have to go now. We're having a boat come and get us.'

'The police have asked us to keep everyone here,' the receptionist said. He turned to me with raised brows.

'Have you a bungalow I can use for tonight?' I asked. The woman who wanted a boat to come for her looked at me and said, 'You're mad.'

I was assigned a bungalow along the beach; back in the foliage, it was explained. When I saw Verve come out from the dining room I approached her. Before I reached her the manager had placed an arm around her shoulders and led her into his office.

I walked outside again and looked at the sea. I had to get over to the schooner. I just needed information, any information. I had no idea what I was stumbling into. There was a big temptation to walk away. The problem with doing that is that six months down the track you realise someone is stalking you, out to kill you, and you can't find the people responsible.

Their tracks are covered, but yours haven't been. You're at a bigger disadvantage than ever. So, walking away is not always the best policy.

The other problem was that to make headway here I was going to have to involve myself. That would mean I needed serious protection. I didn't have real weaponry.

The Queensland police were going to fumble their way through this one. It takes imagination for a middle-class cop to comprehend crime in a state with a coastline that is thousands of kilometres long. With rough country vehicles, light planes and fast boats, it's open slather for illegal business.

Walking around the building I saw Verve with the manager. She was sitting in an office chair, biting the side of her hand, trying desperately to hold herself together, and the manager was talking as he walked around the room. It wasn't until I saw his predator's smile as he looked down on the distraught woman from behind that I knew I would have to rescue her.

Now rescuing people is not insignificant work. It often has dreadful consequences. As many men attempt to rescue beautiful women as there are men attempting to destroy them.

The rescuers themselves are often destroyed because they've offered their services at inappropriate times, or have misunderstood their own motives.

I returned to the foyer, knocked on the manager's office and walked in.

Verve didn't turn but the manager's face shut down instantly. 'What do you want?' he asked. He should have at least asked me to leave, but he was obviously feeling magnanimous, due to the circumstances.

'My dinner companion was shot,' I said, 'and you ask me what I want?'

'Get out, now.' He had the tone of a man who had made many people leave his various offices, homes, bedrooms and lives. His gaze locked with mine. Challenges like this switch me to automatic. I do anything to win.

Verve shifted in her chair and looked up at me. She saw me as a stranger.

'I seem to be in the middle of something here,' I said. 'People I'm looking for go missing, people I meet don't see out the evening. I think it's fair enough that I get to ask questions.' I looked at Verve. 'We have an interest in finding out what's going on,' I said.

'Bullshit,' the manager said and began walking around the table. I grabbed him by his hair and the collar of his shirt and pulled him backwards over the desk. I grabbed his arm and pulled it back and down, letting him feel the tension of it against the edge of the desk: more weight would spring the arm from the shoulder socket.

'Now listen, mate,' I reasoned. 'You're going to leave us in this office for as long as we want.' I let him up, saw the fight had gone out of him, and felt confident enough to dismiss him from my mind. He was a poor bastard doing his job in some terrible bureaucracy that ran holidays for the complaining. There was nothing sinister about him, apart from his sleazy need to dominate those he felt were weaker. He had kids working in the bar for him, and kids don't have the experience to know how damaging speed can be, no matter how many martial arts lessons they've had. You only have to have reflexes a split second faster, and I had them. In five years' time it would be a different matter. By then I would be well past any inclinations to rescue people. Physical courage has a lot to do with physical capacity.

Verve watched him leave the office. She looked up at me. 'What goddam right do you have to do this?'

'I'm nervous,' I said sitting on the table. She stood up and leaned against the sill of the window that looked out on the patio and the pool.

'How close were you to Truman?'

'I met him with Charlie,' she said. Emotion twisted her face with dislike.

'They did business together?'

'I don't know,' she said.

'You don't know? How long were you with Charlie?'

'Six months.'

'Hey, he's a motor mouth.' I had almost given him past tense. But I'd done that once before in another time and you certainly remember never to do it again.

For a moment her eyes looked at me with a new spirit. Her face was transformed. Charlie wouldn't have left this woman for any business or pleasure, and she knew it. She must have known the kind of deals he was doing.

'Charlie and I used to hit the horses pretty hard,' I said. 'Was Truman a gambler too?'

'Charlie was taking a bigger gamble,' she said.

'With Truman?'

'Yes, I think so. He had so many things going though.'

'But they must have been very close for Truman to lend Charlie his cigarette boat.'

'He took it,' she said.

'Truman seems to have plenty of boats for someone passing through. He could pretty much invade the country.'

Verve crossed her arms over her chest and looked down at her legs. They were outlined by the sari. I wondered if she saw her legs with the same perspective I did. I knew someone should tell her about Charlie, but I just couldn't see myself doing it. I was either a coward or just too kind to hurt anyone. Someone said never go with a woman who has more troubles than you have. With that little rocket coming to mind I knew a little more about my motivation in this; knew another reason I wasn't prepared to walk away.

She leaned forward, a glossy wing of hair falling across her face.

'How long have you been doing this job?' I asked. Innocuous questions sometimes prompt an avalanche of information.

'Since Charlie disappeared. Some friends told me about it.' She was still under the tight control of dislike.

'I can't place your accent. It sounds New York, although it has Midwest in it.'

She laughed and uncrossed her arms. 'I always tried to disguise it. I don't know what I've ended up with. How do you know about American accents?'

I laughed. 'The movies.'

'Really?' She had almost accepted me, but stopped it.

'Well, Charlie and I took some good horses over once. We were going to clean up, but they never got used to the dirt tracks, or the American trainers.'

She laughed bitterly. 'So, that was you. He never mentioned your name. He used to say you were a couple of yokels, or something, trying to take on the big time.'

She began to talk to me then. She ran a finger beneath her eye as if it needed scratching. The gesture told me that she was going to lie. 'It was all a mystery to me. I didn't see either of them doing anything really wrong. Truman was always talking about conservation, the environment. Charlie talked about everyone getting a fair go. He hated the corruption here. He said the police here had forgotten they were supposed to be helping run a democracy. I sort of loved being around them most of the time, but Truman made me uneasy. He gave you the feeling he knew so much more than he was telling. I mean he wasn't a criminal type. He didn't want flashy women or show off his money . . . Truman would know who shot him,' she said, and began crying.

'Yes,' I said, touching her back lightly. 'Of course he would. He's just not going to tell us.' Her back was firm, every emotion vibrating through it.

'Have you been on the schooner?' I asked.

'Yes, two or three times.' She threw her head back as if she didn't like my hand touching her. I moved back.

'What sort of times?'

'It was mainly when they heard about new untouched areas of the coast. We'd take it up the coast, look around.'

She heard the chopper before I did. 'They'll be here, the police,' she said, gesturing upwards. I saw how young she was then. She looked up like a kid at kindergarten. I'd thought she was around twenty-six or seven, but I suddenly saw twenty-two or three. My brain ached suddenly. Three or four pulses and it was gone. She really hadn't learned to find out where she stood in the state of things. I knew Charlie would have kept her in perpetual suspension.

Charlie could keep everyone off balance, until you knew that every word from him, no matter how casual, was pitched for effect.

Chapter 4

The landing lights on the chopper highlighted the white coral beach, the shivers that scarred the sea, and the clouds of minor coral and shell grit swept into the whirling palms. The tourists stood outside the Centre, smiling as the chopper rocked gently down on the beach. They were saved. As the rotor blades slowed the manager walked out to meet the coppers. He was stooped, as a reflex to avoid being guillotined. He'd have to be 240 centimetres tall to have had trouble though.

The coppers dropped to the beach, looked at the coral beneath their feet and walked outside the circle of the rotors. There they stopped to hear the manager's story. I could see the detective was irritated that no-one had apprehended the killer. He chose to look at the death scene and detailed the chopper's crew to scour the island for the culprit. They would have no hope. Even if the bastard was still on the island the rainforest could hide a battalion.

I looked at Verve. As the chopper rose, her clothes flapped against her. I looked away because for some inexplicable reason I didn't want to see her so vulnerable. Above the shriek of the engines I yelled close to her ear that she shouldn't mention the schooner, nor how close she was to Truman. She flashed a desperate look. 'Not unless you have something to tell them,' I said. There, I had reassured her I wasn't trying to keep the police from discovering anything, but was just keeping things convenient.

She turned towards me as the chopper hesitated, tilted its nose, and headed for the far side of the island. 'A week ago I told them Charlie was missing,' she said, her hair blowing across her face. 'They weren't interested. You have to be someone before they take a real interest. At least know someone.'

One of the plain-clothed coppers went straight into the restaurant, and the other stayed in the foyer and outlined how things would proceed for the rest of the night. 'There will be other police out later to take statements.'

They were to be kept in the foyer of the Centre until they had all been processed and then the dark, poised hydrofoil would leave. Those who hadn't seen anything were really pissed off. They began arguing, but the police had them marooned on the island. I told the receptionist if the police wanted me I'd be in my bungalow. Verve had been shanghaied for drinks waiting, and I walked to her at the bar and told her where I'd be. She nodded without looking at me.

I walked to the bungalow down along the water. Where the chopper had landed, the water was filled with white dust. I could hear the rig moving back and forth on the back beach, supposedly driving the assassin towards the front beach.

Unlocking the door I smelled the slight mustiness of beach houses I had known as a child, and felt very sleepy. The front window had a view of the water framed by two palm trees. The path of the moon ran straight across the sea to my window.

I remembered walking along the beach with my father. I must have been three or four and I asked him to explain why the path of the moon on the sea followed us as we walked.

He didn't explain it more than to say that it followed everyone.

'Like God?' I had asked him.

'Better than God,' he said.

'Why?'

'It knows where you are all the time.'

'Doesn't God?'

'The part of you that is linked with God always knows where you are. But there are too many for God to check up on all the time. The moon only has to shine for people walking on the beach. That's not too many.'

I could feel myself smiling as I sat in the cane chair facing the sea. I just wanted to be in a new situation and not have to check it out. I knew I was in trouble. You couldn't do the things I had done over the past few days and expect to pass unnoticed. I'd been lucky, and I knew about luck. I'd seen luck run out on people the very moment they had decided to stop whatever nefarious activity they were involved in. They weren't careless, or boastful, or even awake, and yet circumstances shifted for them like coloured glass in a kaleidoscope, and they were well and truly fucked. Charlie's luck had run out. Truman's had. I realised I would hate mine to disappear without my knowing exactly what was happening here.

Most people lived with luck. You had an average bloke who was lucky to find a woman who loved him. You had a business person who thought their successes had come from their keen business sense and initiative, and all the while it had been luck. I had placed myself in the way of luck. I had done the homework, sweated over form guides, videotapes, and the habits of any trainer that began running winners. If luck was to happen to me I was ready for it.

I woke to knocking on the door. I had trouble discovering exactly where I was. I could feel the saliva wet where it had run from the corner of my mouth. I dragged a hand across my mouth and chin, feeling the stubble. The knocking began again. I saw the sea then. The moon was gone but there was still no wind and the surface gleamed like good pewter. The evening came flooding back to me. A couple strolled into my picture frame. The woman was ankle deep in the water. Obviously the hydrofoil was still here. I had nothing to fear, but my mind was fluttering. I walked to the door. 'Yes?' I asked. 'Who is it?'

'Police.'

'Which police?'

'Detective Inspector Updine.'

I opened the door. He had been first out of the chopper and been the one to check out the dining room. I stood back to let him in. He was shorter than me, and broad across the shoulders. But already he had a gut. His brow was malevolent and he wasn't good at his job. Too much anger in the face.

'I left a message for you to ring,' he said. I didn't reply.

'If you'd rung you wouldn't have had a night like this.'

'It's not too bad a night. I'm here aren't I?'

'Stevo Henderson isn't.'

'Stevo is around,' I bluffed. 'Tried to lose me in the rainforest as a joke, the bastard.'

'So he'll be back then?'

'Sure he will,' I answered. 'Just don't let me get my hands on him. What's your interest there anyway?'

'Doesn't matter,' he said.

I leaned against the wooden partition of the front window, my elbows up on the glass, hands on the wood, my ankles crossed. 'What do you want to tell me?' I asked him.

'It's what I want you to tell me.' I could have laughed at him. There was no way he had me. The bush kill was big in Queensland and the Northern Territory. They were hard to solve. Sometimes they were solved—even twenty years later. But I had my story and it was up to him to produce his first. I knew I was playing a bloke who knew he had no evidence—just playing a hunch.

'One of his friends got a call from Stevo.' So, it had been a mobile phone. He'd put it in his pocket . . .

'You don't have anything to say?'

'About what?'

'About Stevo.'

'You were telling me about him.'

'He told his friend you killed him.'

My laugh was loud, but it was genuine. 'And he's still talking, right.'

'And the phone went dead. He said you cut his throat and he was bleeding to death.'

I looked at Updine and shook my head. 'Listen, mate, I know I didn't kill him.'

'And then we find you here, sitting with a bloke who gets blown away on disco night for the middle-aged. You have to tell me exactly, exactly right, what's going on.'

'If I fucking knew I'd tell you, mate.' Mate sounded like whining. It needed to be corrected. 'I'm looking for a friend of mine. Well, a bloke who owes me money. It's an old debt.

But the bloke isn't Stevo, and I hate violence. It's not what I'm about.'

'So how were you going to collect?'

'Shame him into it,' I said.

Updine thought he had my measure now. He began laughing. 'A real tough nut from over the south, right. Shame him into it!' He went to the door laughing, shaking his head.

I needed more from Updine though. 'Now about this bloke Stevo,' I said pushing off from the window. 'He was going to take me into the bush, north of here, down where the rainforest meets the reef.'

'Boong country, mate. Need permission to go in there,' he said.

'So what about Stevo?'

'If you don't know, mate, it's not for me to tell ya.' Updine was one of those coppers who thinks he will never have to explain himself. He had never seen the limit of his power.

'But you'd be looking for him if someone cut his throat? . . . The story makes me very uneasy.' I gave him the last sentence as if I were a terribly considered fellow who needed to follow up the happenings in his life, extracting every inch of significance from them. The naivety of southerners amused Updine. As Queenslanders knew, life was chaos. 'Fuck me,' he said leaving, laughing. And then he stopped. 'By the way, when did you meet this character Truman?'

'Tonight. I spoke about three words with him.'

'Worried man was he?'

'No, seemed to be looking forward to a night of fun.'

'Okay, we'll catch up in a day or two.'

I stood at the door and watched him walk to the beach to make his way back to the Centre. I looked at my watch. Eleven. Jesus, the tropical nights went slowly. I drew the curtains and took a look at my surroundings. The walls were panelled with light wood. The ceiling was high and the floor was tiled in a subdued red. The bedroom was the same. Above the bed was a marvellous shot of a huge manta ray gliding over the reef. Not good marketing, I thought. The reef should be shown as safe and bright. Small tropical fish of the butterfly variety would be in order. Manta rays would make you think twice before venturing out from the beach, no matter that they were harmless, the beasts had the mask work of Darth Vader. Unfortunately, swimming over the reef was exactly what I had to do tonight.

I watched the tourists file into the hydrofoil at about 2 a.m., not much later than the scheduled run of 1 a.m. It was just that they'd had a murder for a floor show. No matter the complaints now, they'd remember and talk about their night on the tropical isle for the rest of their lives.

A few minutes later as I stood above the coral line I saw a figure through the palms. Just a shadow flitting, but I stepped back into a shadow. I had no weapon at all. And then I saw the rounded hip and the short steps. I waited for her.

'They don't know anything,' Verve said, when she saw me. 'There will be more police out to cover the island in the morning. They don't think they'll find anything. Too professional.'

'I thought you'd be just about on the mainland by now.'

'I decided not to go.' She stood in front of me holding one arm above the elbow, looking up into my face. The night had new fragrances. But I looked into her eyes which were cold and curious.

'How do you get back for work tomorrow?'

'No work tomorrow. And if the bungalows are free we get a discount.'

The ball was in my court. If I did the right thing we would get down to regarding each other with some reality, or we would continue on in the remote, safe sort of way we had so far. The problem was I didn't know whether I should ask her to my bungalow to discuss things or let her set the pace with silence. I chose silence.

She turned and looked out over the sea. 'When I first arrived here I thought this was as close to heaven as you could get. The new fruits, the birds, the animals, the heat. All of it cradled in the most beautiful coastline. I'm a Canadian, originally. Maybe that's the accent I'm trying to hide. I was sick of the cold, and summer in New York is hell. It's gritty steel dust and worrying about your . . . safety.' She laughed without humour. She brushed hair from her eyes. 'I met Charlie, then. We had a lot of fun. But I never knew what he was doing.' She laughed. 'He showed me you didn't have to play along with any of the roles people put you in. You know, the images they have of you.'

'Yeah,' I said.

'Eventually I found out how fake it is here. People thinking it's cool to whack themselves with drugs and have fast relationships. Charlie understood all that.' She laughed. 'He gave them even bigger ideas.'

'Yeah,' I said. 'He found out life catches up with you in a big way.'

Her breath was a sigh. 'It seems to be that way.' She turned away from the sea for a moment, looked up towards the main building. 'People come up here to disappear.' She said it speculatively, as if she hoped that was how Charlie had left her life; that he was still alive somewhere.

'Do you want to crunch along the beach and back? I need to know more about Truman.' I could see the police on the beach at the front of the restaurant.

'Why?'

'He could have killed Charlie easy. The best way to destroy someone is to be mates with him.'

She didn't flinch. It had probably occurred to her during the terrible times of doubt. She was part of her generation—seemingly a realist, but with a romantic streak as wide as the soul. I didn't even want to guess what would happen when the two elements finally met. 'I think you're holding out on me,' I said. 'Fuck you,' she said, but it was without enthusiasm.

We were walking on the coral close to the water, and I had missed the moment we started moving. That's the power of unconscious gesture for you. It has the ability to guide you at all times. Thank Christ we mostly override it.

'They talked about gambling. Money.'

'What about gambling?' She thought for a while. Our crunching feet emphasised the silence.

'What it was, I suppose.'

'What was it for Truman?' I already knew how it was for Charlie.

She took a deep breath. 'They were both mad,' she said, accusing their absence. 'I saw that when Charlie left.'

'Yes,' I said. 'Mad about what?' She didn't want to answer.

'Anything,' I said, keeping after the thread. 'Anything they were both hot about.'

'What are you going to do about it?'

'Nothing, probably.'

'Truman was always talking about risking his life. If you could save a little bit of the world, he'd say, wouldn't you? Risk it, he meant.'

I was thinking that this wasn't going to be any little problem for me. If Truman had done his bit to save the world, he had obviously brought some heavy influence to bear on himself.

'I think you know more than you're telling me,' she said. 'Your questions.'

'I just know how things work. Somebody said, all you do is look for the money.'

'You mean where it went?'

'Or where it was supposed to go.'

She stopped, looked at the sea, and yawned. 'I'm going to the bungalow.' She walked up the beach and along a small path. I waited until her light was on. I decided not to worry about Truman's killer. A killing like that is not only a payback but is expected to be an example to all. It would be calculated that it had already done its job.

An hour later I was sitting beside a rock in my underpants. I had my back to a smooth rock that was still hot from the sun of the day, hoping I would decide not to swim out to the schooner. It would have looked inviting in the early morning, any time in fact during daylight. Now the bugger looked eerie, the dark water out there a channel filled with monsters drifting into warmer water to feed.

Earlier, one of the coppers had walked along the beach above the coral line and taken a piss about 20 metres away. I could smell the grog on him, smell the urine. The manager had obviously been doing his bit to try and keep it all out of the papers. Imagine your restaurant having a warning not to sit too close to the windows. That's exactly how it would read in the tabloids. RICH YANK SHOT AT DIN DINS.

Christ, I said to myself as I crept down to the water. Christ. Christ. Christ. The water was blood temperature.

I tried to keep Charlie's remains from my mind. I gently lowered myself into about a metre of warm water. From sea level the schooner was at least a hundred metres off. It looked as solemn as any old castle with doors creaking in the fog. I could see the lowest step of the ladder off the stern dip under occasionally. I watched the surface there because there were no regular waves. Perhaps a creature was rubbing against the bow. Why would the bloody thing dip when there was no apparent swell? Come on, I told myself, you know nothing about boats. I pushed myself away from the shore, breast-stroking so there would be no splash. I knew the moment the bottom fell away beneath me because the water was slightly chilled. I tried to stay in that warm surface layer. The plastic bag with my knife and small key ring torch made me feel very awkward. For some reason I felt it would make a noise under water that would be heard on the beach.

My mind was wide open to any little feeling that touched my body. Twice I thought I felt a swirl of current over my legs. About twenty strokes out the schooner was no closer. Shutting my eyes I expected a large fin to round the stern of the vessel when I opened them. I kept them closed. When I did open them the schooner was there, high above me. That was also disconcerting. I risked splashing to make it to the ladder, quickly. One hand on the ladder I forced myself to emerge slowly from the sea. Some feat. I went over the stern onto the deck. Christ, I thought, I'm not going back. I looked into the water below the ladder. A grey shadow seemed to hesitate below the surface. I'm being a bloody kid, I told myself.

Careful to give no silhouette, I bellied myself across and into the cockpit. A fore-and-aft rigged craft like this one would have cost Truman a small fortune. It was beautifully finished. The wood was in superb condition and the stainless steel fittings would have put a hole in my bank balance. It was a big boat and it'd be hard to search completely before dawn.

The wood of the hatch gave very easily. Having sprung it a little with my shoulder I found the catch by slipping my knife around the edges of it. I found a Mexican screwdriver in the form of the lip of a bucket that was wide enough to fit a corner, and then cracked the latch from the wood. Hardly made a sound, but I lay still, watching the shore lights for any shadows that might cross them. Nothing.

Dropping down into the cabin I instantly felt safer. I snapped on the torch and found a set of navigation maps for the Great Barrier Reef rolled on a table. The seat was comfortable. Being master of this vessel would feel great, unless you had something else driving you. What was it that had driven Truman? Ambition? Lust? Simple greed?

I swept the cabin with my torch, hoping it was Truman's personal playpen. I looked at his books locked behind glass. Bertrand Russell, for Christsake. Thoreau. Gibbon. No light stuff at all. This bugger had been serious.

In the drawer beneath the books I found something that made me sit back and calculate possibilities. Pages cut from Gould's *Birds of Australia*. The four volumes were worth hundreds of thousands. Dealers cut them up like this, the beautiful reproductions from those first editions costing thousands each. Truman had them along, allowing the sea air to plunder the life from the pages. Why? For aesthetic reasons? Reference? Inspiration? My guess was he wanted the real things. He wanted Australian birds—for his own aviaries. If he couldn't have the real thing before him on his travels, caressing these would have to do. He had been in league with Charlie, I was sure. He was the man Charlie was selling to.

Now I wanted to get away. A new sense of urgency was driving me. I traversed the cabin with the small light. Firearms were displayed and locked in racks high over the navigational tables. The interesting one was a high-powered Weatherby. It was reputed to be a marvellous weapon designed for hot cartridges. I stood on the table to take a closer look. The stock was an outrageous custom-made affair of light, creamy walnut, with as many fins—designed for shoulders and cheek—as a '57 Cadillac. The rifle was probably made about the same time. Weatherby had been sold to the Japanese and now made cheaper rifles.

Weatherby rifles had once only fired Weatherby bullets, always a fraction away from regular calibres, so the hunter either had the edge or had been suckered into having to buy the expensive Weatherby variations. Having a close look at the calibre it was about a .300 Magnum. It had a shell damn near as long as the ancient .450 Express for rhino and elephant. If it had been used to kill Truman, the hot cartridge would have driven the heavy slug through three or four other patrons. And it didn't have a fitting for a silencer. There was also a Brno.22, and several shotguns, none of which would have been any use. For my money it was still the hand gun at point-blank range.

Up on deck I favoured diving over the side descending the ladder would have been too unnerving. There was a ripple across the water now, and I felt colder. I looked over to the administration buildings. The lights were out and nothing stirred. I dived, finding the water warmer than the air. It made me feel optimistic about my chances to the shore.

I stroked strongly right up onto the beach, crawling from the water on my elbows and knees.

The touch on my shoulder nearly killed me. People just didn't touch me. I leapt sideways at the instant I saw who it was. I changed my face from fear to pleasure. This woman was not much more than half my age.

She held back her hand as if she had been burnt. Perhaps it was my smile. I found myself apologising. 'Sorry, you scared me.' Her hair was over her face and a knee peeped from a long cotton gown. 'I imagined all sorts of monsters out there.'

'I was walking,' she said. 'And I saw someone dive from the boat. I wanted to see who it was. You're very cold.' I stripped the water from my body with my hands and pulled my clothes on. By the time we reached my bungalow my teeth were dancing. Tropical night, I thought. She pushed through the door in front of me. 'You can put the coffee on,' I said. 'I'm getting dry.'

I heard her fill the jug.

She must have known it was me out on the boat, followed me down. She couldn't have seen my face in the water as I came in, it was too dark. I dried with a large beach towel, rubbing at my hair, left my wet underpants off, and put on my damp clothes. An uneasy feeling.

She was pouring coffee as I emerged. 'You'll freeze,' she said. 'Get into bed. I'll bring the coffee in.'

Something stopped me taking up the suggestion. It wasn't scruples. At least it shouldn't have been. And yet I did think that it would be unfair on her. My lovemaking was not exactly for the innocent. And no matter how much she had learned in her twenty-three years, I had learned a whole lot more. It was to be performed by experienced players. And I couldn't have gone along with hers, me as the amorous friend: there being no guilts or suppressions, just an open physical relationship. I had learned the truth about people while making love. You could go places you could never go alone. And from what I had heard from the women Charlie had left behind, it had all been massive physical exertion for him.

'No,' she said. 'I mean get into bed—alone, I mean. I'll bring the coffee in.' She laughed. 'I'll talk from the door.'

I laughed. 'An older man's vanity,' I said.

'Old,' she said, questioning it with uplifted eyes. I felt the gesture with the eyes was a ruse.

'I'll stay here,' I said. 'I'd feel too vulnerable in the cot.'

'That's a woman's fear,' she said.

She handed me a black coffee. 'You're determined to find out where Charlie went, aren't you?' she said. Her voice was serious, as if she hadn't quite believed me before.

'Yes,' I said.

'What did you find out on the boat?'

'Just that Truman was a bird lover with a lot of guns.'

'He was mixed up in a lot,' she said. 'There were always meetings with people from way outback. They owned abattoirs, or they were health inspectors, or rangers from the south or whatever. I asked Charlie if they were in drugs, anything like that. He never told me. But everything Charlie did always came back to Truman.

'He offered to give me more information, but I began to think it was dangerous being around him. I mean, I know he wanted me, but he didn't offer the information for anything like that, for me.'

'So in the time you were with Charlie you didn't find out anything that could help us?'

I looked at her closely, as if I were giving her a last chance to confess. Priests probably have the same look: hammy to everyone but frightened children. I was ashamed of myself.

'I don't know that we're looking for him for the same reasons. I mean because he's a friend.'

'We are,' I said. 'Charlie doesn't disappear for so long. Not with a bloody boat like that.

He'd ring someone, want to show it off to them.'

'That took me so long to catch on to,' she said. 'The showing off. But he was so good at it. He made it as if the show happened by accident. That it wasn't the main thing.'

'If you just have a name you could give me?' I asked.

'How do you know how long Charlie used to disappear for?'

'Hey, he used to ring me a couple of times a week.'

She walked around the room. The gown was tight around her. A breast swayed as she turned, unbound. I had a momentary vision of white thighs surrendering. But she wasn't aware of herself. 'He never told me he rang you,' she said. 'When he talked about the two of you together it was as if it was in the past somewhere.' I realised the past for her would be say, two years ago, even last year. Ancient times would be her sixteenth birthday.

'Twice a week,' she said, shaking her head as if she didn't believe it. She was a young girl realising that life isn't a movie, or that it was possible that her boyfriend had given her a new disease.

'What's the problem?' I asked. 'We talked about horses we noticed beginning to show form. It was business. Horses make us money. That's how I can fly around the place looking for the bastard.'

'Klima,' she said. 'Alex Klima.'

'I've never heard of him.'

'Why would you?'

'Where can I find him? Who is he?' I felt a knowing dread. It stirred in what may have been my soul. Maybe instinct. It had always been a great touchstone for me.

The easiness she had been beginning to feel with me was gone. She folded her arms, sat on the edge of a chair, and rubbed her feet against each other. I wanted to put my arm around her, soothe her.

She looked at me with a decision made. 'He runs a kangaroo plant inland from here. Slaughters them by the thousand.'

'Dog food?'

'We spent a few days at his place. It was horrible. He beat his wife. Slammed her around the head with his hands and slung her in the corner of the room. When I went to help her, she just whispered, "Go away. He'll do it to you. It's dangerous being here." I took her to the bathroom but she didn't say anything else. She was bleeding, and she started shivering. An Aboriginal woman came to look after her.'

I wanted to look at her closely. But I didn't. I was old enough to know that people often avoided the really bad things by telling you and themselves the pretty bad things.

'What sort of business did Charlie do with him?'

'He was putting money up for something.'

It was beginning to make sense. Well, a glimmer of something.

'Where did Truman fit in there?'

'They didn't talk about Klima. Charlie told me not to mention his name around Cairns at all. He didn't want people thinking we knew him. He was involved in large-scale things, making millions. But no-one wanted to know about him.'

I began to feel uneasy being on the island. Sydney's big time crims were reasonable; in Melbourne they belonged to the Melbourne Club. Things were done with care down there. Killing someone was only business. The crims even wanted their share of the limelight and, if they employed the right public relations specialists, found themselves in the social pages. Your bush criminal is another horse altogether. He's been plotting in solitude for years, taken to the bush because he's so fucking crazy he can't operate in the city and he's planned his moves so many times he's drifted from pedestrian planning to schemes of real genius. He would know how far he could push things. A few cops on this island wasn't going to keep us safe.

These were the bright bush boys I was thinking about, not your average fuckwit who's escaped north because he plans to live in the sun on the few bob he can scrounge from small time scamming.

I knew Klima's sort. He would take added pleasure in killing right under the noses of the police. Building up a kangaroo-slaughtering business takes a special kind of bastard. He would know the bush and the coast like his own needs.

The island had been scanned in the briefest possible way, and at the most only two coppers would have been left at the Centre until the forensic boys arrived in the morning. This was a different ball game we were playing now, and I had been swanning around the place as if I was the smart arse from the south, here to show the yokels how it was done.

A rubber boat on the beach pulled into the forest, a stroll around to the bungalows, a shot through the lock with silenced weapons . . . and we would be trying to protect ourselves with a breadknife or two. I couldn't believe my stupidity.

'I know this sounds stupid,' I said, 'but we need to spend the night in the forest behind here.' This amused her. It lightened her mood. 'You're frightened,' she said, like an accusing child who has finally discovered that grown-ups are not much different from them.

After I had watched the forest out the back for enough time for any movement to be noted—I was good at night, years spent in the paddocks straining to find any movement indicating spring foals were imminent—we took a blanket each and crept out the window over the sink. I also had the breadknife lying along my forearm, the blade caught under my watchband. The small slimline Gerber was in my back pocket. I hadn't given Verve a weapon. I was frightened she would cut herself.

Chapter 5

I led the way under the gently swaying palms into the heavy foliage. Trees towered above us, the sky was missing completely. The blackness had a deliciousness to it, like smelling mangoes. Where thick roots curled away from the trunks through a heavy cover of fallen leaves I began to look for places to merge with the earth. Lying between the roots a probing torch would pass over us. I was in two minds though. I had thought of simply walking to the Centre and hanging around in the vicinity of the cops. But if anyone did want us gone they would be watching the Centre.

Lying between the roots was comfortable. Verve was several over from me, her position partially concealed by a huge tentacle of a branch bent on attaching it itself to the tree for sustenance.

The smell of the rotting leaves was new to me and, although I pushed the blanket over the leaves under my head, its very novelty was stimulating. I rested with the thought I was somehow returning to where I had once been. I began to wonder why Charlie had been running with Klima. Slaughtering kangaroos wasn't his style. Setting up an establishment wasn't his style. Being around animals up for slaughter on a long-term basis would have depressed him.

The moment I heard movement I was awake. My senses were hooked into everything around me. My body seemed to be humming, as if I were carrying new energy. It was an exhilaration. I turned as she stood over me, one bare foot on each root. She stood there looking down. 'I'm the king of the castle,' she said. She shook her head and her gown was swept away from her leg. I ran the backs of my fingers from her knee upwards to the tendrils and the warmth, feeling the firmness of the layers there, the moistness. Her giggle was breathless. I delved into her with slow dexterity. Her moan was loud enough to disturb the forest.

'You'll have to stand up,' she said, her voice thick and low. I rose in front of her, slid the gown from her body. Her eyes had caught whatever light there was in the forest and, looking close, there was an odd tilt to them. Her smile was hesitant as if asking for admiration of her awesome display. Her body was smooth and firm, her skin having a fineness that was not quite believable. I rubbed my face across her breasts, sucking at them, took her round the waist and lowered her. She wrapped her legs around me the moment I entered, the feeling hot and smooth and capable of transporting me. But then it was as if she were holding me away from a deeper possession. I began to demand the further offer. My cock was an instrument of my brain. There was an outrageousness to my demand, a threat of savagery, a subtle coaxing, a few strokes of swift devastation and I was there, further in, feeling her clamping me with an involuntary urgency. For a moment I watched myself standing there with this nymph clinging to me, her nakedness vulnerable to all textures here, but as natural and as timeless as the forest. She stifled her moans in the side of my neck. I almost yelled when I came, rocking, as strong as a young tree in a high wind.

I fell back to the carpet of leaves, totally fatigued. She put her legs apart as I descended, and she stood above me again. I felt the wetness drip onto me.

I woke early in the morning as I heard a fast boat approaching. I stood up, looking to where Verve had been sleeping. She was gone. Her blanket was gone. I picked up my own blanket and walked down to my bungalow, the sunlight becoming strong and already hot. I tossed the blanket inside, followed by the knives, and began to walk towards her bungalow. Then I saw her in the sea, swimming with a strong stroke about a hundred metres out. The surface was flat and silver and she left ripples as if this were a great pond. I waved to her. The sheet of water dropping as she raised her arm caught the sun. I'm in trouble I thought. She's going to sucker me in and then leave when she's finished with me, when she no longer needs me. And I still won't have a clue to what this is all about. The game will become even harder.

The boat was coming in at the jetty a couple of hundred metres down, rocked by its own stern wave. Updine waved to me as he edged along beside the cabin with the docking pole. The gesture nearly upset him.

I walked tentatively across the coral. At the water's edge I stripped off and launched myself with a flat surface dive. Below me the scenery was miraculous. The reef touched the island here. Schools of brightly coloured fish of the most surreal shapes moved across corals of deep green, orange, shady maroon, fertile bases for succulent purple sea anemones, lacy weed that seemed to shudder as I passed over, huge clams, and sea slugs that moved over boulders. All too much. Years of study in the 20 metres I had been able to cover with my head submerged.

When I drew close I saw she was wearing bathers. She looked at me as I swam towards her, hoping that I would always remember this morning. The hills of the coast were in bright detail across the tilting silver gleam of the sea. I stopped to tread water, seeing Verve and myself grossly magnified and surging suggestively beneath the surface I had stirred.

She backed away from me slightly, keeping some distance from my nakedness. I began to think I must have dreamt last night. She said, 'We're not allowed to fraternise with the guests,' and nodded towards the Centre and the wharf. Jesus, had I dreamt it? I began to feel awkward, embarrassed, and had to stop a gesture to cover myself. I could have sunk beneath the water.

'I'll leave today,' I said.

'Really.'

'I'll see your friend Klima; find what he knows.'

'You'll never do that,' she said. She dropped beneath the surface and emerged with her face to the sky, her hair draping back behind her ears, a politically incorrect beauty. Too feminine; too lush.

I saw Updine leave the Centre and begin to walk over the coral towards my clothes. 'Are you having breakfast?' I asked. 'They'll have to supply it to paying guests.'

'Don't feel like having it there.'

'They'll serve it beside the pool or something,' I said.

She flipped on her back and made a shuffle kick that took her further out and away from me. Her bathers were swept up and over her hips and they really were enticing. I could have chased her, stroked her hips, allowed her breasts to float free. 'I'll see you in there,' I said, troubled by the rapidly building apparition I imagined beneath me.

Stroking towards the shore I saw that Updine was sitting down beside my clothes. He was smoking, his elbows on his knees looking around at the glorious morning. The smoke rose straight above him, no wind to diffuse it. Only a copper would be unthinking enough to mar a morning like this.

When I rose in front of him he laughed. 'No wonder she didn't want anything to do with you.' I looked down. My cock, it seemed to me, had almost retreated into my pubic hair in fright.

'I thought you southerners were big blokes,' he said.

'It's got brains,' I said. 'There are big fish out there.'

'Big mouths at any rate,' he said. 'I ran a check on you.'

'Yeah.'

'Yeah.'

'So what?'

'Nothing,' he said.

I picked up my clothes. Updine wasn't a natural interrogator. Most cops could do wonders with naked suspects. I began to walk up to the bungalow.

'You're political,' he said.

'News to me.'

'All that sixties and seventies stuff.'

'Everybody was,' I said.

'At sixteen?'

'Specially at sixteen,' I said.

He was silent and so I looked back at him. 'That's got to be old files. Sixteen-year-olds with files. Jesus!'

'We've got plenty of sixteen-year-olds with files.'

The sun was already drying me so I began donning my clothes.

'Would they have files if dope was legal?'

'No, probably not.'

'Except for the ones who knocked off ripening avocados to string out their dole money.'

'Yeah,' he said.

We didn't seem to have much to say to each other. Still, he tried. He gave me a small push when I was on one foot pulling my pants on with a leg in the air. I hopped sideways, easily, still poised, finishing that leg.

'You're a gambler,' he said looking more closely. 'That's crime in my book.'

'To some people, I suppose.'

'Where there's gambling there's crime.' I could see he was used to pushing people around. It was second nature to him. When I hauled the other pants leg on I looked at him levelly and spat close to his feet. It's an old sporting warning.

I was once an opening batsmen, used to playing balls that were hurled at you at 120 ks from almost 20 metres away, and I found spitting towards the wicket-keeper, as I looked around the field, to be a highly effective demoraliser. The only things you protected in those days were your testicles, your legs and your fingers. A man could still be a man as long as he could stand with his genitals in his hands.

Nowadays brains seem important, but no-one uses them.

If Updine pushed me again his face would be ground into the coral on the beach. The little push showed he was so confident he wouldn't expect a thing. I'd be charged with assaulting a cop but maybe not even that. Trouble on an island tourist resort is not encouraged by the Queensland government. Apart from that I've always found sticking up for yourself is okay in this country. You get away with your life— unless you're black. And even then they'd investigate your death.

Updine walked beside me to the bungalow. 'You know more than anyone else about this,' he said. 'You were the last to see him, hey. I reckon you're in on it. Got him to sit at that table.' Obviously Updine didn't have the imagination to broaden his powers of investigation. Obviously nobody had even told him about the schooner yet, or his people would be crawling all over it. Still, it might just be that he didn't want to look too deeply into anything; he might run up against those other powers in Queensland, the big crime figures. He would have to walk away from the case before he had even enjoyed himself. He wanted it to be the illicit fuck and swift death syndrome.

I walked up the steps to the door, opened it and walked through. 'See you,' I said to him. He came up the steps and leaned on the door jam. 'And if you're porkin' that sheila you've got to be in it. Missing persons tell me we've got to fly down the coast today. They think some boongs found her old boyfriend, a huge bloke. Would you know him?'

'Know him,' I said, facing Updine, 'I'm looking for him.'

'Why?'

'He's a good mate of mine. Knocked around with him for years. And then suddenly I don't hear from him.'

'You better come with us, mate. Identify him.'

'Identify him?'

'Sure. He's dead.'

I've never been too good at showing emotion and so I didn't now, except for a sudden droop to the lower jaw as if a drink was approaching my lips. Never had to practise that one. But it's effective. It caught me too. I wanted to sit on the steps watching the sea and contemplate a finished friendship. I hadn't felt the least sign of grief before this. 'Fuck,' I said, shaking my head as if my vision needed clearing. 'Where did you find him?'

'North, mate. Couple of hours by chopper.'

'I'll go with you.'

'Good. Better you than the girl, hey.'

'Yeah, well I'll tell her.'

I looked over Updine's head to the sea. She was still lazing around out there. Updine shook his head sadly. 'Lot of blokes been through her, mate.' He shook his head.

'You mean it's different for us.' No matter the idiocy of his words I still felt them.

'It gets to women see. Affects their judgement, makes 'em like it too much.'

'You can't like it too much,' I said, rejecting his attempt at sexual camaraderie.

He looked at me affronted. 'Big fucking deal,' he said, for want of being able to think of anything else to say. He trotted down the steps and walked away under the palms with his coat over his shoulder.

I sat on the beach waiting for her to tire of paradise.

Civilised curiosity won her over though, and she stroked cleanly to shore. Her sandals were at the water's edge and she slipped into them while looking at me for the news.

Her legs sort of dimpled at the knees as she walked up to me. She stood looking down but I didn't look into her face.

'Charlie's dead.'

'I knew he was,' she said, and ran past me to my bungalow.

I stayed where I was. She was going to get down into her grief whether I was with her or not. I looked over towards the Centre and saw Updine watching. He wanted to see how things were. He would remember the scene. He was one of those blokes who liked to see people distressed.

I'm a gambler, I told myself, needing to get things clear. I had started out winging it, and still did a lot of the time. But gambling on horses was a full-time job. I was a professional gambler, not a compulsive. The compulsive feels emotion whether he wins or loses. He even feels good feeling bad when he loses.

I ran my fingers through the pieces of coral. They felt good on my palm and fingers.

I knew I was gambling again now. I had put my bets on. Left some lively messes behind as a handicap. There were bastards to nail here. I suddenly knew what I was doing when I left Stevo close to death. I wanted to know what was going down, no matter the risk to myself. I was laying myself out like bait to bring in the catch. I was angry with myself for not spotting it earlier.

I stood up and walked to the bungalow. I expected to hear sobbing or things being smashed, but there was silence. She was lying on the bed in her bathers, staring at the ceiling. Her legs were crossed at the ankles. 'I knew he was dead,' she said.

'You want to tell me how?' I asked.

'We were planning to take Truman for a lot of money,' she said. 'And then Charlie disappeared, without a word. At first I thought he was running from me as well. But I knew he would tell me. And his bank has twelve thousand in it. His statements still kept coming and the money was never touched.'

'What was Charlie doing for Truman?'

'Putting him in touch with the right people. He told Truman he knew the people he wanted. He didn't but he could quickly enough. That was his talent. He knew people who were into everything imaginable. Klima was one of them.' She turned to the wall, her hip above curved legs.

'He used to spend so fast,' she said at last. Even Charlie's spending impressed her.

I sat down on the edge of the bed. 'I found Charlie's body about three days ago,' I said. 'That cigarette boat exploded off the coast north of here.'

She whirled on me, striking hard across my face. 'You bastard. And you're asking me to trust you.' She got off the bed and walked from the room.

I followed her, opened the curtains of the room, and then went out the back door and around the bungalow. At the back, I looked under the floor close to the steps. Nothing. No-one was listening. I walked back inside. She was on a cane chair staring out at the reef water in all its stunning beauty. She had pulled the tops of her bathers down and was idly stroking her breasts. 'It makes me feel better,' she said. 'Do you know what I mean?'

'Always does,' I said.

'Fuck me,' she said.

I looked down at her and she sucked her tongue in a cute way that was also shockingly carnal. I began to move her bathers down her waist and over her hips. 'Rougher,' she said. I tossed her on her stomach and pulled the bathers down over her buttocks. A small groan escaped her. Her skin was prickled and still damp from the bathers. I heard myself groaning as I tossed her legs open, settled my knees between them and pulled her thigh up and over my hip. She was so small around me I seemed to be splitting her, but her hips worked like oiled machinery. Turned on her side like that her breasts were bouncing, and she was giggling at being surprised by the abandon. Seeing her sucking her fingers I took her hand away and put my own fingers in her mouth. Her face curled into a grimace as she was caught by the throb of orgasm.

Some time later Updine knocked on the door. We were sipping coffee at the bench, looking to the horizon. 'Come in,' I yelled. There was a peculiar joy in my voice.

Updine walked into the room and stood with his feet apart, his hands on his hips looking at the sea. 'We're treating these bodies as one and the same case,' he said.

'You are both linked to the victims.'

'Some deduction,' I said.

'What?'

'Deduction,' I said.

'Oh, yeah,' he said, looking at Verve. 'I want you to let me know if you're planning to leave the city.'

'Not until this is all over,' she said. I searched Verve's face for signs of hammed up grief, but she was just grave, noting his words.

He looked at me. 'You'll be tagging along with us anyway. 'We'll be leaving in a few minutes.'

Closing the door behind Updine I looked at Verve. She was biting her lip.

'How many birds was he planning to move?' I hadn't planned to bring up the birds, the decision had been made for me by the same instinct that helped me survive. I was finished with pussyfooting around.

She showed no surprise. 'Not the birds, their eggs. They had to be checked to make sure they were fertilised, and then Charlie and I would fly out with them. When they were hatched he'd be able to sell them for squillions.'

'How long did you have to move them? Eggs hatch.'

'Depends on the bird. We planned on having six weeks.'

'Was Klima supplying the eggs?'

'He was the one who found their breeding grounds.' It was amazing how many parts to the story there were. Well, they seemed like parts when she only revealed it piecemeal, reluctantly. I did admire my interrogation technique though.

A bit of romance, a bit of screwing, and her memory was jogged.

'The money doesn't seem enough for a big player,' I said.

'But you don't know the birds.'

'What were they?'

'Paradise parrots,' she said.

'So?' I said.

'Everyone thought they were extinct. They were last sighted in the twenties.'

'So what sort of money are we talking about.'

'They were priceless,' she said, turning away to the window. There was a catch in her voice.

'What's wrong?'

'The birds were on the boat, I think.'

'You mean the eggs were, or the parents of the eggs?'

'Everything.'

'If there are some birds there are some more. That's the way it is.'

She turned around quickly. 'Don't be dumb.'

'Hey, come on. 'Are there more birds, or aren't there?'

She shrugged. 'How would I know?' she said.

I stood up. 'How much were you going to get for transporting them?'

'A hundred thousand dollars.'

'Not bad,' I said.

'Each,' she said.

'Two hundred thousand then.'

'Each egg.'

She was an exciting personality. Not only was she beautiful, but she had a certain way of telling a story that was enthralling—a breathless reluctance.

'So you began asking yourself how much could you really make?'

'If we got caught we were going to tell the authorities in America just what the eggs were in case they decided to destroy them.'

'In case they thought you had them along to eat on the flight?'

'Something like that.'

'How many eggs?'

'A dozen at a time.'

'Why wouldn't you be satisfied with that?'

'Charlie was always in a hurry. Always wanted more.'

'Yeah, and I know Charlie would never be stupid enough to walk through customs with the eggs strapped around him. And he wouldn't have let you either; so how were you getting them into the US?'

'By boat. All that fishing off Florida, no-one could track all the local boats. Charlie knew people who would take the eggs on their fishing trips. No customs involved.'

'In the yacht.' I gestured out the window.

'Start off in that one. A change to another once we got into the Gulf of Mexico.'

The story sounded true. But it also sounded too easy. Charlie must have been on someone else's stamping ground.

I heard the chopper and went to the window to watch. It was coming in low at speed. It was clear that the pilot loved the scenes from *Apocalypse Now*. I would obviously enjoy the flight. Updine was already at the door.

As we left the bungalow he faced Verve and, with a close look, told her that the victim's family were flying out from New York. Some heavy pressure was about to descend. They were rich and Truman's brother was the US ambassador to the United Nations. 'All the fucking stops are out on this one,' he said, with enthusiasm.

I looked back at Verve but she had already turned from the door. Circumstances had taken a quantum leap. I knew there was more of her story to emerge, and I wondered if I would be a fucked-out physical wreck before I had the whole of it.

Chapter 6

We approached the beach very low, flicking across the water in a path parallel to our shadow. On the white beach in the curve of the bay there were some Aborigines upwind of Charlie. And for an instant I saw buildings off to the north-west, tucked into a bend of the river. The roofs were in camouflage greens. Stevo certainly hadn't thought to show them to me, had in fact kept me away from the area.

Behind me the forensic boys were exclaiming over the virgin beach.

As we closed with the shore I saw that the tarpaulin still hung from the tree, but now it was shapeless. The pilot was going to plump us down directly in front of what I now saw was Charlie's body laid out some metres from the hanging tree.

Updine was quick on the uptake. He saw why the Aborigines were upwind of the body and tapped the pilot's shoulder to indicate that. I could see Updine's face in profile and it was a man withdrawing. He had no pleasure in this work. He could see it was going to be all headaches. Gone was his enthusiasm. The quicker he could offload this homicide the better. He would whack in a very low-key report which his seniors would realise was from an incompetent, and he would quickly become a faceless bureaucrat and not be considered as spokesman when the international pressure built up over the next few weeks. He wouldn't be heard from again until he had arrested some Aborigines on charges everyone knew were doubtful. Thrown in the bag would be a couple of assaults so he could claim victim compensation. The police had realised that it was much easier for them to be victims than anyone else.

I felt safe with Updine on the job though. He didn't want to do the hard work. He wouldn't use real facts to try and throw a rope around me, just a hotchpotch of clichéd circumstances. A lot of investigation was done that way. Find a recognisable narrative that gloves the available facts and you lock up your case.

The chopper hovered and touched the ground. A sandstorm erupted around us until the engine began to slow. The group to the north strolled casually towards us. Stepping out of the chopper the smell hit me. Charlie was certainly on the nose. 'Aaaah fuck,' Updine said beside me. I walked towards the approaching mob and Updine followed me. The two forensic boys walked off towards Charlie. I hadn't had a chance to talk to them and didn't think I ever would.

'Who found him?' Updine asked the first bloke who came up. It took courage to be the first Aboriginal to talk up to a cop for they were usually targeted as the troublemaker, and often inexplicably died. I realised it was Mick, but didn't greet him. He looked different away from the streets of Cairns. Here he was easy with the bush. He was in long khaki shorts, a dark blue singlet and a shapeless cotton hat. He was in his twenties. A strong bloke. The rest of them had a similar style. You knew they had been eating from the sea and not from the cans that used to be the staple diet.

'Bloke from another tribe, boss. Gone along way now.'

'Who reported his find then?'

'Me.'

'How long has the body been here?'

'No idea. He really stinks, man. Don't want to look. He's a white man.' Updine swallowed what seemed to be an insult.

I looked back at Charlie as Mick nodded back towards the body. Updine's forensic team were there wearing little white masks. Photographs were being taken and some collecting being done. There would be no recognisable footprints in the sand.

Updine was still going for the simplest solution.

'This bloke from the other tribe, what was he doing along here?'

'No idea, man.'

I looked at the other faces of Mick's tribe. They were all open, looking independent, knowing they could disappear into the rainforest for weeks at a time.

'Any drugs back in there?' Updine asked. 'Got any plantations. We'll find them. We'll ask for satellite shots of this whole place.' Updine looked hard at Mick. To match the gaze would have been rude and so Mick pulled out some sunglasses and donned them in a very cool, precise way. He could have been a copper himself, just off the set of *Miami Spice*.

'What's your name, Jack?'

'Mick Seerino.'

'What the fuck is that sort of name?' Updine asked, shaking his head. 'Italian. Can I get you through the mission?'

'No mission now, mate.' Mick handed him a card.

I remembered that the Italians had come into the canefields in the thirties and forties. It was the Black Hand then. Not the Cosa Nostra or Mafia. They didn't get a toehold then because the cane cutters refused to be stood over. Five decades later, however, our bureaucrats and law enforcers had been accepting the word of prominent Italians that there was no Mafia. The fact that members of the Italian community were shotgunned on a regular basis didn't seem to stand for evidence that there was.

Updine went on with his in-depth investigation. Did anyone see anything funny? Hear anything? Know of any drug dealers? Did they see people coming here by boat?'

'It's a wonder he's still here,' Mick said. 'Some big salties about. Some kids missing down to the south.'

Updine turned back to Charlie's resting place. 'Where did they get those little masks?' he asked himself quietly. The forensic crew could have been tropical beach bandits in their medical masks.

'Don't know,' I said.

'What did you say?' he asked, unaware he had spoken aloud.

'I think I'll stay here,' I said. 'I don't want to go near the stink.'

Updine looked strung out. I was sure he would take bribes and protection money with great panache from gambling dens, brothels, and hoteliers catering for under-age drinkers, but out here in the bush, with massive crocs, and half-eaten cadavers, he was pretty close to a little boy lost.

He started talking as if he were assessing the situation. 'He was obviously tortured before he was killed,' he said, as if he was so in sympathy with the air around us it was telling him things.

'How do you know?' I asked. 'You haven't looked at him yet.'

'Cutting somebody's legs off and slinging him up in canvas shows whoever did it was a fucking maniac.'

'Wanted him to be found anyway,' I said.

When he turned to look at me his eyes were flicking from side to side. He wanted an escape route. He wanted a story in his head before he viewed Charlie's deteriorating body. 'Hey,' he yelled to his forensic people. 'Where do I get a mask?'

One of them pointed to the chopper and called, 'Cargo.' The two of them were pretty laid back. They treated Updine as a piece of unnecessary baggage, but he refused to acknowledge that they were trying to do that.

I walked with him to the chopper. He got the mask from the small cargo hold, obviously felt his hands had been dirtied by whatever else it contained and walked down to the water's edge to wash them. I pulled myself up through the open door of the chopper and sat there with my legs dangling out. An armalite rifle was clipped just beyond the door—a very accurate and destructive weapon that was once lauded as having a tumbling bullet that created such hydraulics in a person's body that even if it only took a finger off, the pressure in the brain would be massive enough to kill. It had been reported in a weekly news magazine during the Vietnam War—all bullshit.

Thirty metres out from where Updine was now scrubbing his hands furiously at the water's edge was a sandbank. Water depth was only 6 or 7 centimetres there, so when the big salty crossed it he was very obvious. Water sprayed away from his twisting, armoured body. It barked once like a choking dog.

Updine was transfixed, watching its approach. And then his feet began to move in a backing-away stumble that his brain was unaware of.

'You better run, mate,' I said.

He took my advice. He turned and ran for it. I had to stop an urge to grab the armalite. The animal was magnificent, up high on its legs like a galloping horse. It seemed it would catch Updine. Why would I harm the creature just to save a bullying hypocrite? It had obviously been taunted by Charlie's body and was considerably irritated.

At the moment Updine turned towards the aircraft, a peculiar pleading in his eyes, I closed the side door closest to him. I imagined Charlie laughing at my audacity. I had a perfectly legitimate excuse, the croc might climb into the chopper. Updine didn't even notice my move. His brain was running on what was possible. It didn't want to think about rapidly closing escape doors. The brain had simply told him to expect the inevitable, in the way of bad dreams we never remember: there was no-one to blame.

Unfortunately Updine's instincts were right. The croc was a bit doubtful about the aircraft, and so when Updine crossed out of his sight, he gave it away. Usually crocs make that one savage burst over a few metres. This was an unusual reptile, a deep thinker, or maybe it was just had a passion—to eat.

The creature spread sand as he turned back to the sea. In the water he seemed to disappear. Even though he didn't go over the bank to the open sea you couldn't tell whether he had gone north or south. The water couldn't have been much more than 15 centimetres deep over his back, and yet there wasn't a ripple on the surface. What a design.

I let Updine in the pilot's side door. Or I was going to, but he had evacuated and looked at me sheepishly, his knees on the door frame. I told him it was normal, and that he had better dig a hole in the sand that side of the chopper, deep enough for the water to flow in it. 'You'll have a sort of wash basin.'

'Christ,' he said, panting. 'That fucker could be back just like that.' He tried to snap his fingers but they made no sound.

'Yeah,' I said. 'I'll tell you what I'll do. I'll empty a mag from the armalite into the water. Spray lead; keep them away, and you can really douse yourself. If he comes back,' I said, smacking the clip home and pulling one into the breech, 'he'll be dingo meat.'

'Can you shoot?' he asked.

'Sure can,' I said. I walked down to the water's edge and gave the water half a clip in a 20 metre arc. 'You're safe, mate,' I said.

He didn't really have an option. Even he could see we'd leave him behind in the bush rather than have him in the chopper for the ride back.

I took out the half-empty mag and turned it over to take the second that was taped to it, facing out. Taped magazines are usually only seen in street-to-street fighting or on terrorist weapons. The Queensland coppers were becoming ambitious.

'This rifle's right,' I said. 'Fully automatic. Just don't get in the way if he comes. You know, keep well down, so I can shoot over your head.'

He walked down to the water's edge, his back to me. I risked a glance towards forensic. The taller bloke was holding his stomach. The pilot had walked out of the jungle.

Updine was not bashful. He scrubbed thoroughly. He nearly wore his trousers out with handfuls of sand. His brush with death had taken away any inhibitions he had about his plump nakedness. I gave a dark seaweed shape to his left a few rounds, BBBBBBBRD, and Updine burst out of the water and tore up the sand. His head and body were thrown backwards as though he was allowing his legs, the croc's target, to escape first. His cock was thrust forward as an offering to the approaching jungle. He wasn't looking behind. 'Jesus, I'm sorry,' I said. 'I was sure I saw the bugger.' He swivelled his eyes sideways as he ran, saw my smile, and collapsed on the sand with relief. He struck me as a man who didn't want to die.

Slowly he dragged himself to his feet, the sand falling away in sheets. Then he began screaming. 'You goddam fucking arsehole, you did that on purpose.'

'No,' I reasoned, 'you've got to be careful. I mean it's safer that way.'

I knew I had made an enemy. He walked up to me really close.

'Bastards like you pay,' he said, his panting making his words barely audible.

'No, I never do,' I said. 'Plenty of people have tried to make me pay, but they get so angry they misfire; their timing is never right.'

'You buggers are always at the races,' he said. 'You can't keep away. Fucking slaves to it. I'll find you with your arse out of your pants at the races.'

'Where mate? Paris? New York? Roma? And you better do a better job on your own pants, mate.' He grabbed the armalite from me and waved the pilot down. I walked up the beach, with a little white mask on, to identify Charlie.

Charlie had dried out in a peculiar way. His face must have been against the canvas while he was bundled up, because his jaw and upper lip was set off to one side in a grotesque sneer, his mouth open and full of teeth, and his darkened tongue, in the manner of a wicked vampire that has been sucking blood and been zapped that way, was protruding.

In case people think I'm a callous bastard about old friends, I have to tell you that I believe once the spirit has departed the flesh there is nothing left to honour. Charlie would have hated looking the way he did. He would have been the first to walk away from the sight he was now. Not that I was walking away. I could do with forensic clues to his murder. And anyway, if there is anything in the spirit life, Charlie's would have been rolling in the sand, laughing at Updine's confrontation with the croc.

I looked at the work the forensic boys were doing. I was uneasy about them. It was not the thought that they might be after me, it was more that I understood they couldn't be trusted to do their jobs with any sort of honesty. I knew they worked in a milieu of corruption, but I had always thought that scientists were above any sort of skulduggery. Surely their professional dedication to truth placed them above the uneducated coppers they worked with.

'What's it look like?' I asked them.

'He's dead.'

I looked at the comic. I think he was Ivan.

'He was a good friend of mine,' I said.

'We can't tell you a thing,' Ivan said.

'We've got nothing,' Dick said. 'But I'd guess he was full of water.'

I looked up at the tarpaulin. 'What's all that then?'

'Someone has put him up there away from the animals,' Dick said. 'They wanted him to be found. Or else they were coming back for him.'

'He's been here a while if he's rotted through?' I asked.

'I'd say a croc was after him . . . from the rip in the canvas.'

I walked down to where the pilot was talking to the Aborigines. They were laughing together. I was anxious, eager to be away. There was nothing here for me.

I held up the hand of friendship as I walked up. It was a wave in the sort of a greeting a North American Indian might give, palm forward on an upright forearm: How! Don't know where I got hold of it.

'How are the Sherlocks going?' the pilot asked.

'Has Updine ever solved a case?'

'Wouldn't know?' he answered. 'They just hire my chopper. In the season I spray sugarcane.'

'Any chance the croc'll be back?' I asked Mick.

'Nah, real shy boy. He's out there thinkin' how dumb he was.'

I sat down next to Mick. 'The coppers never get the right bloke,' he said. 'They just get someone who they reckon could have done it and beat the shit out of him.'

I looked up at the gulls wheeling overhead. 'I saw some parrots out on the island,' I said. 'Very fast, and they streaked through the foliage. Never seen 'em before.'

'Lots of parrots here, mate,' Mick said, tossing his head back into the jungle.

'Do any bird-nesting?' I asked. The term took me by surprise, back to my childhood. I remembered the feel of warm spriggers' eggs in my mouth as I climbed down from nests. On the ground I'd prick each end of the egg and blow them, watching the white and then the yoke bubble and hang from the egg. I'd taken the eggs of spur-winged plovers and maggies, risking the spurs and strong beaks for the prizes. The only valuable things I had were memories.

I lay back on the warm sand, my hands under my head. I remembered running across the irrigation paddocks, ducking at the last minute as the plovers dived at me, hearing the clicks of the spurs, finally taking refuge beneath the willows or the gums close by. I knew I had been living then.

That sort of excitement as a kid can keep you looking for more.

Still with my eyes closed to the blue of the sky, I asked, 'Is there any money in them, Mick?'

'Sure is,' he said. 'Not for Murrays though, mate. Long time ago whitey asked us to catch birds and gave us nothin'. These days they come here and not say anything about what they're doin'.'

'You can kick 'em off,' I said.

'Not government fellas.'

'They do it by themselves?'

'They find where the birds are, then other blokes sneak in and get 'em.'

I wouldn't have got anything out of these blokes if they hadn't seen me humiliate Updine. Perhaps I'd done it on purpose; unconsciously known what to do.

'The dead bloke, ever seen him before?' I asked. I was playing along to find out if he had told his mates about me. Their various gazes didn't falter. He hadn't told them.

'Nah,' Mick said. 'He came in by sea.'

'Yeah,' I said, relaxing.

I stayed in that pleasant area that arrives just before sleep, hearing the voices around me as if they were far off.

Later I turned on to my side and looked over the sand to the forensic squad. They were placing Charlie's remains in a body bag. I dragged myself back to awareness. Through the foliage I saw a faint gleam in the forest. I moved my position again. It was a four-wheel drive, identical to Stevo's. My body hit alert. I stayed where I was. I was too close to the group for anyone risking a shot at me. My brain began speculating. How the fuck?

'How do you blokes get around?' I asked Mick over my shoulder.

'Got a vehicle, mate.' He nodded in the direction of the four-wheel drive.

'Those yours, the buildings back there?' I asked Mick.

'No buildings there, brother,' he said.

Updine began walking down the beach towards us. 'Hey, you boongs,' he called, 'come and lift the body to the chopper.'

'No,' Mick said. 'Fuck off.'

Updine knew he was ratshit on this beach. He waved fuck you to our little group and turned back.

It was a funny feeling carrying Charlie. For a start he was bloody heavy, but his body moved like jelly on our shoulders. A bloody nightmare feeling.

Updine went back to talk to Mick. I guessed he was telling him that there'd be a squad of coppers back to search the bush.

Chapter 7

The American ambassador John Marshall had caught up with Verve by the time I got back to Cairns. Marshall had been in Vietnam, South Africa, and for a time been the ambassador to the UN. All this I knew because he was a recent arrival and the press had done some considerable fawning. Naturally he knew Truman's brother, having preceded him as the UN ambassador. Now Marshall was in Australia for a stint, which meant he had stuffed up at the UN. I wondered how deep it would all go. Those who have manipulated the trouble spots of the world tend to develop unholy liaisons. Often they develop a taste for business opportunities for themselves. The fact he had rushed to Cairns so quickly made him an instant suspect. He was putting his hand out for something.

The official angle was that Truman had obviously been an identity, an indulged and straying son of a wealthy and influential family, and they had brought their force to bear on the government to investigate Truman's death. The family wanted some bastard to sweat over this one. But what I had suspected had happened was that a bureaucratic opportunist and privateer had become involved. When I rang Verve she was breathless and asked me to come over.

'Do you want a lawyer?' I asked.

'Of course I don't,' she said. Her voice contained excitement I would normally of thought of as sexual. I sensed it was the closeness of real power stimulating her.

Charlie may have looked to her like some sort of saviour, but here now was a man from her own continent, swanning in and taking over, making things happen, kicking butt. I thought she'd probably head back home in a few weeks, making her experiences here seem like a horror story from her earlier life. I didn't want to lose her. I wished I could discover some anchors to Verve's character. All I knew was that she was frank and honest only when she didn't feel threatened, which was most of the time. That wasn't enough to hold her.

When I arrived she was ready to leave. She was dressed in a pink silk dress that was not quite a negligee. 'Do you really want me along?' I asked.

'He wants you along. He said I should bring you.'

In the car I told her she shouldn't open up too much until she knew the game that was being played.

'Hey,' she said. 'You were at the table, I wasn't.' It was almost as if she were going to enjoy my attempt to extricate myself from all this. I put this down to her youth.

One of Marshall's servants opened the door of the suite. His eyes flashed at Verve. For a moment I thought I saw recognition there, but decided I was too edgy. It was only a response to her style. A typical young diplomat, a slight sneer to his lips, eager and enthusiastic to his superiors, as I saw when he took us through to Marshall.

Marshall was a tall black guy. He knew his power and he wasn't going to pussyfoot around. He had a sheaf of papers in one hand and a cigar in the other. He was walking around the room talking to himself. He waved us to chairs. I perched on the back of one, staying about his height. His speech was directed at a conference phone and he was only organising some reports to Washington. It may have been a call to impress us. But he shut it down pretty quickly.

'Well,' he said to me. 'It seems to me that you can solve all my problems.' He smiled at Verve who smiled back. For a moment I thought he was acting for her benefit. Or for mine.

'I'm only interested in solving my own problems,' I said.

He looked at me. 'Careful,' he said.

I looked at him carefully and decided to enlighten him.

'I've got no need to be. You're here to do a job for Truman's family, that's all. You're doing it because they're rich and influential. There's a young black barman here,' I continued. 'If he turned up dead, you wouldn't make a phone call. So, let's cut the horseshit here. What do you want?'

He strolled with his hands behind his back, like some self-important white guy. He looked around suddenly, turning on one heel.

'Let's get through it quickly then. You tell me about Truman . . . how long you knew him?'

'About five minutes.'

'Smart boy,' he said with a smirk. 'Okay, you can go. Verveine and I will talk.'

'Sure, if she wants me to go.'

'You'd better go, man. Right now.'

'Fuck you,' I answered.

'Rick, Melvin,' he called.

'They touch me, they're fucked. You have no rights here.'

'Diplomatic rights,' he said.

'Not the right to interrogate Australians, or manhandle them. I'll have a lawyer wake up the press in Sydney for me.'

Rick and Melvin appeared. They looked at Marshall. If appearances meant anything they were tough, and ready to do anything he wanted. I remembered during a president's visit an Australian driver carrying presidential security had been ordered to drive through protesters. He had refused. The security operatives had left the car, hitting the protesters hard, knocking them down, bleeding.

Verve looked at them over her shoulder. 'Stay,' she said to me. It seemed she had made a decision on who to go with here. I smiled confidently towards her.

Marshall was certainly pissed off. He could barely contain himself, but he nodded his aides from the room. 'Remember Truman's family,' I said. 'You have to satisfy people, tell them how and why it happened. I don't think you have a hope. Not with your attitude.'

He sat down then like a competent bureaucrat who has sensed things swinging away from his control. He would try and coax them back. 'Verveine,' he said, soothingly. 'Could you tell me about Truman? What you know about his activities here. Your relationship with him.'

'We didn't have a relationship,' she said. 'He was a friend of an old friend of mine.'

'Who is also dead.'

She nodded her head, her hair falling forward. She hooked the back of her hand beneath the fold of hair and flicked it away from her face.

She told him about Truman's friendship with Charlie and that she thought there was obviously something that linked their deaths, but she was unsure what.

Marshall leaned forward, sliding his hands over the desk towards her. 'What do you think they had in common then? I would have thought nothing.'

'They talked about boats. They sailed a lot; laughed a lot.'

'I don't know that laughter is a good basis for a relationship,' Marshall said, rather sarcastically.

'It's the only one; only worthwhile one,' I said.

'Shut up,' he said to me. I knew then that further down the track I would find him deeper in this mess. He didn't want to know anything more from me. I was someone he could discount in the larger scheme of events.

'In this country,' I said, 'when you tell someone to shut up, you have to be prepared to back it up.' I went to his desk, picked up a paper weight, and before he moved, slammed it down on his Mont Blanc fountain pen. I knew he would get the symbolism. At least feel it in his testicles.

'What fucking right,' I continued, 'gives you the idea you can talk to us as if we're shit?'

Verve was already standing. I asked her with a gesture to the door whether she wanted to go. We walked to the door together.

Outside the door Marshall's staff stepped back reluctantly, awaiting further instructions.

At the door I looked back at him before closing it. The smashed pen with a pool of ink around it was all I remembered.

It was dark outside the hotel. Tourist merriment was in the air. I thought a nice seafood meal somewhere by the water would be something different. There is nothing quite as rejuvenating for the spirit as eating by the sea; whether in a flash restaurant, or dipping into wrapped fish and chips on the sand with a bottle of wine, it doesn't matter. After the day I wanted warmth and music, and a friend to share it all with.

It wasn't going to happen. As we walked away from the hotel I saw Updine step from a police car at the kerb. I didn't acknowledge him, and didn't mention it to Verve. I had been aware of how her hips and thigh touched mine as we walked, and it was something I didn't want to spoil. The bastard mightn't even see us. He's to report upstairs, I thought.

An Aboriginal bloke moved from the rear door of the car in front of us. I saw his face was wide open with effort. Updine wouldn't have seen it coming because the speed was easy. The knife went into Updine's belly three times. The first hit him somewhere vital for he gurgled and staggered. The third stab was actually holding him up. Then the knife was out. The black bloke looked at me, skittered the knife over to my feet, and was across the road and away. Verve had been looking in a shop window and didn't see. I put my arm around her affectionately, to guide her.

A small kid pointed to Updine leaning against the police car, his legs splayed out, the blood running down his shirt just under the flap of his coat.

'Look, Mum,' the kid said.

'It's only a joke,' his mother said. 'Come on.'

'It doesn't look funny,' the kid said.

Verve and I stayed looking in the window at the T-shirts with the mass of Picassoish figures.

In the window reflections I saw the kid looking back, his arm fully stretched as his mum pulled him along.

The driver of the police car had been looking across the road at a handsome woman in an expensive cabriolet, and he was unaware of Updine propped against the other side of the car. His fingers drummed on the steering wheel. I moved into the shop with Verve. A few people looked at Updine but, deciding not to say anything to anybody, passed on. As Updine was literally doing. He should have died on the beach, a gourmet meal for a member of the endangered species. Nothing like beer-soaked fat.

'Keep walking,' I said to Verve as I saw we could walk through the shop to the carpark. She didn't reply, just walked. I wasn't going to mention Updine's passing to her. If questioned she would be truly innocent, someone I might need as a witness to my own unawareness. The look on the killer's face had been calculated. Had I been supposed to panic, some shit like that, and involve myself by becoming another witness to a murder? Fuck 'em. Unless they had a shot of me looking, I was in the clear. Nobody could have calculated Updine would leave the car as I was emerging from the hotel. Jesus! Of course they could. These things can be easily organised by powerful people.

They would have told him grab Speerman when he hits the pavement. And then they would have someone hit him, Updine. Christ, what a long shot. And the effort; the plaiting of influences and circumstances to get such an operation up. What were they going to win? Have me surrounded by doubtful circumstantial evidence, supported by the suspicion of having witnessed so many murders taking place within a few metres of me.

I decided as we hailed a cab that someone knew I hauled Charlie's body from the water, knew I had sent Stevo bye-byes, or tried to, and knew I was getting closer to whatever they were trying to hide. I had a feeling that somebody wanted me to wear something—for them. They wanted me uneasy enough to manipulate.

At the motel we went straight to my room. Verve showed me on a map where I could find Alex Klima's property, a couple of hundred ks inland.

'When did Charlie last see Klima?'

She shrugged. 'Don't remember.'

I looked at her now without registering any attraction. Why couldn't I still desire her even though I was in serious danger? It's like that with everyone. Even long friendships can dissolve in the face of fear. They certainly do in the face of ambition.

'Was it weeks, months?'

'Weeks.'

'Was it about these birds, the parrots?'

She crossed her legs, and the smoothness of the skin, the shape, the challenge, whatever it was, reversed my whole theory of how danger tore at relationships.

'No, I have no idea. They didn't tell me things.' I believed her. Hadn't I just protected her from seeing Updine's demise?

I stood beside her and stroked the line of her neck. She smiled up at me. I flicked her dress back from her legs. She leaned her head back over the chair and uncrossed her legs. I leaned over and parted them, slightly. I wasn't sure her vulnerability was real.

Before I left for Klima's property I needed Verve safe. Short of putting her on a plane south I didn't have much idea. Like the head of the National Crime Commission I was deeply suspicious of coppers. They weren't in it to protect citizens, they were in it for retirement funds.

In the bathroom I removed the louvres and reached up to the roof guttering for the plastic package there. It was a .38 Smith and Wesson Special, a hand gun used for rapid centre fire on pistol ranges. Beautifully balanced, low loadings made it remarkably accurate over 30 metres. You could also load it with .357 Magnum bullets for hardier but less accurate results. I loaded it with Magnums. Once I had actually decided to take protective measures the fear picked up. When the phone rang my veins moved.

The voice was beautifully modulated.

'Angela,' she said.

Truman's wife. She hadn't been satisfied with the ambassador's report. Her voice was friendly. Judgements had, so far, been suspended. Could we talk to her? she asked as if she were only bent on capturing me for a social engagement. Before Truman's trip to Australia, she told me, she had become very close with him again, but had heard little for months, except that he hadn't wanted her to join him.

'You'll have to come here?' I said. Take a wealthy person away from their opulence and it does wonders for their comprehension.

Verve sat watching television. 'Visitor coming,' I said.

'Yeah,' she said.

'Truman's wife.'

'I heard.' I touched her shoulders, they were tight with tension. She leaned her head back against me. It set me on fire again.

'You want to fuck now?' she said.

'No time.'

She walked into the bathroom and I saw her foot lash out at the plastic bucket. It bounced off the tiles over the bath.

I speculated on how well she had known Truman. Had she been generous with her affections?

Angela was quite a presence. Tall, draped with a linen suit of extravagant proportions. She looked cool, chic and expensive. The motel room immediately seemed nastier. She smiled and took a seat with the same ease she might at the Hilton. Here, just maybe, was a supporter.

Offered a drink she asked for a Jameson, and I spun the cap off a small bottle and poured it for her. 'No ice,' she said, 'a little water.'

She turned her warmth loose on Verve. 'Please tell me about Truman and what he was doing here?' she said. If there had been room on the couch she would have patted it to have Verve beside her. Verve walked to the window and then back towards the bed. She was trying to find an approach to help her deal with Angela. I knew Angela would have more luck with Verve than I had. She could almost have been Verve's long-lost mother. She was that good.

'I loved him,' Angela continued, 'although we were separated. He will always be part of my life, part of what I am. I couldn't ever forgive myself if I didn't try and discover how it all happened. I might be able to set things in place again . . . for myself I mean. Perhaps for his friends.' A beautifully considered performance. Off pat though. To some it would give Truman's death respectability. Listening to her I could almost imagine his brains hadn't exploded over the dining table.

I watched Verve. Her face was lighter than it had been. She realised the interrogation wasn't to be conducted on a brutal demand basis. People overwhelmed with relief often drop into a stream of consciousness and begin to tell everything. A lawyer's nightmare. Verve sat in the chair beside the phone and crossed her legs. 'We're trying to find out what the two of them have been up to,' she said, finding a tone that matched Angela's. 'I feel such an idiot. I was with Charlie and Truman often, but I never discovered what either of them were doing. And we were good friends.' Not bad. Just the right tone, as if the two victims were just naughty boys who had been caned.

'How was he, when you last saw him?' Angela asked, an edge to her voice.

'He was excited,' Verve said, herself a little too eager, and I realised she wanted to unburden herself. I moved forward to catch her eye, but I was too late. 'He had discovered the birds . . . '

'Aah the parrots,' Angela confirmed. We were well along now, I thought. Why hadn't I been able to have that effect on Verve?

'You know about those?' Verve asked.

'His aviaries are splendid. People barely know they're in a cage when they're viewing his birds. They cover hectares.'

'Is that how he made his money?' I asked.

'Oh no. He was collecting birds that were nearly extinct. He was going to save the various species.' She attempted for a little pride in her voice here, but failed.

'Do you know who he was dealing with here?' I asked.

'All he knew was that some corrupt bureaucrats were planning to market them. He was going to deal with them. Pay their price. So I don't understand what could have happened.'

I became anxious to help this woman. She gave the impression she would be appreciative of information, that I could be a great friend of hers. Gone was any suspicion that she may be a player. Fortunately I always suspect my feelings of goodwill.

'He was paying a lot for those parrots,' I said.

'Not as much as he was prepared to pay. He loved them. He sent me film of a pair in the bush. They were most unique. They moved around their environment like fish; swaying through the branches, dancing with each other. Birds are the fish of the air, after all. Well, these were anyway,' she said as if she had already dismissed them, realised her mistake and attempted to recover. 'They gave you a marvellous feeling. Paradise.'

'What did they look like?' I knew what they looked like now. Stray feathers and broken egg shells.

'A very light green chest,' she began to recite as if she had learned from rote, 'fading to a blue green colour; black wings slashed with scarlet, and a scarlet belly. The head was topped with black, scarlet cheeks, and then fading to blue. The call didn't sound anything like a parrot. It had a sad note, almost that of a song bird.'

'I've seen them,' Verve said. 'They fly, even in a small cage, without damaging their wings. They're very precise.'

I looked at Verve. She was admiring Angela.

'Where did you see them?' Angela asked.

I saw Verve hesitate, only slightly, but I knew she was going to lie. 'Charlie took me to see them on Truman's boat.'

'Which boat?' Angela asked.

'The long, fast one.'

'Anybody know where the boat is?'

I stopped a grunt of laughter. Didn't her friend Marshall know, or hadn't he told her?

'Only Charlie would know,' I said, 'and it's very unlikely he will be able to tell us.' I didn't think the light humour out of place. I understood Angela was honing in on the parrots. Her voice was casual now, no hint of hardness in her inquiries, but they were that all right, inquiries about priceless parrots, not about Truman. Then again they were the only lead that might take her close to those responsible for Truman's killing.

She looked across to Verve. 'You don't have to be frightened about talking to me,' she said. 'I'm amassing quite a few helpers. You'd be looked after; kept safe.'

Verve looked at me. There was an appeal in her eyes: you make the decision. I shook my head, ever so slightly.

'There is someone else involved,' Verve began. 'Well, I think he's involved. He was definitely a staging place for the birds. He had a huge cage in a large old barn and the roof could be opened, like a giant roller door.'

Angela stood up. 'I think we've found the link,' she said, with a maternal smile. She looked at Verve. 'I don't think you're safe here do you? I have people and I have the place. Absolutely nothing could happen to you there.' She didn't want her to say another word in my presence. Verve would be whisked away into a cocoon of protection.

'Verve and I are going south for a while,' I said.

A flash of irritation moved across Angela's face like a wispy sea breeze.

I turned to Verve and gave her a wink, let her understand that none of any of this was serious stuff, that we were going to use Angela.

'We'll keep in touch with you,' I said. Angela moved to the door quickly. She had no practice in handling rejection.

We walked down behind Angela to the limousine. Three men lounged around close to the car. When I took Angela by the arm, catching her off balance mid-stride, one of them moved like lightning, but catching herself easily, she waved him away. 'I hope you'll keep me posted,' I said in a whisper. I had been hoping her flunkies would try me. Not for any particular reason. Perhaps only to establish myself as a player.

She shrugged my hand away, and looked me straight in the eye. She had sensed my compulsive challenge. 'I know how you operate. But I don't creep around pretending I'm someone I'm not.' Her look was contemptuous. She had spotted the difference between us. She had been rich so long she thought that everyone should buy enough protection to slide through life hassle free. She didn't know that some people hid most of themselves most of the time, just to survive.

She stepped into her car; smiled at Verve as a flunkie closed the door. The limo crackled down the drive over the gravel.

Chapter 8

We had to move fast if we were going to beat Angela to Klima's. The four-wheel drive I hired had 500 ks on the clock. I had told them we were just going to drive up to Port Douglas, look at a few beaches, motor through the canefields. They had decided we looked like we were used to comfort and wouldn't be hard on their new vehicle.

We drove straight up into the hills to the plateau above Cairns. Up here were the dress circle dwellers, the professionals who could afford to get away from the heat close to the sea. At this height, rising air created a breeze, and when we stopped to look out over the city and the sea, I guessed the temperature was 10 degrees cooler. In summer it meant the difference between living and expiring. Verve hadn't been keen on the prospect of a trip to the hinterland menagerie, but now she stretched, leaning back in the seat, her hands raised in the air. 'Oh, I enjoy getting away from that town,' she said. 'Up here nothing has a hold on you.'

There was barely any traffic on the winding road and Verve lay with her head in my lap. She was asleep in moments.

On the plateau the thick forest country gave away pretty quickly to avocado and banana groves, grazing country with grass at least a metre high, and winding banks of trees that followed waterways into the distance. I settled into a driving mood. I tossed in a couple of tapes I had bought; Cajun music, with its crazy violins and rocking drums, and the wild yells of the vocalists sounding as if they already had blood in their throats. The right sort of music for this country. Verve stirred, and bending forward and over her I saw a small smile on her face. We hit the Tablelands around nightfall.

It was a pleasure to negotiate the winding roads. The modern four-wheel drive bears no relation to the early Land Rovers and Toyota's I had used for bush work. This thing was really suspended, and it hugged the curves like some old sports car, but without the stiffness and hardness.

When I felt the fatigue I drove off the bitumen. Several banks of trees and bushes from the road, we were completely secluded. Verve made no effort to wake as I lifted her into her seat and wound it down to recline. Not many people look good after several hours sleep. She retained it all.

I took a leak over both number plates, threw dust on them, and then peeled off the hire car stickers low on the bumper. Not that there would be many who would be around to identify the vehicle.

Finishing that job I stretched and looked up into the night sky. The heavens were pulsing. The only word for it. There was not a square centimetre of night sky unoccupied by stars. Living close to cities for so long I had forgotten the immensity of the universe. I took a dozen oysters from the esky and downed them with beer and herb bread. I washed my hands in the melted water in the bottom of the esky. In the heat of the evening my fingers were only chilled for an instant. Looking over the tailgate I saw Verve's face in profile. I took the remaining oysters and opened the passenger door. 'Hey, time to eat,' I said. She smiled before she opened her eyes. 'I'm whacked,' she said.

'You need to eat something,' I said. I dangled an oyster close to her lips, catching its salty juices in my cupped hand. Her tongue slipped from her lips and I laid the oyster across it. She retrieved it like a long-tongued lizard with an insect. We repeated the action half-a-dozen times without her opening her eyes and then she turned her head to one side and fell asleep. She snuggled into the seat as I tipped back the driver's seat.

My eyes opened sometime after midnight. I was totally alert. In front of me Verve was softly lit by the parking lights, moving to the music she had slipped into the tape deck. Seeing I was watching she stroked her stomach and breasts, a wicked twist to her lips. I smiled at her, lifting the back of the seat to spectator position. Holding one breast she moved her hand under the fabric of the shirt and stroked it.

I moved to open the driver's door but she held up a hand in a gesture to stop me. Her body moved in a sway to the music as she undid the button on her jeans and ran the zip down. Without one awkward movement, and still rocking gently to the music, she removed the jeans from her hips and legs, stepping from them when they reached the ground.

'You're gorgeous,' I whispered.

She wore those silky French knickers, wide on the legs. Her fingers dipped into the legs of her knickers once in a while. When she lolled her head back in time to the music I stepped from the car and walked behind her. She danced, rubbing her buttocks against me while my hands roved. She was marvellously gone and I entered that spirit with her.

Birds woke me in the dawn. There was a chirring sound like a cicada that was split by a high-pitched keening. And then bursts of a trilling, kree, kree, pitched high. Not birds that I had heard before, and I would probably have disregarded them but for my inspired interest in the worth of some of them. I strained to see them in the branches but all I caught a glimpse of were some brown birds with flashes of white running down their wings. Not at all like the song.

Verve and I raided the esky again for cold water to wash with. She was friendly but gave no hint of the sexual obliterations of the previous night. We talked as if we were boy scout and girl guide fixed on getting our camp tidy. I knew the meanderings of her perversity were as lost on me as mine were on her.

Through the trees in front of us the hills rolled away into the distance, a blue range close to the horizon. I pulled out, bucking the machine back on the road.

A few kilometres further on there was a small food stop. It was a brown house on the side of the road with a verandah covered in signs advertising local tourist destinations. I would have missed the sign for Mexican food except it had the look of a small tearoom in the Dandenong Ranges around Melbourne, so I looked a bit deeper.

We found there was none of the advertised Mexican food, but eggs and bacon were cooking. When I asked for a couple each he cracked four more onto the broad hotplate, standing, scraping at the surface with an egg slice. He waved it occasionally as some blowflies buzzed around.

'You know the Klima place?' I asked.

'Give it a miss,' he said.

'Yeah?'

The bloke paused for a while before answering. Out in the backblocks, conversation was slow, something to dwell on and enjoy. When

I first came north I thought they talked slow like that to take the mickey out of someone from the south. But it's their usual rhythm.

'Yeah, he's a fuckin' maniac. Excuse me.'

'What's the story on him?' We sat down at one of the tables, a faded laminex job, bordered with chrome that was rusting. He can't do too much damage to eggs, I thought.

'What's it to you, hey?'

'Looking it over.'

'He'd never sell, mate. Got a big roo business goin'.'

'It's not real roo country is it?'

'Every bit of it's roo country. And he trucks 'em in those frigerated trucks.'

'See much of him?'

'Yeah, a couple a days ago. That bloody Porsche a his. Kill himself or someone else, the stupid bastard.'

'So where's his dog meat factory, round here?'

'Who said dogs meat?' He slipped the eggs on a plate that had the thickness of paper, and then drained some bacon out and laid it across the plate. The bacon fat was as thick as my finger, it was already congealing. The real bush tucker.

'It's a classy operation, then? For novelty restaurants or something?'

'Not round here. Who'd eat fuckin' roo meat?'

'It's supposed to be healthy, no fat, no cholesterol.'

When he laughed he showed a few gaps in his teeth. 'Fuckin' healthy? Jesus!' he said. 'Fuckin' roo meat healthy? They skin 'em in the dirt, hose 'em down, cool 'em. It's got be a day's drive to get 'em on a plane. Mate, I wouldn't want to eat that shit.'

I slipped into the eggs. Verve lit a cigarette, changed her mind and butted it out in one yolk. With my mouth full I continued questioning. 'You worked for him, did you?'

'He's got a big turnover. Not many stay round. He's a nasty prick.'

'How'd I get to see him?'

'You wouldn't. Not with that rig out there. He only takes to buggers who got nothin'.'

'Philanthropist.'

'Nah, don't think he goes for kids.'

He closed up then. Threw some coffee at me without asking if I wanted any. It was white and sugared. He decided not to give Verve any, and she decided not to ask for any. 'Five bucks, mate,' he said. He must have made a lot of money from the tourist signs. Bacon and eggs shouldn't taste like his.

I sat in the rig for a while wondering if I wanted to go ahead with this. I looked at Verve looking off to the side. She didn't seem to care where she was going. So what if Klima killed Charlie? What was I going to do about it?

My mind scrabbled around a bit with that question. I could feel it ducking for cover, avoiding the straight, clear answers that I always expected from myself.

All at once I'd made the decision. The reason I was here was the birds. My mind threw it up instantly. I wanted Charlie's share. I smiled to myself. I wanted a lot more. It seemed to me I had been waiting a long time for a justification like this. The circumstances were right. I wanted revenge. I was going to kill Klima. I felt like a general who after years of inactivity could begin annihilating the enemy again. Minute drops of adrenalin began to feed into my system, strengthening arteries and giving my heart a deeper beat.

I had never known the feelings of such extreme ambition.

No wonder people became addicted to it. No wonder they could lie, cheat and murder to hold on to whatever they had.

As we got close to Klima's place Verve began to come to life. There was a nerviness to her. She bit one side of her finger constantly.

'Don't you bite your fingernails?' I asked.

She laughed across at me, obviously relieved that I wasn't so nervous I didn't not notice things.

The property was a sprawling one—40 000 hectares on the verge of the dust country. It had been overused, grazed out, although I didn't see one head of stock as I sped down the track to where I thought I might find the homestead. It was twenty minutes in from the gate. I was glad of the four-wheel drive. Two dry creek beds were steep and damaged. There must have been another road into the place because dry properties needed heavy trucks in pretty regularly, on the basis that most years, no matter how well they might start, could quickly become drought time, but Verve knew only this one. Farmers didn't realise that to keep this country viable you needed to nurture it, with considerable care: light stocking to preserve the environment that supported them. Instead, with a gambler's lust, they bought big and hoped for lucky rainy seasons and mild summers.

The homestead was red earth rendering and corrugated iron. Vehicles monopolised the shade of the young trees that must have taken real effort and energy to water. And then to the south I saw the cattle yards. Dust from mustering hung over hectares of ground. Closer I saw the steel yards were on heavy concrete, and young weaners were being marked there. They were separated from the other cattle, run into a crush, had their pouches slit and their knackers squeezed out and sliced away.

No-one appeared to notice when I parked close to the other vehicles and wandered over. The cattle were bawling so profoundly it was hard to hear anything but the occasional shout over the melee. They must have penned around four hundred head. Their condition wasn't too good, although they were doing everything but give them food to make them healthy. A young bloke with a pack of toxin on his back was hovering over thirty head in a race, trying from all angles to insert his nozzle in the mouths of the beasts.

I waited outside the yards, watching the activity. Verve had stayed in the car and wound up the windows. I wouldn't see it happen, but a stranger in the back country is reported to the boss pretty much immediately.

I watched the bloke at work on the young cattle. He saw me and began to ham it up. He was a sort of squint-eyed bastard with a Yank ten-gallon thrust back from his brow so he could work in close. He gave me a wink and when he had slit the pouch he bent over, sucked out the gelatinous nut and lolled it in his mouth. The young, soon-to-be bullock, struck at him with a back leg that bonged on the steel rails.

Behind me a mad voice said. 'We do that to some of our visitors.'

'You wouldn't have a mouth big enough,' I said, turning around, seeing a mouth that could only have been slashed with a steak knife. I continued. 'I tell ya what, it's the first time I've seen a hydatid cyst sucking on a knacker.'

'Hah, hah, hah,' he forced. The sound was loud, devoid of merriment, and obviously it was a warning. Apparently it was his normal laugh for all the other blokes started laughing, whether they had heard the exchange or not.

'We've got a fuckin' comedian here,' he yelled. It was impossible to tell whether he was stating this as an insult or he was going along with me. I was inclined to think the former. I looked at his men, the half-dozen close by, to gauge their reaction. Nothing more than one sly glance. It was enough. I looked like being entertainment.

'I'm looking for some real shit poor cattle to ship south to fatten up,' I said. 'Looks like I've found 'em.' I smiled around at everyone like a dumb yokel, wanting to be included in the joking. No-one laughed.

The slit-mouthed one began tightening his crazy face, focusing the eyes that seemed to loll in their sockets. 'I sure as hell don't sell anything to smart arses.'

I stepped up close to him. So this was Klima. I smiled at him, noted the filth in the creases around his eyes red with bullshit. He was big but his hips were too narrow to have the real knockdown strength. 'That's just for the hicks, mate,' I said. 'I buy birds, for appreciative customers. I'm told you're the bloke to see.'

He turned, walking out of the yard and I followed him. About 50 metres from the yard, beyond the cars, he stopped. He stood with his back to me. He was obviously in a rage and he needed to turn to me with an answer. He would at least want to know who had told me.

This was dangerous ground, for him. Should he talk to me, pretend he would sell to me, or just stop me from going anywhere? I stayed about 5 metres from him. If he turned with annihilation on his mind he would have to be quick.

After a few moments he turned. I found it difficult to comprehend the change. His manner was hearty. 'You'll have to forgive me,' he said. 'I'm stuck out here with illiterate morons for months at a time and I forget how to treat normal people.' The charm was extraordinary—for its insincerity.

I smiled at him. 'I thought I'd upset you in some way,' I said. 'I'm a pleasant sort of bloke myself. I like to know the people I do business with. I'm not like some of the bastards who rip you off the first chance they get and then pretend not to know you a year or two down the track, when you're trying to collect your money.' For his benefit I mimicked just such an individual: 'You must be mistaken. I've never seen you before in my life.'

He shook hands with an easygoing grab. 'I do business with some of the wealthiest people in the world,' he said. 'I've got to warn you, I'm expensive. But my birds are in the best condition.'

'Jack Speerman,' I said, letting go his hand.

'What are you after?' he asked. 'We've got some red-tailed blacks. Good stock.'

I looked at him sharply. If he was trying to test me I wanted to show I was up there. On the other hand it could just mean I was a businessman with sharp reflexes.

'And how expensive are you?' I asked.

'I'm talking fifteen grand,' he said. The red-tailed black must be a relatively unimportant little item.

'I'm talking eggs, and lots of them.'

'You have that sort of operation?'

'What else,' I said. 'I started collecting and flying them out myself. Now I hate flying.'

'Come up to the house. Have a drink. We'll talk this over.'

'Sure,' I said.

'How did you get into the business?' he asked.

I laughed. I was tempted to tell him Charlie's story about the brolga eggs, but I plumped for lizards. He may have heard the brolga story already. 'I took out some blue-tongued lizards and frill necks,' I said. It sounded ridiculous, but I always work on the principle that if you can think of it somebody else has done it. 'Found I could pay for a holiday. You know, just in a business briefcase. Ridiculous thing to do for a small return.'

'Leave your car here,' he said. 'I'll run you back later.'

'It's okay, you might trust your hands but I don't. I've got precious cargo in that wagon. I'll follow you up.'

In the vehicle I asked Verve if he had seen her, knew who she was. 'No,' she said. 'He was too worried about you.'

Klima drove in a leisurely way, giving himself time to think; or perhaps it was to alert someone at the house. I was glad the four-wheel drive had tight windows because the dust didn't begin seeping into the vehicle until we were close to the house. Again Verve stayed in the vehicle.

The house and its surrounds were functional—just. The overhanging roof was corrugated iron which sloped down low, making verandahs all around. The inside walls were faced with some sort of chipboard, but it was old and it didn't welcome a second look. It was a big house with at least three huge rooms, two of them seemed to be bunk rooms and the third contained a huge table and kitchen bench. Off to one side was a billiard table with a ripped cloth. It was dim inside and Klima had to turn on the bare light that hung from somewhere up in the rafters. The kitchen window was covered in spider webs. A bush with small thin leaves rubbed the outside of the window. A jutting blind was covering for the bush. Over the chimney piece were half-a-dozen rifles, their breeches open. This last fact, coupled with the torn billiard cloth, gave the impression that recreation here was taken seriously.

Klima sat on a high kitchen stool and pointed to a rickety director's chair for me. It didn't mean a shit to me whether I was above or below his eye level.

'You know,' he began. 'I only do business with people who come to me with recommendations. I get a call, someone says so and so will be contacting you. Now you're out of the blue, mate. I have to think you're a cop. Or somebody who wants to knock me off.'

I started on my spiel. 'I don't like anyone knowing my business, except the people I do it with. I don't want other people I deal with knowing I do business with you. And you won't get any other names from me. Life is too fucking precarious, mate. You might have cops in this with you, customs people, whatever. You might want to do them a favour. The government might want them to crack down on smugglers. You know how it goes. I don't give you my real name, and I probably don't have yours.'

He turned on me, vicious. He'd show me he didn't give a fuck. He had twenty blokes within screaming distance. 'Yeah, well now I want one name. Who told you about me, or we don't do business? And maybe you don't leave here.' This was the stuff I loved to hear. Threats gave me an edge most people could never have imagined.

I laughed. 'You know, the bastard has disappeared. I was here a few weeks back and this bugger contacted me, said we could do business, and now I can't find him. That's the best I can do for you. Big bloke he was.

Klima kicked the leg of the table, not aggressively, more speculatively, the way a truck driver kicks a tyre for pressure. If it bounces back, hard, it's okay.

'I don't know who the fuck that would be,' he said.

'He was about to do business with me.'

'He told you about me, even though he was going to be the contact between us? I don't understand.' He was getting impatient. He stood up from the chair and walked towards the guns. I stood up instantly, leaning forward to be able to cover the distance if he reached for one. The movement saved me. A blow directed at the back of my head hit my shoulder. I turned, grabbing the hand which held a waddy. It was the Nut Sucker. I pulled his arm across my body as I stamped at his ankle, grabbed his neck with the other hand, and slammed his face into the table.

Looking up I saw Klima working the bolt on a three-0. I put my foot in the sucker's back and pushed him towards Klima. It saved me no time at all. I dragged at the Smith and Wesson under my shirt tail. I had it up firing as he levelled. I shot Nut Sucker in the back and dived for the bench as the old military rifle seemed to explode. The slug from it would go through the walls and still not stop for 8 kilometres.

I had the gun on him before he worked the bolt again. Stupidly I eased off, thinking I had him under control. He was fast but I had managed to keep him in that corner away from any cover. I was on the wrong side of the bench though and the wounded Nut Sucker slashed at my hand with his knackering knife and opened up my wrist. I changed the gun to my left hand but Klima was running and out the door.

Stepping from behind the bench I looked down at the form feigning a cringe on the floor. He was ready to spring again and I walked backwards towards the door. I heard Klima starting off in his ute. I was in a trouble. He had about a dozen people out there. Nut Sucker began to smirk because he understood my position. The wound in his back was off to the right so he was probably okay. He knew he would pull through. I shot him in the kneecap although I had been going to blow his head off. I was just not up to killing outright.

I ran outside and checked the vehicle. The passenger door was open. Verve was gone. I looked out along the verandahs, ran for the western side. Nothing. A corrugated iron tank on a sagging stand, and bush off the back between the house and the iron barn-like building to the west. Running back, checking the activity off in the mustering yards, I saw several men were looking towards the house. If Klima had Verve I was in bad shape. I ran inside again, my eyes slow to adjust to the light. The Nut Sucker hadn't expected my speed so his lunge was late. He was coming at me again when

Verve struck. I saw from the corner of my eye exactly what she was doing. The carving knife was held in her fist, the back of the blade against her forearm. With her elbow locked and all her weight in the shoulder she punched down across his throat, practically severing Nut Sucker's neck. I knew I didn't have to worry about her.

I grabbed a shotgun and rummaged for cartridges. I took a high-powered rifle and walked over to her. I held the shotgun out. She didn't take it at first. She wiped the blood from her face with a dish cloth. The excitement had drained her strength. She took the gun in weak hands.

'I think you know how to use this,' I said.

We ran for the four-wheel drive. Verve was in the passenger seat before I had made it through the door. She lowered all the windows and slipped the cartridges into the magazine of the Browning. I was bleeding from the wrist, but it was one of those veins that people slash for a quick death, only to find they're still bleeding an hour later. I would be okay if I could just get the fucking vehicle moving. I reversed away from the house. My hands slipped with the blood on the wheel as I tried to spin it.

I turned the wheel with the spokes and headed for the track. I locked the wheel with my knees and cut away a sleeve which I wrapped around my wrist. Verve placed the barrel of the gun on the floor and held it there with her knees. She took the sleeve and wrapped the cut firmly, slipping my knife down the back of my wrist as a splint. The hand gun was in the holding tray between the seats. The drive was going to have to be a fast one.

In the wing mirror I saw the workers running for their vehicles. I had a rough track in front of me, most of the old heaps that were in pursuit wouldn't travel well here. And then I saw some of the cars were headed on another track, parallel to this one, but about a kilometre over to the west. It'd be easier going there. They'd probably meet me at the gate. Let the bastards try.

I had to slow for the first creek bed, and that put the crowd on the other track ahead, marginally. I made distance again on them though, and then the second creek bed. I hit it too fast. The wheel spun in my hand, my head hit the roof, but the wagon was user friendly and it took the road up the bank of its own accord. The crowd on the second road were ahead again, and I couldn't make distance on them. They were making it on me. The gate I had to go through had only a cattle grid to negotiate so I'd still be rolling. But if they could catch me on the graded tracks, they would be all over me.

I began laughing with relief when I saw the next move from my pursuers. Three hundred metres off the gate I saw that instead of turning east to catch me they turned to the west. They were running too. They weren't chasing me at all. They were escaping—from me, or what they imagined would be reinforcements. Klima had just told them to skedaddle. What the hell did they have on the property? Not fucking birds' eggs, that's for sure.

Chapter 9

Thirty kilometres away we turned into a stand of trees, threading through them so we were concealed from the road. My heart had slowed and my breathing felt comfortable. Death had loomed and I knew now that it was time to stop winging it. From now on I wouldn't move unless I knew there would be a benefit.

I stepped down from the vehicle and looked at the wrist. Still wrapped in the shirt sleeve, the blood had dried. I would need water to moisten it. To remove it dry would start the bleeding again as the crust was pulled away.

'Leave it,' Verve said. 'It'll be clean. It bled long enough.'

I opened the tailgate and sat there listening to a hot afternoon. It was still hot in the shade. Verve tossed off her shoes and stripped away her jeans, settling back in the seat to sleep.

These moments in the bush were deja vu for me. I fully expected to hear a rooster crowing. Their calls from the backyards of country towns punctuated my days as a kid when time hung on my hands. It was almost impossible to beat such dreariness. I remembered asking myself, where is the time going? Once I sat on a wired-in verandah, crook with the measles, and lis-

tened to what a day was. It was all the noises
I had heard in my life until then. Screen doors
slamming, dogs barking, milk cans being turned
on the cement floor at the dairy, a whistle from
the sauce factory, far off a school bell, a bakelite radio on a kitchen shelf. Would I ever
remember this day when I was adult? I asked
myself then. Thirty years later I was still
remembering it. Those long afternoons had
forced me to look for excitement.

Hunting had been big with me. Ferrets down
the rabbit warrens behind the shearing sheds;
daring myself to sit on horses I could capture
in paddocks out in the bush near Dead Cow
Lane; snaring ducks under water like I had read
the Aborigines did, breathing through hollow
reeds. Anything at all to stop those afternoons
going on forever.

I dragged myself from the past. I knew we
had to return to the homestead. It was imperative. They had left so suddenly there would be
material left behind. Nobody ran like that,
unless there was something serious to run from.

After drinking from the stock of fruit juice
packets we had brought along, I opened the
back doors of the vehicle, stripped off my shirt,
folded it and looked at Verve. She was dead to
the world. I placed the Smith and Wesson on
my belly, and slept.

I woke with a nasty, panicky feeling. Without
opening my eyes I put my hand around the gun
and felt better. I filled the magazine with low

velocity bullets and spun the cylinder. It was late afternoon and I was covered in a sweat that made me nauseous. A thin pain flitted through my head with every move. If tetanus was coming on this quickly I didn't stand a chance. For years I had kept up my shots because working around horses made you especially vulnerable to lockjaw, the bacillus breeding in a profound way in the lower intestine of the animal. I felt Verve's hand fall away from my shoulder where it had been resting. My eyes snapped open. She was still asleep.

On dark we were back at Klima's place, pushing through the top four fence wires with the bull bar, hearing them each snap away with a quick whine, and driving over the lower two.

I opened the sun roof and stood with my head out so I could look far into the night, and asked Verve to take the wheel. We crawled along. I wasn't sure how far the motor would carry in the stillness. About 3 kilometres from the homestead Verve parked in between two bushes, the only cover available on this side of the house.

Leaving the wagon, we walked along the fence line because a watcher doesn't bother looking there. The eye naturally takes in the centre of any paddock. There was no moon, although the sky was bright enough for me to see several hundred metres ahead.

'I don't know why we're doing this,' Verve said. I had expected her protest earlier. It was like revisiting old places you didn't want to see again.

'I think there's something here,' I said.

She shook her head. 'There's nothing.'

'How can I know that if you don't talk to me?' I said.

'I just don't want to talk,' she said.

'Why not.'

'It hurts.' I looked at her. The way she had killed the Nut Sucker told me her visits here with Charlie had left her wounded. She had killed him for revenge.

About four hundred metres from the house I sat down with my back against a big straining post and watched the house. Verve squatted beside me. I could make out the front door hanging open, but that was about all that was unusual. A small breeze stirred the dust in the front yard. No dogs anywhere.

I felt if I stood up and walked down to the house Nut Sucker would meet me with a three-0 in the doorway. He would have sewn his neck to his head and he would be dripping blood over his rifle stock. A stupid thought—he would be stone dead on the floor. Verve had opened both his carotid arteries. That frightened me too.

Maybe I wouldn't need to go into the house. I could secrete myself somewhere with a couple of firearms and wait for their sneaky return.

Finally we crept around the house to the aviary. A truck with a water tank was parked in the shadows. I could see a huge pump on a trailer behind the truck. Closer in I saw a thick hose ran from the pump into the aviary. Beneath silver metal paint the aviary was actually constructed of wood, with several huge sliding doors to the south and the west.

I searched in the back of the truck for a Mexican screwdriver, found it in the form of an old-fashioned crowbar, round and thick and incapable of being bent, and then stopped myself. What the hell was I doing? If there was anyone left they would come running at the first sound.

I forced myself to check the house. Verve stayed with the shotgun in her arms and I walked straight to the back door and kicked it in. I leapt through the kitchen, switching on lights as I went. They had left the generator running. Nobody. The blood was curdled dark on the floor near the bench, but that was the only sign I had been there. Nut Sucker and the rifles had gone.

I walked out of the house towards the aviary, jammed the hand gun in my belt at the back, picked up the crowbar and inserted it under the padlocked hinge that locked the two doors. It sprang easily, but the doors wouldn't give. It seemed that the sliding rails were chocked, so I placed the wedge of the bar between the doors and heaved sideways. I felt the bar beginning to give, shortened my grip downwards, and then felt the door shift from its runners. I stepped back in case it had some falling to do, but there was enough space for me to slide through. I looked at Verve but she just shook her head.

Inside was pitch black. I moved off to one side of the doors and squatted down with my back to the wall, listening. There should have been feathery shufflings at the noises I'd made. Night birds are wary of slithery intruders. There was total silence.

I stood and moved forward several metres. I found the wire of the huge cage and began walking around it, carefully. There are plenty of variations of treading on the upturned rake.

The only object I encountered was a hard, steel wheelbarrow. The scents were fresh though. Some plants were flowering. I risked a match. Dense, high foliage confronted me. I touched some leaves through the wire. They were coated with dew. I shook the match as the flame touched my fingers and tried another. Off to the east was the huge brick wall of the coolroom.

Water pipes ran up the walls and into the cages about 25 metres up. I turned a tap and looked towards the cage. I heard a soft shushing. The water was misting, a warm draught of moisture passed over me. Still no birds moving.

I walked around the huge cage again striking matches every few metres. I found an incubator—cold—off in a small alcove. I slid the trays. Any eggs had been removed.

'You were right,' I said to Verve when I emerged.

'You can't find out what went on here just by walking around,' she said.

'If only I could talk to witnesses,' I said with an undertone of accusation.

We walked back to my wagon. Already I was feeling fatigue again. I eased the seat back and watched the house over the sill, the Smith and Wesson in my lap. I lowered the windows a few centimetres only. If there were sounds about I wanted to hear them.

'It was the sex here,' Verve said. She made it sound as if the sort of sex here had never been done before.

'Everyone gets caught out by sex,' I said. 'You learn.'

'Not like this was.'

I waited, looked across at her, but she'd decided not to go on. Forcing such conversations only buries the subject deeper.

In the morning I woke to the mournful cry of a crow. I opened one eye and saw it swoop from a tree and head for the stand near the house.

It had to be around seven. The crow had obviously been about his work for some time. For a moment I felt vulnerable and apprehensive. Nothing was moving though. The front door of the house was still open. The whole place managed to look desolate.

We walked over to the house and while Verve showered I fossicked for food. There were eggs and tomatoes still in their supermarket packaging. There was milk in cartons and about a gallon of ice cream.

Hearing Verve still in the shower I drove the wagon around the back of the house to the aviary.

Inside the aviary it was dark and still. I found a door into the cage, opened it, and stepped inside. I had to push through the undergrowth to find the small artificial lake, dry.

The birds hadn't been here for some time. Even the funky smell of all bird cages was fading. This little exercise had produced nothing, except the knowledge I was dealing with a highly volatile and frightened group of operators.

The whole place had been designed for abandoning.

Moving back to the door of the cage I brushed against two bushes that were dying. I didn't think too much about it. They must have dried out, but at the gate I thought again. Everything else was alive and flourishing. Nothing like birdshit for fertiliser.

I pushed away their branches to look at the earth around their trunks. It was drier than other areas because it had been disturbed. I pushed at their trunks with a foot. They were loose in the ground. A few minutes digging with a short-handled shovel and one hand, pushing on the handle with my stomach to rest the wounded wrist, was enough to clear the loose dirt away from a small rocket launcher wrapped and greased under plastic, several rockets, and something else further down. The smell was of putrefaction.

I began scraping further, knowing what I was going to find. There were at least four bodies snugly buried. I could tell because each arm I exposed had a right hand attached to it. They were face to back. Very efficiently buried to save space and time. And they had been there for a while.

I began covering them again, standing the trees up in even more solid positions—inserted down between arms and backs. I took the rocket launcher and the things that made it function, and turned on all the misters. I felt the trees would thank me for this.

I placed the rockets and their launcher in the back seat.

It seemed to me the weapon was evidence that influential people were involved. It would be virtually impossible for an average crim to have one. They would need powerful friends.

'What is that?' Verve asked. I told her. 'It was probably used on Charlie,' I said.

'Fuck,' she said.

'Did Charlie talk about taking the place over out here?' I asked.

'Yes,' she said.

'Tell me about it.'

'I told him he was stupid to try. I didn't want to know about it.'

'Did he have other blokes in it with him?'

'No idea,' she said.

I walked across to the loading dock and ran up the brick steps to the side of it. The jemmy took care of the lock on the lever handle that was attached to bars that ran to wedge locks at the top and bottom. The door opened with a whomp, pushing back against me as the air escaped.

The air was stale, old, fetid. Not a beef smell at all, slightly sourer. That was strange to me because kangaroo meat can be sweeter than beef, and has none of the fat decay about it.

Switching on the lights I was confronted by a vast empty space. The floor was rubber that had the texture of old linoleum, the walls also some sort of rubbery composition. At one end there was a raised area almost like a stage, but the motor was there. Long lines of rails traversed the room well below the ceiling, about 2 metres up. Hundreds of roller hooks were at the far end of the rails. Off to the left were the freezers.

I swung the first door open. Empty. I had expected white frosted walls, so that was strange. The next had four plastic supermarket bags off to one side. I glanced inside them. Men's clothing, work boots: from the four bodies I guessed.

The third was equipped as a laboratory. It was extensive, impressive with its stainless steel benches, small portable freezers, racks of tubes with seals good enough to withstand any expansion due to the freezing of contents. There was a huge microscope, and high on the wall was an air purifier. It wouldn't have been out of place in an AIDS research laboratory, where clean air is essential. All in all the place was far better equipped than anything you might expect from a grazing company dabbling in the artificial insemination of their stock.

Outside the sun greeted me like light from heaven. I had been submerged in the charnel house for too long.

The air was sweet from the eucalypts in the aviary. I thought of the rainforest that ran down to the ocean, the water that was so clean you could see the bottom 6 metres down on a windless sea. My one wish was that I could see it again.

I glanced south between the house and the aviary, and froze.

Two vehicles were travelling towards the house, about 2 kilometres away. I ran into the back door to get Verve away. She was watching the vehicles, the shotgun over her shoulder as if she were a hunter out for a casual day's quail shooting. When I called to her she turned her head slowly as if I were an unwelcome intruder.

'Verve, you okay. We leave now, right?'

She ran out to the wagon. I ran, feeling the Smith and Wesson bruising some muscles in my back. Stuff it.

Slamming the wagon into gear I started moving, slowly. Telltale dust would be just as bad as a glint of metal. In the undergrowth beneath the trees I reversed quickly over some low foliage, and then rocked over a small ditch and into the thicker foliage beyond. Dust rose around me. I had only just stopped and turned off the motor when I heard their motors die and several doors slam. Their dust came over the house and mingled with the dust I had stirred.

To arrive like that they must have either known they would be welcomed, or have known the house was empty. I stepped out of the wagon, opened the back door and looked at the launcher. It was so covered in wrapping and grease it would be at least half an hour before I would have it close to firing . . . if I knew how to load it. I didn't expect to find a book of firing instructions in that little lot, but I had pulled apart enough firearms to have a general idea. I looked at Verve watching me.

She shook her head. 'I think Charlie was killed by the stuff being tested by the Americans in the jungle.'

'You mean by mistake?' I asked, as I watched the house for movement. I'd read about the Americans testing their new technology. It was the night-fighting lasers and radar that enabled them to move in darkness, with digital vision displaying the jungle and its occupants on a pulsing screen over their eyes. Every infantry man was a hi-tech warrior. His vision could even be broadcast to his command centre for analysis.

'Not by mistake,' she said. 'Charlie said the Americans wanted the birds, too.'

'Which Americans?'

'I don't know. He just said some heavy security people thought birds were better than drugs.'

I kept an eye on the house. I certainly didn't want to get caught by Angela. 'When we're away from here,' I said, meaning tell me later.

I crept back to the first bank of low shrub. I counted six intruders. They checked the house first, and then returned to the vehicles for cans of flammable fluid. I saw Angela walk over to the aviary, stop to look at the damage to the doors. She closed the doors leaning a shoulder to it as she worked the lever. She turned around, stood on the loading dock and looked directly towards us. I almost flinched away. Some people do have a sixth sense, but most refuse to recognise their ability. I hoped she was one of those.

She was certainly a stylish woman. She had her arms folded, but one leg was relaxed apart from the other in the way of a ballet dancer resting. Her jeans were a snug fit, and she had a black T-shirt under a light jacket. Her hair fell in thick waves down either side of her face. When it encroached too far she flicked it back with a toss of the head or a hand.

She looked up and I followed her gaze. High in a thermal were two wedged-tailed eagles. Giant birds, their wingspan making about 4 metres across, they had an eyesight that could watch me watch the others. Did they see me as hunter or hunted? As a kid I had been hunting in the bush when the ground in front of me moved into the air. Its cry was like a screaming cat. The bird had been feeding on a wallaby. I had a twelve gauge over my shoulder but I didn't move. The magnificence thrilled me. I doubt I would have shot it even if it had attacked me. As it rose in the air I saw that stray feathers gave it an untidy look. What else could you expect from high altitude winds or silent drops from the heavens at over 160 kilometres an hour? Now an egg from these beauties was worth tens of thousands of dollars. According to Charlie, the thing most collectors didn't realise, was that there were still thousands of the birds in the mountains of New Guinea. Not as rare as was imagined.

I dropped my eyes from the soaring flight of the eagles and saw Angela walking towards me.

I didn't move. Should I step out from concealment and claim the comradeship of a similar journey: looking for her husband's killers? Or should I grab her as a hostage to guarantee our safely leaving the area?

I needn't have worried. A voice called that everything was set, and she walked back around the house. I could smell the fuel. I walked backwards to my vehicle. If the explosion reached the stand of trees we would still be protected. Verve and I covered our faces.

The two buildings went up with an explosion that no-one would have expected. The heat scorched through the windshield as I started the wagon. But the trees didn't catch. Christ, it could have been one of those fires left over from the Gulf War. It had that look of permanence. I moved the wagon back to the very edge of the stand of trees. The intense heat might just atomise the fuel in the engine's delivery system, and we'd be stuck for an hour or two. Still be here when the help arrived from nearby properties.

Leaving the wagon I walked to the south of the stand to watch Angela and her crew driving down the track. Ten minutes later we pulled out and headed south, and the long drive back to Cairns. The outback is not a good place to hide unless you have the camping gear and a well-concealed destination. People who live 80 kilometres apart tend to note all movements they see, and they use choppers to round up their wayward stock. Anyway, I felt like swimming pools and cool bars. I had lost the country habit. I didn't have to be around fires anymore, didn't have to stay to fight them.

Fires could be a sickness. You woke in the early morning feeling the intense heat and the low humidity and knew this was a day you would fight fires. You didn't want to leave your bed. You rounded up all your stock though, and brought them into holding yards. You cleaned the guttering out, stuffed the down drains with tennis balls or socks, filled the gutters with water, along with the sink, the hand basin and bath; checked the water pump to make sure the protective hood was clear of debris and that the power lines would be the last to burn; and then sat down to a salad lunch and waited. Even if there was a clear blue sky, by noon you could smell that acrid hint of smoke in the air. And then the fire radio crackled into life in the kitchen and you were living one of those days from hell.

Charlie's boat had obviously been taken out with something. Despite Verve thinking it was an American navy thing I still opted for the launcher. But being Charlie he would have seen it spiralling in with its smoking exhaust, and taken to the drink. Imagining he was still going to live, the shock wave from a missile would have been beyond his experience. He would have died thinking he still had a chance.

Bird smugglers had used to be, according to Charlie, just a whole bunch of freelancers doing their own thing. But with rocket launchers involved, and more deaths among smugglers than the creatures they were smuggling, it was obvious there were serious criminals wanting to control the industry.

It occurred to me that Alex Klima was not the type. He had the rage all right, but his style was too cramped. The real boss wouldn't have attacked me and wouldn't have run;, would have prolonged a game of teasing deceit. Klima had chopped off the playing too early. He was only imitating someone else.

And what was his relationship to Angela and her late husband?

I looked across at Verve. She was back listening to Ry Cooder, her eyes closed.

'They had a laboratory in there,' I gestured back to the direction of the property.

She sat forward in her seat. 'Charlie mentioned there were experiments.'

'What sort of experiments?'

'He laughed about it. They wouldn't have to smuggle eggs at all. They'd smuggle bits of the birds, and implant them later over there, in other eggs, or test tubes or something.'

'You mean cross parrots with chooks, stuff like that.'

The image of that caught her. She began to laugh. One of those nervous sounds, close to hysteria, that can be triggered by the poorest joke—if you've just been scared to death.

'Where's there?'

'Somewhere in California,' she giggled. 'God, why am I doing this?' she managed.

'He didn't say exactly where?'

'Noooo,' she groaned. A wild burst of laughter had her writhing again. I caught her laughter for a moment.

Every new thing we discovered altered the possible scenarios I carried in my head. The state-of-the-art lab, the US navy testing new equipment in the rainforests, the rocket launcher possibly linking them with Klima, the navy possibly killing Charlie. I had to make sense of those links. I hated to be burdened by unanswered questions.

Verve was quiet now. I thought of the Nut Sucker, his head turning away from his severed throat like a grotesque imitation of a carnival's row of laughing clowns. 'Why did you kill the Nut Sucker?' I asked. She burst into shrieks of laughter again, rocking around in her seat. It could as easily have been tears.

It was a long-delayed question because I had been trying out various ways of approaching it. Now I waited for her to answer me. After several kilometres her laughter subsided.

'He had it coming.' She jacked her seat up. 'It's not something I want to think about.'

'Charlie taught you how to do it, didn't he?'

'Yes. But I used to help Dad with the killing on the farm. It wasn't like that though. You just cut smoothly, you didn't strike.'

'Did you ever see Charlie do that?'

'No, he showed me after he had been drinking one night.'

'Was he expecting trouble? You know, the serious stuff, killings?'

'I don't know.' The voice was petulant, something I would have expected from a young girl.

'We're right in this now. I have to know it all.'

'We were talking. He wanted to show me how to protect myself.'

'Talking about what?'

She turned a level look at me. 'I was raped. I was raped out there.'

'And Charlie wasn't around?'

'No, he wasn't.'

'Did he revenge that?' Charlie was a romantic. I knew the rage he must have felt.

'No. That piece of shit we killed was a part of it.'

We travelled in silence; my mind was rapid with speculations. Behind that was a growing feeling of confidence I knew I shouldn't have. I couldn't place it for a while. Then it struck me that the launcher in the back seat was like a security blanket. I stopped and hid it in the hollow trunk of a tree, jamming it down, feeling the plastic rip.

'Tell me why Charlie would have been killed by the navy?' I said, when I swung back into the cabin.

'I don't know. He saw them, that's all.'

'Where did he see them?'

'Where he was found I guess?'

'You spoke to him?'

'He had a mobile.'

'So he was in the jungle there when he saw them?'

'Yeah.'

I looked at her. 'You could help me with this,' I said.

'Well I s'pose he was in the jungle.'

'Come on. He didn't just ring you and tell you nothing.'

'He said they had cut inland for several kilometres. They seemed to know where the birds were.'

'So Charlie grabbed the birds and took off in the boat?'

'I s'pose,' she said.

'Fuck this,' I said. I was angry that she hadn't taken any steps with me, angry she wasn't giving anything.

'Look,' she said, bringing both hands down hard on the dashboard in front of her. 'I know I should have known how it was going but I was enjoying myself and not seeing what was happening. Really dumb.'

'Hey, you're seeing how it was now. You can help, for Christsake.'

'It's too big now,' she said. 'I can't believe how big. And I'm scared of being squashed.' She began to reassemble her emotions and compose her face, leaning back, breathing deeply.

'We're going to find out how big,' I said. 'They must have seen the boat though . . . if they landed on the beach.'

'He would have had it up the creek. Near the old abattoir. Well it's a river sometimes. During the rains.'

I could see Charlie making his move, creeping down to the bay and opening the boat up, risking as much as he had when he killed the pirate on his way to Japan. It was just that a cigarette boat isn't as fast as a heat-seeking missile.

Chapter 10

Close to Cairns I looked across at Verve. It was a shock. I tried to stop the surge of feeling for her. The affection, the love, was irrational. The effects spread like wind across water, filling every part of me. I didn't care what she had done or who she was. Even the despatching of the Nut Sucker was only a small problem for me. The real hurdle was that I knew she didn't have any real regard for me and, because of this, I could never trust her completely. It was intimacy with an unknown force.

Winding down on the road to the town I watched several jets coming in over the mountains, like giant toys held hovering over a toy city. Great swathes of sugarcane country swept to the north. To the south, the huge river mouth where the American warships were anchored. My only path to the secrets they held was through Marshall. Or was he simply a parasite feeding off them? Using their personnel as instruments to take an entrepreneur's hold on the illegal bird trade.

I began re-examining my motives for being here, simply because, on the one hand I wanted to leave this town, with Verve, immediately, and, on the other, I wanted to finish those responsible for Charlie's death. It felt right that I should be here causing trouble.

I needed to talk to Verve before we descended into Cairns. I put on a Miles Davis tape and shook her gently. She woke and looked across at me, smiling. She grimaced when she saw we were back in Cairns.

'This is how it is,' I said. 'There's Klima; there's Marshall, and what appears to be his personal navy, and Angela. And the cops. We know some are flirting with the others because they think the others may be better organised or have better resources. That's how I see it. Do you see anymore than that?'

'Doesn't give us much of a chance,' she said. I had hoped she'd be more forthcoming.

We were running through the small farms on the edge of town. There was poverty here like anywhere else. The cane's lushness disguised it.

'We can't take the high ground here and go to the press, because we're in too deep ourselves.'

'So?' she said.

'It's not going to be easy,' I said, feeling as if I was speculating to myself. She stretched in her seat as if I had suggested a holiday away from it all.

My motel was still there, something of a surprise. I had half expected that Angela would have removed all trace of Verve and myself. I wondered if Angela may have even fired the place for Klima, if they were now working together.

The receptionist was as congenial as ever. 'We're supposed to ring the police the moment you arrive,' she said.

'Feel free,' I said. Verve gave a look at the ceiling.

She giggled. 'What have you been doing?' she asked Verve with a look of heavy significance that ended in a grin.

'Not enough,' I said. 'Could you give me a few minutes? A call to make.'

From my room I called Angela's hotel and was told she was out for the day. I told them I would speak to the room number. No answer. Not even a flunkey to take care of messages. She must have been moving as fast as we were.

I rang reception. 'You could tell the cops we're back now.'

'Why do that?' Verve asked.

'Show them that we're not trying to hide anything.'

They arrived ten minutes later. I watched them from our window. I could see Updine's replacement knew he was out of his depth. He was nervous and obviously wanted to assault everyone he saw approaching him in the motel courtyard. He was having nightmares over knife-wielding kooris.

Finally he knocked loudly on my door.

'It's open,' I called, and he stepped in with his two companions.

I saw he had his hand on the gun tucked into a holster under his cotton coat, but when he saw me in a chair with a drink, he pretended he was tugging at some clothing. He was a big, solid man with fading red hair and a face that had been crisped by the sun. His head was blunt and tough, the lips sort of numb-looking and immobile. He said he was detective inspector Albert March, and that he wanted me to go with him to police headquarters to be interviewed.

'You can do it here,' I said.

'Get your coat, mate. We're going.'

'Are you arresting me?'

'I'll think about it,' he answered.

'I'll go if you're arresting me, otherwise I stay.'

Verve walked into the room from the bathroom dressed in some very understated and elegant gear that showed the promise of her more than the substance, and the cops were moved to wariness.

March asked me where I'd been, as if the answer might be the only reason he would need to arrest me.

'The hinterland,' I answered. 'Touring around, looking at the country.'

'You and that American's wife get together?'

'No,' I said. 'I did talk to the American ambassador about Truman, but I couldn't help him.'

He signalled his two juniors to leave. They were completely uninterested in proceedings, but found their dignity had been injured by the request. They weren't going to get anything out of all this except work, but a cop's dignity is all he's got.

'We don't want to know about the American ambassador,' he said. This meant Marshall was using his influence.

'He's here to sort things out for the wife?'

'I wouldn't mention you've spoken to him,' he said, the threat contained only in the information. He hadn't bothered with a threatening tone. 'What he's doing is none of your bloody business.'

'Is it yours?' I asked.

He was looking around the room, walking with his knuckles resting on the backs of his hips. His glance at Verve totally deferential. 'We don't know anything about that.' It was obvious he didn't want to know either. He changed the subject. 'Exactly where have you been?'

'Looking at the birds in the rainforest, talking to birdwatchers. Well, they said they were birdwatchers.'

'What were their names?'

'Now just wait a minute,' I said. 'I don't have to answer any questions here. I'm only telling you this to put you in the picture, right? I'm doing you a favour.' Then I walked close to him and held his elbow. I could feel his tension. 'You don't have to tell me about the ambassador,' I said. 'But if he's in this, just nod your head.' He nodded his head. I had caught him with a gesture. I had done the male to male thing: let's get straight about things out of earshot of women. I felt I knew redneck Queenslanders because I had grown up with redneck Victorians.

He sat down in front of the dressing table, the mirror reflecting the back of his head. He looked at me, rubbing his hands as if they were cold. He got up and walked over to the window and gestured me to follow him. 'Excuse us,' he said to Verve. He put a hand on my shoulder as he whispered. 'These birds are worth several billion dollars a year in business.' He spoke soberly. The figure impressed him. 'If you want to be safe, you co-operate. Do you understand me?'

I spoke with his whisper. 'I thought it was the other way around; you know; co-operate and you're dead. And the billions sounds like bullshit anyway.'

He looked at me sadly. He'd found a know-all: still, he knew how to deal with them.

'Whose estimate is that?' I asked, to postpone his thoughts of violence.

He glanced at Verve and continued his confidential whisper. 'Some wildlife people have been watching certain areas of the rainforests and bushlands, noting the number of eggs and birds disappearing, and figuring the same is happening all over the country.' He had been impressed with whoever had given him the information, for his voice had taken on a lecturer's cadence. 'We have very rare birds here, and overseas collectors are hungry. Even the mid-range birds are worth $25 000 a piece. These prices are downplayed in case it encourages people to take up the job.'

He was so impressed with all this information he had needed to tell someone about it—even someone he disliked.

'But that's not money we're losing, right,' I said. 'If there was no smuggling there'd be no money anyway.'

'It's the birds and animals,' he said without emphasis. The birds and animals were the last thing on his mind.

'So why is the ambassador up here from the capital?'

'No idea,' he said.

'You don't really want to solve this one, do you?'

That pissed him off. I understood. He had to go through the motions. If he found someone he could land with some charges, fine. But if not, don't worry. The government imagined a lot of that money was going directly back into the economy. The whole bloody state of Queensland, and a good portion of New South Wales, could look healthy with that sort of money being spent. It was the same with drug money. Queensland had a booming economy, helped by small farmers and their secret plantations.

'You've got a choice,' he said. 'You can come along now without any trouble, or we can kick your arse.'

I leaned towards him, looking for his eyes. Charlie could do this stuff magnificently. 'I deal in information,' I said. 'I'm not a player in the game. I sell information.'

He was scornful. 'Information? You call racecourse bullshit information?'

I couldn't not argue with him. 'Look, if you know certain trainers don't put electrolytes—minerals and vitamins—into the veins of their horses and the day is going to be hot and muggy, you don't back their horses. That's what I call acting on real information.'

'So what have ya got on the birds?'

'I don't have the slightest interest in bird smuggling.' He didn't believe me.'

'Your mate, did,' he accused. 'And now you're here.' He stepped back now, including Verve in the conversation.

'Hey, he owed me money.'

'Ah yeah,' he said. 'They told me. The successful gambler, and that's gotta be a bloody contradiction in some way.'

'So, part of gambling works this way: If I give you a horse to back you put some money on for me.'

'Which means what, in this case?'

'I'm not one of those to be charged.'

'It won't be up to me.'

'Like hell it won't. You're doing the leg work; you don't even have to mention me.'

'Hey, names can get handed down from above. What can I do about that?'

'You and I don't have a deal then. It's that simple.'

He smiled at me. 'But I know you're the sort of bloke who makes deals,' he said.

I smiled at him. 'You don't, you know,' I said.

He stood up, stiffly, and walked to the window to peruse the courtyard, changed his mind and headed for the door. He was almost upright when he reached it. 'I'll probably get most of the information I want without making any deals at all. If I don't, we could probably talk.' He gave Verve a shifty look, as if he hadn't wanted her to hear such dirty politics.

'I don't think so,' I said. 'You probably won't be around that long.' I hadn't meant to say it. He had been confused by us, uncertain of his moves, but he knew a threat when he heard it.

He was back to me in two strides. 'Don't try and fuck with my head,' he warned. 'I'm ahead of you already, mate. You have no idea the stew you're cooking in right now.'

His face was nasty, the lips sneering and the head thrust forward like a fighting cock levelling for balance before it lunged with spurs.

'Hell, you're fucking with your own head. I don't even have to help it along.'

He was unsure whether to call his friends back and have me for resisting arrest, but I saw him calculate that I wasn't Aboriginal or a derelict, and that some smart arse lawyer would appear from the south to take care of me.

In the doorway he said, 'I feel sorry for you.'

'Yeah,' I said. 'It's hard being on the side of justice.' I think my words were lost in the banging of the door.

'You sound like you know what you're doing,' Verve said, doubtfully.

I realised how glad I was he hadn't come with a search warrant, or if he had, that he hadn't remembered it. Police on the take always forget the basics, figuring they don't need them.

I checked the Smith and Wesson, emptied the bullets, spun the cylinder and reloaded. I tossed the gun to Verve. She caught it casually. 'Who taught you about weapons?' I asked.

'My father,' she said. 'He was a gun freak.'

'We're moving,' I said. 'I want a hotel where the cops feel uncomfortable just crossing the lobby.'

Outside the evening was beautiful. The tropics were for nightlife. Not the night sleaze of tourism, where drunks roam the city looking for anything at all to shift the loneliness from themselves. Not one car followed us for more than a block.

'Did Charlie ever make any runs with his eggs?'

'No,' she said.

'Did he ever have airline tickets to anywhere? You'd remember that wouldn't you?'

'Jesus he'd never smuggle birds by commercial airline.'

'Why not? Too dangerous?' I laughed.

'There's so much to do. You've got to keep them alive. They dehydrate in a plane. In the toilet you have to give them water with an eye dropper. If you put them out the anaesthetic kills half of them. They only take small amounts compared to anything else. Not even the vets can calculate it. And stuffing them in those small plastic pipes is inhuman.'

'Have you done it?'

'No, but Charlie asked around. He wanted to find out if it was viable early on.'

We took a room in a hotel complex that looked out over the sea. Verve hardly commented. At her age I hadn't been able to afford luxury at all. It made me wonder.

It was in fact a great place. The sofa was overstuffed and, in the style of a chaise lounge, could accommodate a passionate couple. The walls had prints of traditional oils that had been painted in the late nineteenth century for the tastes of southern graziers. Flocks of plump beasts being shorn or herded through rolling country by a hearty stockman with a whip over the shoulder. The carpet was good enough to fuck on without hurting knees or buttocks, and the wallpaper was pastel and mild enough to be by Laura someone. In fact nothing that would challenge comfort, physical or mental, in any way at all.

'The food can be good here.' Verve said. 'In the dining room. I hate room service stuff. It's straight microwaved glub.'

'You've been here before?' I asked.

'Of course,' she answered.

'Okay, the dining-room,' I said.

She shrugged on a dark jacket and walked to the door. In the lift she swayed against me briefly.

In the lobby I said, 'Why don't we eat Thai tonight? Give the hotel a miss.' She nodded and walked across the foyer to the entrance. I was a few steps behind. For some reason I was aware she took the suggestion as a command, one she welcomed.

Several men looked at her face as they walked into the hotel. I'm lucky, I told myself. But I didn't have that feeling. On the track I always made my own luck.

The doorman flagged a cab. Verve's hip was against mine, and once she rested her head on my shoulder. Small gestures that tend to inflame those who are not familiar with intimacy. The Thai restaurant was crowded but the walls cocooned the sound, so our conversation was only for our table. I had chosen an outside restaurant because I didn't want her to feel she had a quick refuge in the hotel room from the questions I wanted to ask.

'I found four bodies buried in the aviary,' I said. 'Do you know anything about them?'

'Charlie told me there had been a massacre there,' she said easily. I didn't say anything. But it certainly explained Klima's troops running off. They probably thought they'd be next. I looked around the restaurant. Finally I looked at her. 'Why?'

'Charlie thought Klima was going to cut him out. He hired some people.'

'Hey, if Charlie was hiring people he'd win. He was a meticulous bastard. It doesn't make sense.'

'He put them up there to look after things. Those were the four you found. When he couldn't contact them he ran.' She hesitated a moment. 'He didn't tell me he would run. He didn't want me with him.'

'Lucky for you,' I said. I took her hand. 'Can't you just tell me these things all in one hit? I mean we could save a lot of time.'

She removed her hand. 'I don't want to know about some things,' she said. 'And I tell you about them when they come to me.' She flicked her eyes as tears formed. She then looked over my shoulder, and forced her eyes to dryness. Finally she breathed deeply the way you do when you're about to plunge into icy waters.

'Klima raped me and left me with the others.'

I couldn't bring myself to look at the waiter when she came to the table asking for our choices. Verve had to suggest more time.

I said, 'I hadn't realised Charlie had sunk low enough to compromise other people with bastards like that.'

'You don't just dip your toes in,' she said. 'You know that. I don't have to tell you, for Christsake.' She was angry.

'Did he work with Klima after that?'

'Of course. He cooled down. I just didn't go there again.'

She was leaning back with a glass in one hand, supporting her elbow with the other. Her brilliant purple red lipstick gave her a vampish look that was too old for the rest of her features.

'Now how about Truman?' I said. 'Did you screw him too?'

She banged her wine glass down. The stem broke and it spilled, but she didn't give it a look. 'You bastard,' she said. 'I didn't screw the others. I had no fucking say in it. Do you understand . . . you fucking idiot?'

The waiter was mopping the wine and Verve could hardly cope with her rage.

'Hey, I didn't mean it,' I said. The waiter left for another glass.

'You bloody meant it. I'd like to see you out there as a woman. There'd be no swanning around pulling those dumb acts of yours. By Christ I'd know what you'd be. You'd be sitting at home with the first prick who asked you.'

We silently and mutually agreed to leave the restaurant.

Warm rain fell out of the sky as we walked from the restaurant. As we waited for the cab, I saw an ugly creature looking at Verve's ankle. It had moved out from a stand of cane near the tea tree fence close to the door. A huge cane toad, squatting, looking as if it might take her foot in its mouth. 'Move away,' I said. 'They've got poison glands behind the head.'

When she saw it she let out a kick with her high-heeled sandals, catching its soft neck. It hit the fence with the solidness of football and didn't move. 'I hate the bloody things,' she said.

Queensland kids play a sort of baseball with cane toads, a species that had been introduced to the country to take care of the beetle that ate the sugarcane. Now toads were spreading right across the country, killing anything that fed on them, and taking the food of the small mammals, many of which were close to extinction. Klima was obviously a genetic descendant.

I put my arm around her in the cab back to the hotel. 'Hey, come on,' I said. 'You weren't telling me anything.'

Her shoulders stiffened. I removed my arm.

At the hotel we decided to eat. The food moved into my stomach like a healing balm. Verve appeared to be at ease now, something I didn't understand. She could do this, throw away her anxiety without talking about it or resolving it.

We went up to the room and she entered and stepped back to let me in. I walked to the window to look over the bay. Verve was in the bathroom for a while, and when she came out I saw she had brushed her hair and had freshened her lipstick. Her perfume was a musky fragrance.

She walked over to me and I found the desire of my youth. Neither worried about how our clothes came off as long as it was fast.

Naked on the bed there was a hesitation, she seemed to want to cover herself with a quick turn of her leg. I wasn't sure whether it was to tease me, but I held back, needing to know exactly how it was all happening, not wanting to force anything. I looked at her face and saw she was in her own world, teasing herself.

Later there was a quick knock at the door. I was out of bed in a moment. As I walked to the door I discovered I was holding the Smith and Wesson in front of my testicles. I took a deep breath and moved it away.

'Who is it?' I asked.

'Angela.'

I grabbed a hotel gown and opened the door.

Angela was about to barge in, following the opening door like a bull at the edge of a cape, but she stopped up short.

'Oh, I'm sorry.' She was looking at Verve who was walking naked to the bathroom.

'It's all right,' I said. 'I'm back.'

She still wasn't sure. 'It's not that important,' she said, but her gestures assured me she wasn't about to leave. Her style rivalled that of a buccaneer, so it was impossible to have her go away. Some people have the ability to force issues, influence others. It's labelled charisma, but the word is inadequate. Charlie had once had the same magic.

She called through the bathroom door, asking Verve if Klima had contacted her.

'No, why would he?' Verve called back. 'He wouldn't even know I was here. I mean, he doesn't really know me.'

'Whether he does or not,' Angela said, quite prepared to gloss over the fact she was calling Verve's word into doubt, 'he'll be trying to contact you over the next few days.'

'Time for her to leave,' I said.

Angela looked at me as if I were mad. 'She's quite safe here.' She sat down in one of the stiff-backed leather chairs.

'I think none of us are safe if Klima knows where to find us,' I said.

There was the tiniest flinching in her face.

'Why would he bother looking for any of us?' Verve asked, returning in some of the clothes she had worn to dinner. She was playing the game she had played with me. She sat down at the ornate iron-lace table near the window.

'Because one of his places has been torched,' I said.

Angela was amazing. She looked at me straight and cool; the sort of glance that said, really, tell me more, that's interesting. I almost imagined she had a twin sister, and she was being kept in the dark about the dreadful goings-on.

'I saw it go up,' I said.

Verve broke through the gaze I had levelled at Angela. 'You, didn't do it, did you?' Verve asked Angela. I looked at her.

'No,' she said.

'Well, whoever it was, destroyed a lot of evidence.'

'What sort of evidence?' she asked.

'Enough to enable the cops to link everyone in with bird racketeering and murder, just stuff like that.'

'It sounds as if it may have been quite deliberate,' Angela said. She pushed her loose sleeves up her slim arms and grasped one knee in both hands.

'I don't really know,' I said.

'How far away were you?'

'Not much more than a hundred metres.'

She leaned back in her chair, one arm shifting to lie along the back of it. Angela's searching look was from someone who was completely curious. There was no hint of panic, fear, or doubt: if she had been seen it was only another small problem to be surmounted.

'Who lit the fire?' she asked.

'You did,' I said.

'I see,' she said looking down at her crossed legs. 'What did we destroy?'

'The aviary of course, the cool store, the laboratory, the house, which contained so many blood stains Klima would have been arrested on suspicion of running a death camp there, and all the clues to how the four people died who are buried beneath the ruins of the aviary.'

'But the bodies are still there?'

I leaned against the wall near the bar and crossed my legs at the ankles. 'You were in a hell of a hurry,' I said.

'I needed a bargaining position. The newly arrived widow in town doesn't exactly pack a lot of fire power. They need to know I have endless resources; that I am not going to wait around listening to crap. I can stay here as long as I like, and make it as hard as I want for everyone.'

I didn't believe her. It was a reasonable scenario. One I had thought over myself. But the words came from a person who was geared to roll over everything. She was a glossy little power plant. She wouldn't have needed such a gesture, her presence would have been enough. She would have known that.

'Yeah, well I think you probably did them a favour. They all left the day before, for good. Have you spoken with Klima?' To my mind she had set fire to Klima's place to cover for him, to hide evidence.

'Yes,' she said.

'Are you with Klima now? Or are you with Marshall and his mercenaries?'

'You've come a long way,' she said.

'Do we cut the bullshit now?' I asked, suddenly hoping that she may have all the answers.

'I'm not with anyone,' she said.

'So why is Marshall up here? He's supposed to be investigating your husband's death.'

'Truman's family wanted that.'

'He knows nothing about the birds, wants to know nothing?'

'Only as far as it links with Truman's death. He doesn't *want* the birds, if that's what you mean.'

It was then I felt something was about to happen. I've always placed faith in my sixth sense, purely because I know it to be a tangible thing.

Verve had been silent. She was either in awe of Angela, or she wasn't prepared to reach conclusions. She walked to the window, her arms folded, like a kid who has decided not to participate in adult conversation.

Angela rose to move to the bar, the folds of her linen dress parting slightly along the length of her leg. It didn't happen again. Did she know how to use the effect, by taking an extra broad step, or had it been just something that happened? It seemed important to find out.

I was so restless I stood up and walked into the bathroom. As I was about to shut the door the hall door burst open, and two men walked into the room with automatic weapons. I hadn't turned on the light, and I was invisible to them, even when they moved fully into my view as they crossed the room. The two women said nothing. I couldn't see their response because they were beyond my angle of vision.

One of the weapons was flicked from side to side, directing the women in the casual way of a stockman working a cattle dog. I would have liked to have seen Angela's reaction to that. My heart began a life of its own. I thought I was cool, but it began running as though my blood were adrenalin.

I stood up on the bath. As the first of the men passed close to the door I stepped down quickly, whacking his hand with the Smith and Wesson, the weapon dropping to the floor. I stood behind him, my arm around his chest. I had him as a shield to cover the second gunman. To get at me he would have to shoot his mate. The prospect of that seemed to bewilder him.

The bastard I held began to regain his balance. I whacked him with the butt behind the ear and he slumped heavily forward across my arm, leaving my chest exposed. I could barely hold him. I didn't take my eyes from the second man and pretended my exposed chest wasn't important. He was young, anxious to shoot, but with the brains to know he was safe if he did the right thing. 'Down,' I said. 'The gun. Down.' My voice was on a dead level tone. I glanced at Angela, for a moment thinking there might be serious danger there. She had positioned herself behind a standard lamp, as if it might deflect bullets. Verve was breathing through parted lips. As he placed the gun on the carpet I moved to within a metre of him. 'On your knees,' I said, flicking the hand gun downwards. As he kneeled I kicked him under the jaw, dropped the burden, and picked up the second gun, a silenced Glock 9 mm. The weapon surprised me with its weightlessness. Much of it made of plastic, it was an innovation in hand guns.

The second gun man showed signs of waking again and I whacked him solidly behind the neck. His nerves responded as if he had been lying doggo and his feet began to flutter.

'You know these two?' I asked both women. I ran quickly to the door and opened it a shade. Two of Angela's people were lying in a small alcove away from the door. They looked dead but I didn't have time for a second glance.

'I think we should all get out of here,' I said.

'I'm staying,' Angela said. I stuffed the Glock in my waistband on my right side. The Smith and Wesson I tucked in the back, the base of the butt upwards and facing the way my right hand would come to draw. It might seem awkward but that way you didn't have to turn the weapon away from your body as it came around your side. It was pull, point and fire.

I walked to the door, and Verve followed me. 'What about Angela?' she said.

'I think she'll be fine,' I said, looking at Angela. 'She has some serious influence here.'

'What do you mean?' Angela asked.

'That ambassador mate of yours only has to show up, and whatever you say will be believed. I know these Queensland cops.'

'But these people were looking for you.'

'How do you know? What you're going to find is your people dead or bashed out here in the corridor, so you're going to be the focus of all this. They'll think it was the same people who blasted Truman.'

'I'll tell them about you,' she said. She was angry, pointing at me as if I was her enemy.

'They know about me,' I said.

Outside the door two women and a man were warily approaching what they could only see were two pairs of feet poking from the alcove. They looked at me as I emerged with Verve into the hall. I had an expression of wonder on my face. The two former bodyguards had the looks of stressed puffer fish. One face looked vaguely familiar. They had been garrotted, the fencing wire corkscrewed together at the backs of their necks. 'I'll tell them downstairs,' I said as I headed past the group to the elevator. They didn't look at us, and would probably forget our presence.

In the lobby I casually bought a newspaper, looked around the paperback shelves for one of those little masterpieces that grow there occasionally, and then walked out into the night. We were two blocks away, walking easily, when the first police car flashed by, without a siren. An unusual approach for a police car.

The only time a siren wasn't used for an emergency was on a covert raid. Or did they know what they were supposed to find?

We manoeuvred around the streets, window shopping, taking direct or reflected looks at just about everyone in the area. After negotiating several alleyways quickly I felt comfortable that no-one was following us.

We walked down to a small hotel on the seafront that catered for bus tours, and booked in. Our room looked over the tidal mudflats, but I didn't watch them for too long. Verve put her arms around me and unbuckled my belt. When I turned she backed away and pulled the curtains closed. For a moment I felt a fatigue that frightened me. She sat on my lap and rubbed her breasts across my face. 'I feel safe with you,' she said. I picked her up and laid her on the bed.

Moving inside her, my face locked to her neck, I felt myself grow smaller. She was away already. It wouldn't have mattered whether I was there or not, or who was making love to her. I pushed myself up on my arms, away from her. She had turned her face away from me. 'Look at me,' I demanded, and tilted her face up although her eyes were closed. Her lost face was so enticing I began strengthening again. She opened her eyes and smiled just before the spasms hit her and her face crunched down as though she was being hurt.

Chapter 11

I woke, rang for coffee and the morning paper and checked the hand guns. Weapons have a soothing effect on me. Genuine serial killers have sexual excitement when they hold a weapon.

When room service knocked I asked them to leave it in the hall and sat off to the right of the door for five minutes. Enough time for any gunman to lose his cool and try and kick the door down. I opened the door, the gun close to my head as I leaned out. The hallway was empty. I placed the gun on the tray and backed through the door. I poured the coffee but Verve only grunted at my offer.

Nothing about last night's violence. Angela's diplomatic contacts had either stopped the story, or the police hadn't reported it to their press liaison group.

I glanced over the political stories. Nothing but rhetoric. I put the form guide to one side. Even a quick glance at it would take me away from the trouble I was in and that was dangerous. A feeling of dread sat under my ribs, that feeling of inevitability that tends to stop people planning or fighting.

Verve finally woke beside me. She lifted a smooth leg and slid it across me. I ignored her. She sat on me. 'Lick my breasts,' she said. 'Suck them.' She rose over me and I slipped my hands around the back of her thighs as she threw her head back, arching against me. 'Let me,' she said, as she sank her sliding warmth down and around, smiling at me, showing me I was doing what she wanted.

Later I swept aside the curtains expecting to see the mudflats, but I was stunned by the vast high tide, glistening silver in the morning light. Off to the north some mangroves edged into the water. Clouds were low on the horizon, but standing close to the glass I could already feel the heat building outside.

As I was about to shower I glanced at the paper on the floor and a story on page seven caught me. A man had hung himself in a hotel shower recess. The name enlivened me. Les Strachey. I would have recognised him last night but for the bloated physiognomy. A notorious Sydney underworld figure, according to the tabloids. And he was. An efficient little hit man who worked for Esben Robe, another notorious Sydney underworld figure, who was untouched by the law because he ploughed his money into a variety of legitimate businesses. I didn't believe Strachey had suddenly gone freelance. No-one left the employ of Robe unless Robe wished it, and there was a sort of permanence to their leaving. Strachey as Angela's bodyguard meant only one thing. She had Robe's backing. And one thing I could predict from that was a bloodbath. Robe was used to annihilating his colleagues, taking over their businesses, their criminal environments. I wondered how his involvement tied in with Marshall's. An Australian crook against a representative of the most powerful warrior nation in the world? Or were they working together?

Robe had been a large meat exporter at one time. Almost ruined a good portion of Australia's meat exports with his meat-substitution rackets. Was he also behind Klima?

My mind began to play with these questions. I had thought Robe was only Sydney based, but his tentacles obviously reached this far. Bigtime criminals all gravitate towards slaughterhouses in one way or another. There is more crime in an abattoir than any other single place in town. Drugs in carcases; meat-substitution rackets: kangaroo meat replaces prime beef; more dealing in drugs and stolen goods than in any bar; meat inspectors bribed; and plain outright theft and marketing of meat, hides, vehicles and possessions.

Robe was involved in everything. Illegal gaming, prostitution, drugs, stolen goods, and very straightforward protection rackets. He even dabbled in the arts. Apart from investing in theatre and movies, he purchased paintings and sculptures, and befriended down-at-heel writers and poets. He was personable, and loved to taunt artists and writers about their inability to fend for themselves. He often advised the recipients of his grants how to invest the money for continuing benefit. This way, he had ensured, on his demise he would be more famous than Gough Whitlam. Maybe even Ned Kelly. After all, there were many underworld slayings marked down to him personally. Apparently he loved to kill.

This was deep tidal mud. Wading through it changed my whole approach to our survival. Robe had enough power and influence to have a blanket solution thrown over his problems, once he had discovered the extent of them. He rarely acted hastily and, he didn't leave untidy ends capable of talking.

I walked into the bathroom and read the story to Verve. I told her about Esben Robe. She was dismissive.

'I've never heard of him,' she said. The young can always delude themselves into imagining they are safe because they are emotionally satisfied and alive.

'So, what does that mean?'

'Go on,' she said.

'When you think of crime in Australia, you think of Robe.'

She didn't reply at first. 'What can we do?'

'Nothing I can think of, except look after ourselves. Disappear.' I was giving her a chance. My instinct was to stay in the game.

'Impossible.'

'Have you got a better idea?' I asked.

Verve stepped out of the shower and wrapped herself in a large towel. 'We should talk to him.'

'Well, we have been in a way. He's obviously hitting it off with Angela. Anything we've said to her as gone to him.'

She looked away from the mirror. 'I remember Truman saying his wife looked after the American side of the business.'

'I think you know more than you're letting on,' I said. 'Why are there so many killings if the birds no longer exist? Or are there little bits of them in a freezer somewhere? The laboratory at Klima's was for dissecting . . . If there are no more birds . . . '

'There are many species that can bring good money,' she said quickly. 'There is a problem with how to catch them. You have to have the right people. They have to know birds. Know how to find them.' Her voice was tough.

We walked to breakfast at a place half a block away. We passed the huge dining room attached to the hotel. The glass doors were propped open, and it stank as if a heavy smoker had belched on waking. I began outlining a plan. 'They don't know where we are at the moment, but they'll catch up to us today. It's just a matter of checking every hotel and motel in town. We're about to begin walking around in ever-decreasing circles, unless you let me in on all you know.'

She didn't say anything. I began to suspect she had been trying to fuck away my curiosity. I was watching for any response from her at all.

'People have been dying all around us,' I began. 'My only suggestion is that we hide for a while. This is a very small town.'

She looked at me. For a while she must have imagined me an honourable and fearless man; the person who was going to make it all right for her. I had honestly seen myself in that role, but the enemy was on too many fronts; there were too many unknowns. I levelled with her. 'I'm beginning to panic,' I said. 'In town here, they'll catch up with us.'

'Why won't they out there?' she asked, nodding vaguely to the south.

'Because an urban thug would lose himself in a hectare of rainforest without any trouble at all.'

'So, then we disappear, is that what you're saying?'

'No, we don't disappear, we just fade into the woodwork.'

'What's that mean?'

We turned into a breakfast nook and took a table. There were a few people reading the papers, and some tourists eating before they took a bus to a crocodile park, the big avocado or a boat trip to the reef.

'We camouflage ourselves. We're still there, doing whatever we decide we want to do about all this, but we're nowhere near where they're looking for us.'

'We could take the yacht,' she said.

'Hey, you're joking.'

'No,' she said. 'I've sailed yachts all my life. On the lakes.'

Through the window I saw two vans pull up. Not together, but they were sufficiently new and clean to have been recently hired or bought. This was paranoia. Not that it wouldn't have been a completely valid mental regime for me to live with.

'The yacht would be a dead giveaway,' I said.

'How do we disappear?' she asked.

'It's going to be . . . ' I began. Verve's mobile phone rang; she picked it up from her bag and listened. It unsettled me that I hadn't known she was carrying one. She handed it over to me. 'It's Angela for you.'

Angela was slightly breathless. 'Where are you?' she asked.

'How did you know Verve had a mobile?'

'I've been looking through Truman's things.'

Verve was looking at me as if she wanted to know how. 'It was with Truman's things,' I said. Verve relaxed.

'Where are you,' Angela said. 'I'd like to join you.'

I looked across the road at an Italian restaurant there. 'Il Posto,' I said, reading the red neon.

'Where's that?' she asked.

'I don't know,' I said. 'I don't know the streets here. It'll be in the phone book.'

'See you in five minutes,' she said.

I pressed the aerial back into the mobile and handed it to Verve. 'She thinks we're at the coffee shop over the road,' I said. 'Why don't we watch what happens?'

Verve picked up her bag and slung it over her shoulder. 'You honestly think that's the way it is?' she asked.

'Yeah, it could be,' I said, as we watched the coffee shop. I'd give her a minute. The back of the van opened. They had obviously traced us to this street anyway, which was not reassuring. Four men emerged from the van and walked into the coffee shop. One carried a sports bag and the others had bulky, casual jackets.

I looked over to Verve. 'See how close they are?' I said.

'Shouldn't we move?'

'No, they'll probably do a tour of the streets. If we're not where we said we were, we must be running.' I don't know why I felt so safe. The men emerged from the restaurant a few minutes later and without even looking over to where we were sitting in the window, jumped into the van and headed off down towards our motel. Aaah, so that was it. They had already traced us to the motel and followed the directions to the eating houses they had been given by the receptionist.

I stood up and walked over to the cash register close to the door. The waitress hadn't brought our bill so I asked for one with a scribbling gesture when she emerged from the kitchen, her arms burdened with dishes. I memorised a cab number from a card taped to the side of the cash register and went back to the table. Verve rang the cab on her mobile. A few minutes later we were at a car hire firm near the airport.

I chose a low-powered four-wheel drive because a turbo used too much fuel and was awkward to control in the hard going.

We stopped at a wayside store and stocked up with avocados and mangoes and some tinned stuff. I wished I had lifted the old Weatherby .300 Magnum from the yacht. Its wallop had enough tonnage to buckle the hide and brain of the biggest croc. We'd have to sleep in the wagon.

Several hours north, in deep rainforest country close to where I had emerged after leaving Stevo in the mess of my making, we stopped. Verve had been sleeping fitfully, waking suddenly to spring forward in her seat and, comprehending where she was, falling back into a doze.

We were in a small clearing close to a forest creek. I just sat behind the wheel staring into the forest. Fatigue had caught me. Verve jumped from the wagon and went down to look at the view down the creek. I envied her ability to handle pressure. All she had to do was have me drive her to the airport and she was gone, the danger removed. And yet she was here. I didn't believe she was here for me. It meant she still knew more than she was telling.

I stepped down from the vehicle and wandered over to her. Our conversation was desultory. Our presence in the bush so unexpected it seemed stupid. The deep silence was cut with finely tuned bird calls. I asked her to identify them. 'Charlie knew them all,' she said.

'Yeah,' I said, meaning he's no longer with us.

Verve hoisted herself onto the mudguard. 'Charlie was really impressed with what he said Truman was doing.'

'What was he doing?' I asked.

'Charlie said he spent millions in Africa trying to save rhinos. He conducted an experiment on an enormous scale. If the rhinos were being killed for their horns he thought dehorned rhinos would have to be the answer. He found some of those poachers, showed them how to use dart guns with anaesthetising chemicals, cut the horns off with chain saws, and handed them over. Half an hour later the monsters would spring to their feet and trundle off. But Charlie said he couldn't change human nature so quickly. The poachers were really hunters, so it didn't catch on.'

I was profoundly tired, but knew better than to rest on the mossy bank of the creek. When

I turned back Verve was sitting on the roof of the vehicle, gazing off into the forest.

'Klima wouldn't have understood they were trying to save anything,' I said. 'Maybe not Robe either. They'd only understand the money thing.'

'So, do we just continue heading north?'

'I have no idea,' I said.

'You don't want revenge for Charlie?' she asked, lying back on the roof. 'Or the money?'

I looked at her. There was nothing dramatic about this. I had known what I wanted. There was no need to explain it. I wanted her and the money, and if I could pay back someone for Charlie's death so much the better. The honesty of it refreshed me. 'Tell me about the money,' I said. 'The parrots have gone, and neither of us knows anything about birds.'

She rubbed her hands as she looked at me, turning them over within themselves, musing. 'Truman trusted Charlie completely. He said he knew he was a buccaneer the moment he spoke to him.' She slid off the roof, brushing the seat of her jeans. Walking towards me she put a hand against my face. 'Are you going to stay?' she asked.

She looked up into the higher realms of the rainforests. 'You know there are whole worlds up there. Small birds, animals, insects, thousands of undiscovered species, and the forests are disappearing before we even discover what they are.' She looked at me for a second before looking up again. 'That's Charlie, word for word. He said if the forests went and we couldn't save the life there, the creatures that lived on that life would evolve into something dreadful because they would need to live off us.'

'We don't need to be here,' I said suddenly.

'You know why we're here,' she said.

'Well it's in the general direction of where Charlie was found,' I said.

I was thinking I should have tortured that little Stevo bastard out here. Leaving him had been a mistake. I had simply thought torturing somebody for information was beyond anything that I had ever imagined. I could kill someone, fine. I moved around the vehicle, looking down to the water, as if it could be of some help to me. Obviously I had left the bastard in agony. I could do that, but the concentrated agonies, the intimate whisperings to the torture victims, were particularly abhorrent.

'I'm the only one in the dark. You know about the money, Angela knows about the money, and I'm on the edge of everything, not getting a look in. We can run around like this for a while but they'll catch us . . . especially if you know where the money is, or how to get it.'

'Fuck you,' she said. I knew then she would run out on me the moment she thought she could handle things herself. I couldn't believe she was so stupid. The moment she tried to trade or make a demand, she would be laid to rest somewhere out on the reef. But I knew I couldn't walk away. And she knew she had me; that I would be around as long as she needed me.

As evening came down a pungent essence alarmed me, but it was Verve rubbing some sort of anti-bug ointment around her neck and up and down her forearms.

I climbed into the wagon, wound down the seat almost flat and closed my eyes.

When I woke the jungle was dark, moist, the air heavy with the breathings of night-flowering plants, almost too sweet and succulent to be pleasant. A tree frog squeaked and grunted. Some people think frogs are like the canaries down the mines last century. When they died the miners knew to run from gas. Our frogs are dying but we have nowhere to run. A lizard skittered among high leaves and a bird woke in fright and whispered away through the high foliage. Verve slept on beside me.

The morning sun turned the ribbon of fast-moving creek to a turbulence of gold. It was a surprise to realise the movement was completely silent. Above, the dark foliage was silhouetted by embers of red. Birds swooped and climbed to the songs of others. A cockatoo squawked, indignant at the nearness of the creatures it had held in contempt for eighty or ninety years. 'Listen,' I yelled to it from the wagon, 'we've got a price on your head—twenty-five grand.'

Verve woke immediately.

'So, you're better,' she stated.

'Yeah,' I said. There was something missing. I was no longer as sharp as I had been. It was as if I had taken two steps back in my awareness, my capacities.

'So how are we going to play it?' She stepped down from the vehicle and stretched.

'I propose we kill everyone until we have it all to ourselves.' I was only half-joking.

'You can't kill them,' she said, walking around to my door. Her eyes were the cold blue of the sea touched by the wind. 'We have to sell what we know.'

'What do you know?' I asked.

'That we have to find out who we should sell to. The strongest ones.'

'If we are going into the marketing business,' I said, 'I have to know what is for sale.'

'It's a lot,' she said.

'Tell me,' I said.

'You didn't tell me about Charlie,' she said. She knew she didn't have to tell me. She was the boss now. I'd be around because I wanted her.

We drove back to Cairns to auction her knowledge to the highest bidder. I knew now that some paradise parrots had survived. And Verve was the only one who knew where they were. My role was to market information. The energy I had was the same that took me over when I knew I had a horse with enough running ability to pull off a betting coup.

Chapter 12

I discovered the next day that if I watched one of the abattoirs in Cairns we could get close to Robe and Klima. It didn't take much in the way of guess work. If Klima was running an export scam, substituting kangaroo meat for beef, he would have to put it through a legitimate abattoir. I simply checked the company records and came up with Robe as one of the directors of the local company. Robe had owned it for years. If you ran a crooked business there was nothing like a legitimate one of the same kind to hide it.

Verve and I moved out of the hotel. Or at least we didn't return to it. I caught up with Mick and asked him if there was a chance of our bunking with a koori household till things were over. He found us a run-down fibro shack back from the beach just to the north of the town. It didn't seem such a bad place because it had a mango tree in the back yard and some avocados growing up a small lane. He reckoned we might have to put up with some racist shit but told us to mention his name if it looked like really developing into anything. He even organised me a job at the abattoir.

Two days later I was at the tail end of the reluctant group of workers moving into the plant. I found facing the stink and physical slavery of this daily work a very good reason why I should think of another method of getting close to Robe.

After a week I knew I was getting nowhere. Robe simply didn't visit his northern holdings on a regular basis. I had to hang around until he did.

Being unskilled in the meat trade I had landed the worst job of the lot, and keeping up with it had occupied most of my depleted attention span so far. It was the worst sort of rat hole. It had so many entrances, exits, and foul places to hide in, if any clean-skinned young tax investigators or Italian-suited detectives were enthusiastic about busting Robe, their zealous approach would be dampened after gazing at the meatworks for a few minutes. Even if seeking bribes, they would find a more congenial place to approach him.

I worked as part of the skin-cleaning process. Robe was not into new mechanical techniques. He liked loyal people around him, and I had discovered all the good jobs had gone to someone with connections to Robe or his family. The union had been kept out that way. No-one was stupid enough to vote for union membership.

My job was one not even wanted by friends of second cousins. I had to oversee the regularity of the skin-cleaning operation. When I mean oversee, it meant I had to do all the work of supplying the various machines with skins, and this meant no respite, apart from a morning tea break, lunch and afternoon tea break. There were hours of hard physical labour in between.

Under the corrugated iron roof I had on a rubber apron, rubber boots, overalls, and rubber gloves, all supplied by the company, and as the day warmed up so did I.

I stood under a huge revolving drum, 10 metres long and many metres wide, and it was a sort of washing machine for loosening the dirt, blood and tissue, on the skins. They were flung out at about two a second onto a conveyor belt. These skins travelled towards me and I had to load them onto trolleys, fifty wet ones a vehicle, and push them to five other machines which soaped rinsed and squeezed the skin.

Each of those machines had an operator who worked as fast as possible so that I would get behind and they could have a quick break and a smoke before I turned up again. The trolleys had small metal wheels. Those wobbly wheels splayed and played when loaded with skins and often disappeared into cracks in the floor. They skittered towards the cracks like a recalcitrant supermarket trolley. Somebody would have to pay for this humiliation.

The morning Robe turned up the slaughtermen were singing. He stopped the car to discover what was happening. I recognised the song then, a hymn, 'Onward Christian Soldiers'. They were driving the cattle up into the killing yards. I watched through sweat dripping over my eyes as Robe laughed, slapped the steering wheel, and drove on.

I was so desperate to get away from the job I felt like following his Rolls, grabbing the bastard as he stepped from the car and sticking him. There were plenty of knife-wielding suspects around here. I persuaded myself it was not a good idea. I was wasting my time here wandering around looking for secret aviaries in my lunch breaks. No-one even noticed what I was doing. For the moment nothing illegal was going down.

On that last day of my working hell, as I sat on the cattleyard fence south of the cleaning shed, drinking an orange juice, and wondering how many bugs were landing in it, the side gates were opened again and two huge refrigerated rigs were driven into the lane and down to the cattle pens and cool store. I wandered along there to the canteen. When they swung the truck doors open one of the drivers stuck his fingers in his mouth and blasted out a whistle. Knowing he had my attention he waved me away. I did so, obediently, but not before I had smelled the meat in the rigs. It was a sweeter and older smell. Two loads of kangaroo carcases. Klima's handiwork. Evidence of a nice little substitution racket, or simply dog food. I didn't need to know, either way. The driver's wariness, though, pointed to something illegal.

There was a problem. If Klima and Robe were working together, who had killed Angela's guards? Strachey hadn't been much good at protection. His forte had been hiding himself behind rose bushes in his victims' front gardens and shooting them in the head with a .22 as they walked by.

Later in the morning, as I was standing in a lake of bloody water, the skins dropping, quivering into a trolley, and I was shifting them to balance the load, I heard the trucks start up. They had to back and turn over bluestone cobbles. I risked going to the door for a breather. Fill my lungs with something other than the fog of atomised blood and water in the shed.

I was joined at the door by one of the skin pressers who lit a smoke and began to regale me about the sheila up at the meat store who would fuck a few of us blokes if we dobbed in a few dollars. 'Jesus,' I said, 'why don't they pay us?'

'They don't want it as much as we do,' he said. 'You be in it?'

'Right now I couldn't make the moola for a dead sheep, mate,' I said. 'It's not on.'

'Aaah shit,' he said. 'If I've gotta spring any more dough the misses 'ud know what I'd been up to. She's real quick on the uptake.'

I was certain I was going about the whole thing the wrong way. A week and I had nothing. Now Robe was here I could at least follow the bastard. If he left and I didn't follow him I'd have to stake the place out for another week.

'I tell ya I'm really fucked off with this work, mate,' I said.

I looked behind me and saw the pile of skins was about to topple. Did I want to save it, or was I going to let the pile just keep building until it covered the trolley? I decided on the latter. I walked back into the change room, stripped off the wet gear, didn't bother with a shower, donned my jeans and T-shirt, walked out again still fitting on my shoes, squelched my feet into them, and headed up for my motor bike. Looking back I saw the pile of skins building all around the trolley. The hill of them had obviously fallen several times. The other operators were waiting for me to come back from wherever and have to work like hell to catch up. As I turned I heard the switch being thrown and the barrel came to a jolting halt that echoed through the building and out the door.

Getting onto my bike I felt like a kid nicking off from school. I was ready for someone to come running, chastise me even. I kicked up the support bar, kicked down on the starter and rode towards the gate. The bike had been an indulgence. I hadn't ridden one since my youth.

I convinced myself I needed one to pass as the genuine abattoir worker.

One of the guards came out. 'You can't leave, mate. You won't get paid.'

I stopped the bike and sat there. 'Big fuckin' deal,' I said. 'Open the fuckin' gate.' I blasted out of the stinking hell hole, feeling the wind on my face.

The sea was glorious. I walked into it in my clothes, not caring that the big sea lizards would be attracted by the abattoir smell that had infiltrated my skin. It was warm and because of the lack of wind the sediment had filtered to the bottom. Moving slowly forward with my head underwater, my eyes open, I seemed to be enclosed in a great cavern of liquid glass. I turned back towards the beach and stripped off to my undershorts. On the sand I lay in the shadow of a palm, my clothes spread out to dry beside me. That was the good thing about the beaches just north of Cairns, they were pretty much deserted, except for some black blokes who were drinking near an upturned skiff.

I rode to our fibro shack. Verve was dancing to a sound track from *The Hot Spot*. She grinned at me as I rode up.

'Hey, you're home early.'

'Think I've got the answer,' I said.

'Tell me?' she asked.

'Our strategy is not too brilliant.'

'I feel like eating,' she said.

Our food was mostly from the market near the airport, but when we ate out it was fish and chips because hired gunmen from the south ate at the best restaurants. We headed off into town on the bike.

I sat with some unemployed kids on the bench outside the fish shop while Verve ordered up. Like me, they were from the south. They asked me about jobs. I told them there was skin handling going at the local abattoirs. 'I'm not part of killing animals,' one bright-faced boy said. 'None of us are.'

I pointed to the fish he was eating. 'I eat other predators,' he said. 'Otherwise I'm a vegetarian.'

Verve came out of the fish shop. 'Let's go,' she said.

'Sure,' I said, standing. She slipped her arm into mine. How easy life would be, I thought, if I could enjoy these simple pleasures each day. Living the simple life, however, didn't find you such an exotic companion as Verve.

The fish and chips were upmarket in the sense they were cooked in light oil, the fish battered in the style of Japanese tempura. The simple life had gone, replaced with food you could enjoy.

'We need to get Robe on territory he doesn't know,' I said.

'We lose surprise,' she said. 'That was one of the main things we discussed; getting him on his own ground.' I had forgotten. I was getting soft. The back-breaking physical labour in disgusting conditions had taken away my sharpness. And after only a week. What happens to those attached to the job for life?

They were waiting for us. I spotted both cars because they were clean, had darkened windows, and were travelling together behind us . . . slowly, keeping pace.

I knew we weren't dealing with Robe or Klima. Their mob would use cars that fitted in pretty much with the surroundings. Here they'd have an old white Toyota four-wheel drive or a rusting Holden. Something no-one would give a second glance. These two black cars with impeccable paint had immediately caught the attention of the kids on the bench. Wondering which celebrity was gazing at them had quietened them, and they were feeling a bit humiliated.

At the corner of a lane beside a dry cleaners I whispered to Verve to run. 'Get to a phone and call the police. Throw things at windows. Just draw attention to yourself. Go.'

She took off as I drew the Glock 9 mm. The lead car accelerated, turning towards the lane, and I fired four rounds into the engine block. I was surprised by the balance and lack of recoil in the hand gun. The car lurched to a stop in the middle of the street. The other limousine pulled up behind it. No-one moved. I began walking down the lane after Verve. Was it all going to be this easy? I looked behind me as I heard doors slam and two men begin to follow me down the lane. The remaining limo reversed and squealed off down the block.

I walked slowly towards the street, glancing back, letting my followers know that any sign of haste from them would produce a nasty response. Finally I made the street. They had caught Verve. She was already in the limousine, seated comfortably, facing Marshall, the door open so I could see her. Two aides stood by the door. One made a discreet gesture. I tossed the Glock into a rubbish bin, and walked towards them. Ridding myself of the weapon took the edge off the aides and they didn't search me before I stepped into a seat beside Marshall, facing Verve. I still had the Smith and Wesson. The door was closed and we were in a cool and shaded cocoon. I could barely hear the air conditioner. Marshall wasn't looking at either of us but seemed to be staring through the windscreen into the middle distance.

'I need information,' he said. He turned with a frank and inquiring look. The limo moved off, taking a road along the waterfront.

'I have a small army here,' he continued. 'But events are becoming rather more complicated than I had anticipated.'

I waited. I looked at Verve. Her tan and the heat in her cheeks gave her the colouring a make-up artist would spend hours trying to achieve. 'I need your help,' he said. Bullshit, I thought.

'Our interest in this is of a diplomatic nature.'

'What happened to the other body,' I said.

'Sorry?' he said.

'Only one body was hanging in the hotel last week. Where was the other?'

'I have no idea,' he said.

I smiled at him. 'Hey, man,' I said. I mimicked the accent because I was irritated. 'You're being diplomatic now, ain't you?'

'I want this finished with.'

'So do I,' I said.

He looked at Verve. 'I can tell you about your friend. He died in an explosion in a boat in which he was running arms to Fiji. He was an arms dealer and he was stopped.'

'That's horseshit,' I said.

Marshall ignored me. 'I'm giving you this information because I want you to help me.'

'What do you want?' I asked.

'We have discovered that certain people are trying to break our trading agreements with Australia, and we need to know who they are and how they're operating. Cargoes of kangaroo meat landed in the US always create a hell of a row.'

'Where are they operating?' I asked.

He smiled at me. He was very good. He could patronise without showing a hint of it. 'You're quick,' he said. 'Your authorities are so corrupted; the kangaroo slaughterhouses are closed down and started somewhere else. Every cop in Australia must have his hand out. We want to make sure there are convictions.'

I almost laughed. But I nodded, indicating serious concern. He was pitching a story that would sound so credible to those brought up on television. Here was a grave and concerned bureaucrat who was putting forth valid reasons for a course of action. If you didn't know about the bodies, and the criminal types Marshall was prepared to run with, you would have no reason to disbelieve his motives. If we were nice to him we might be safe for a few days.

'So, you just want the locations.'

He nodded. This couldn't be all he wanted. He was days behind Angela.

I told him about Klima's place. He stooped for a briefcase, snapped it open, and asked me to draw a map on a pad with an embossed US government letterhead. I sketched it roughly, giving hours' driving time rather than kilometres. 'It's a big beef cattle run,' I told him, 'but they've been chilling roo meat there as well.' Let him find out operations there had been cancelled.

'Is that all you have? I understand there are several locations?' He looked at Verve. She looked back without speaking. Her look was a blank stare. Get lost.

'Where are you dropping us off,' I said. 'Just about everyone in town knows you picked us up. We'll be too conspicuous.'

'Airport,' he said, slipping tickets from his inside pocket. I was tempted. Why not fly out forever? Except I knew it wouldn't be that way. Within weeks we would be running for our lives. And we wouldn't know whether we were about to be killed for simple expediency, or vengeance. Robe or Klima could be ordering our deaths from their respective cities, and I didn't think Marshall would want us to live long either. He had the resources of US security to track us down. Here, we were close to the action while it was confused enough not to have any parties focus entirely on us . . . and at least we knew who we had to avoid—everyone.

'It's a good idea,' I said, taking the tickets and smiling at Verve. We were approaching the airport. I looked over her shoulder at the driver. He seemed oblivious to whatever was going on.

'You only get on a flight if you tell us all we want to know.' His smile was nasty. He was gloating. 'You're piss scared. You've been hiding out. Frightened to even get out of town.'

As I pocketed the tickets I drew the Smith and Wesson and, below the vision of the rear mirror, pointed the weapon. I smiled at the way his crutch attempted to withdraw against the leather upholstery.

'Yeah,' I said for the driver's benefit, 'I was telling Verve we should leave anyway. At the airport we pulled up at the departure depot of a local airline. 'Could you confirm the tickets?'

I asked Verve, slipping my rent-a-car credit card from my wallet and handing it to her. I gave her the tickets as well, so that those in the car behind would imagine things were going well. She stepped out and closed the car door. I moved over to Verve's seat, the gun still concealed but pointing at his face, which seemed to be a big relief to him.

'You know,' I said. 'I've been mistaken about all this. I thought it was all about bird smuggling. You can get it wrong can't you?'

Marshall didn't say anything.

'I've got more information about birds than I could have ever imagined,' I said.

'What have you got?' Marshall asked.

'The whole thing, really.'

Marshall looked out the window, wondering how to avoid humiliation. 'I'm interested in anything you've got.'

'Why would you be?' I asked.

'There's a great deal of money involved.' I could see him calculating. Should he sucker me along with an extinction of species story? 'The money,' he repeated. I was silent. 'Several billion dollars.' He was desperate to impress me.

'I don't believe it,' I said.

'It's right.'

A four-wheel drive drew up beside us. Verve smiled down. I looked at Marshall. 'I've got to go.' I stepped out of the limo as the driver understood things were all wrong. Verve flipped open the door and I jumped in. We headed out of the airport road network and north into sugarcane country. The limousine loomed up behind us and the following car was attempting to pass us both, but on the narrow road of occasional farm vehicles it could take time. 'Slow right down,' I said, 'and just do as I ask.' It was ridiculous to attempt to outrun the big cars. 'Okay,' I said, 'into the cane.'

Verve slammed on the brakes, skidded down off the shoulder of the road, crashed across a small gully and into the cane. Her vision down to only a few metres she didn't hesitate. The limousine would break its back on such a manoeuvre. We turned south, the cane whacking against the undercarriage with the rhythm of a fast train, and headed towards Cairns. We took the cane route as far as we could, only once having a farmer's house on stilts loom above the plants. No-one attempted to follow us to remonstrate.

On the outskirts of the town we took the road to the west. We could disappear anywhere here. Twenty metres off the road we were invisible. I would have liked a day to mull over the conversation I had had with Marshall, consider the probabilities of his interest, but it had to be action and reaction if everyone was to be kept off balance long enough for us to survive.

Down a bush track I saw a welcome sign. It spelt out overnight lodgings and as much fruit as you could pick for your breakfast. We turned onto the gravelled drive and pulled up at the front of a beautiful old Queenslander. It was high off the ground on its three metre foundation stilts, and had a wide verandah all around. Off to the north was a grove of avocados. I could smell the perfumed sweetness of mango.

It was run by a middle-aged Dutch woman who looked younger. It was the tired voice that betrayed her. She was suspicious of me and was about to reject my offer to stay when Verve stepped from the vehicle and enthused at the view out over Cairns and the ocean. I hadn't noticed it. She took us in but was very short with me. She had run a guest house in Noosa but was now looking for a more peaceful existence. 'If I don't want,' she said, 'I take no-one.'

That night I moved restlessly around the room. The polished boards were surprisingly cool. Outside the trees were still. A light rain fell in the early morning. Once I looked down at Verve's small body and wondered how it could generate such energy. I touched her hip and she flinched, a small gasp escaping her as if she were crying in a dream.

Chapter 13

Coming down off the plateau in the morning I rang for Robe at the abattoir on the mobile phone. The receptionist was friendly, but struggled with a cover-up. 'We don't have a Mr Robe here,' she said.

'Tell him,' I said. 'that the paradise parrots still exist. I'll ring him back in an hour. He'll know exactly what I mean. If you don't pass this on, he'll be very angry, and your brains will no doubt turn up in your little meat shop out there.' The rudeness was enough to have her give him the message, purely on the grounds I should be punished.

I rang again when we stopped to look at the view before going further. Mr Robe would ring me, the receptionist said. Could she have my number please?

'Tell fucking Robe that if he is interested, he'll answer at this number in an hour. If he's not, I'll go elsewhere.

An hour later, boiling with indignation and wasted time, I rang again.

'Connecting you,' she said.

'Yes,' Robe said. 'Who is this?' His voice was mellow.

'I have a deal for you,' I said. He didn't respond. 'My group knows where there is a small breeding ground of paradise parrots.' Still no comment. I hung up. He would have to learn to contribute to conversation.

A few minutes later I rang again. 'Damn,' muttered the receptionist when I asked for Robe. Obviously she had been blamed for the line falling out.

'What the hell happened?' Robe asked. His voice was tough.

'I don't like talking to myself,' I said.

'Oh,' he said.

'Yeah,'

'We'd like to meet with you in Port Douglas.' Again the silence.

'Can't you talk while you think?' I asked.

A quick laugh. 'No,' he said.

'No, you're not interested in the birds, or no you don't want to meet us in Port Douglas? You know, it's just north of here?'

'I don't talk to people who delight in giving me lip.' He obviously took pleasure in using a combination of society dialogue and the Australian idiom.

'You'll miss this deal,' I said.

'I can put you onto the person who deals in this business.'

'We'll only do business with you,' I said.

'I'll meet you here in town,' he said. 'We could have a meal . . .'

'Lunch,' I said. Criminals of Robe's stature tend to want to do things at night.

'I like Thai,' he said. His voice was unexpectedly warm. The toughness had seeped from his voice. He only felt at home with things he could eat.

'Fine,' I said. 'I'll call you when I've made the bookings.' I clicked him off. Verve was chewing the inside of her lip.

'Why are you doing this?' she asked.

'For you, for money. Take your pick.'

'I don't like it.'

'We can pull it off,' I said. I was feeling the excitement I had organising a racing coup. It was a feeling that hid any thought of consequences. You rode with your ability to change things. You knew which buttons to push and when to do it.

'Pull what off?'

'We can take the birds. Set up our own operation. We have the birds, we only need transport . . . Truman's yacht . . . and we could float into Los Angeles and find the contacts.' I hesitated. I knew the best way to get away with this was double-crossing Robe. We'd have to pretend co-operation, lull him into complacency, until the time was right.

'No,' she said.

I looked at her. She didn't look back. Her face had a tenseness, drawing her features into a new look, almost like a mask, and when she turned to me her eyes were depthless, like a clear pond. 'I'm frightened of Robe,' she said. 'I don't like it.'

'Tell me another way.'

'The breeding area in the rainforest,' she said. 'We could move it. They could never find them. Just take the birds and go. We don't have to even talk to them again. Just wait them out; wait till they go away.'

'That's what we'll do,' I said. 'But we can't afford to have them moving against us. If we're close we'll know what they're doing; we'll know if they fall for our story, and we'll know if they move against us.'

'What could we do then?'

'New plans,' I said. I held back on what it could really mean: killing the competition and making a run with the birds.

I phoned a Thai restaurant on the waterfront and booked a table, although I was aware of Verve's agitation. I phoned Robe as we descended into the town. His receptionist took the time and the place. We had about an hour.

We visited a local boutique ship's chandlery where we bought wet weather gear for camping and binoculars powered to 15 x 70, then on to a boat-hiring firm. I left Verve in a boat on the river, and then parked the four-wheel drive down near the yacht club.

I walked the area as a tourist, watching the restaurant, but failing to mingle with the crowd. They were Japanese—I stood out like a barbarian come to plunder. I walked towards the beach, and stopped to look at the view. I was about a hundred metres from the restaurant. I took my paper to a bench and began reading in the sun.

I saw Robe arrive, followed by two other cars at a discreet distance. One parked with a clear view of the entrance as Robe's car dropped him at the door of the restaurant. The third car then followed Robe's car out of the cul-de-sac.

The parked car interested me. I slipped across the road under the trees and walked casually over. It had only one occupant. Level with the driver's window I stopped as if something in the paper had the power to stop me in mid-stride—highly unlikely these days. I looked down at the driver. He was assembling a 35 mm camera with a long lens of some quality. Looked about a ten power. I reached through the window and grabbed the camera. I whacked it against the rim of the driver's door. It fell to pieces. I hit him in the side of the neck and reached for his mobile phone. I put it in my pocket. There was another camera in the seat beside him so I took it and walked to a nearby bench. A tourist observing the action was about to raise his video camera. I shook a finger in his direction, smiled, and he took the hint.

Back on my bench I assembled one of the cameras, checked it for film. I took a few snap shots of the view.

A few minutes later Angela arrived in a cab and quickly entered the restaurant.

Off to the right a young bloke in a stylish leather jacket ran along the pavement to the photographer's car. The photographer obviously pointed in my direction because the Leather Jacket began to run towards me. I snapped him as he came. I nearly misjudged because he looked further away in the view finder than he actually was. When he was 5 metres away I tossed him the camera casually, which caught him off balance: it was valuable and shouldn't be dropped. I punched him hard to the heart, and whacked him across the face with my elbow. He was good though. He kept thinking. He didn't drop, and he held the camera. I kicked him in the nuts. He lowered himself to the bench while I removed a short-barrelled .357 Magnum from a coat pocket lined with stiff leather. No hammer catching material here.

I took the camera he had carefully placed on the ground and walked down to the restaurant. It was a pleasant place, dominated by the sparkle off the harbour. I spotted Angela who had been seated with her back to the door, and Robe who glanced up at me and then stared as I approached with the camera. I took a chair from another table and spun myself into their table. It all had to be reasonably fast.

'Esben,' I said with a mock heartiness he didn't immediately suspect. He had one of those ugly dials that are made genial by mobility and enthusiasm. Just now though he was grave, his face locked into a grimace of a smile which disappeared when he said, 'Who are you?' Obviously he couldn't smile and talk at the same time. Hitler had the same problem. A phrenologist of the old school had noted it as a peculiarity of those who fornicated with the dead. Aaaah for the old, accurate sciences.

'I'm Jack,' I said.

'We were just discussing the shares each of us should take in the venture,' Angela said. I looked at her in admiration. She had calculated it all. I was here for a cut of whatever was going. This marvellous embracing gesture nearly fooled me: three perfectly reasonable human beings coming to the table to discuss the way the profit would slice.

'I don't want to waste time,' Robe said. 'What have you got that you think I'm prepared to pay money for? Tell me straight, no bullshit, and we might be able to do business.'

Robe's words were pronouncements he expected to be obeyed.

He was a heavy man, a coating of seal fat over muscle. He had made his lips thin by sucking them when he was sorting out trouble. When he spoke there was a gleam of gold in a lower tooth.

'I believe I'm the only one who knows the whereabouts of the birds,' I said.

'You might have the produce,' Robe said, making a very dour effort of admitting we had the goods, 'but that doesn't get you very far.' Perhaps he thought you only needed the organisation and the goods just arrived miraculously. I put this to him.

'Smart arse. I could finish you in this country, like that,' he said to me, and then looked at Angela as he flicked his fingers. His small eyes were tight with malice, his voice low and rough.

'Hey,' I said to Angela, 'he must mean kill me.' I looked back at Robe. His face had pinked and his eyes threatened.

I lowered my head when I spoke to him, setting my shoulders as if I, physically, might come off the table and nail him. 'You're a mug to throw this one over. It's foolproof. We're only dealing with you because we thought it might take some unwanted excitement out of the operation.' The tension was palpable.

He leaned towards me, looking up. 'I'll find out where the fucking birds are,' he said. 'You're not leaving this place under your own steam.' He nodded to the door. 'We'll have you squealing like a stuck pig in about thirty minutes.'

'You know,' I continued, taunting. 'You need better people than you've got,' and walked away while he couldn't wave his people at me without a lot of witnesses catching on to what was about to happen.

Outside there were two cars tight to the entrance. I saw them as I left the dining area. I picked up one of those sugar pots with a sharp metal spout from a vacant table and held it to my side. As I left the front door I drove it into the arm of the leather coated invalid who was coming to collect me with his team. I pulled back my linen coat to show the hand gun to his team mates. They were too smart to shoot. The sugar changed from white to crimson as the blood flowed into the bowl. I darted towards the river. Four men began to sprint behind me. I looked at a group of Japanese tourists with video recorders who were watching open mouthed. I waved to them and pointed to our pursuers. The heavies saw the video cameras, hesitated, sort of slowed, embarrassed, awkward, their brains fused by the thought of being filmed.

I arrived at the wharf as Verve turned the boat up against the timber. I ran down the steps of the landing. She turned the boat, and within thirty seconds we were heading out into the wide river at twenty knots.

The boat was an aluminium 18 footer, and I had no idea of its abilities in open water. We needed to hide at sea for the remainder of the day. Only minutes later we rounded the short peninsula to the south of the river, a piece of land of which it was rumoured was once owned by Elvis Presley. We were out of sight of the yacht club, but our destination was unambitious: the first beach where we could anchor and land.

My hit-and-run guerilla tactics began to depress me.

Verve slowed the boat. What did we do for the rest of the day? Plan A had been to deal with Robe. That had failed, so we moved on to plan B—escape. But now we had to work on the details of plan B. Beneath us the water was so clear we seemed suspended on glass; the ripples' distortion like a warped mirror. The beach ahead of us was inviting, and meant we were easy targets. Even if we could drag the boat into the foliage it would leave a tell-tale scar on the virgin sand. But I felt we were safe for a while. To pursue us after the chase through a crowd of tourists would be too risky. The police may have even been called.

We headed for the beach. It was a nice run in. We anchored in about a metre of water and dropped over the side with a few essentials held over our heads.

Before we made it to the sand Verve's mobile phone rang.

It was Angela. I gestured that I wanted to listen in. Verve was reluctant but turned the phone at her ear so we were head to head.

'You must realise that Truman set everything in motion. The birds are surviving because of Truman. I only want to continue his work.' I pulled my head away slightly and looked at Verve. 'Bullshit,' I mouthed.

Verve smiled into the phone. 'You might only want to continue Truman's work to save the species,' she said, 'but we're after the money. Saving the species is secondary.' I raised my eyebrows at Verve and shrugged: not a bad reversal.

'I can pay you,' Angela said.

Verve was struggling for an answer. 'I can't hear you,' she said, finally. 'There's interference. 'Give me your number and I'll ring back.' Moments later she clicked off the phone.

I didn't say anything, just lay back on the sand, watching the boat bobbing.

She looked across at me. Her legs and arms glistened with oil, and sunglasses made her smile enigmatic. 'Truman started with a bird called a Gouldian finch,' she said, finally.

'Yeah,' I said.

'It's pretty rare in the wild. He thought he could save it. Smuggled it to Japan, where it flourished. Somehow the Japanese evolved a new kind of Gouldian finch, sort of genetically engineered a new one. Not a lot different apparently. Charlie said the Japanese are like that. They want to make things slightly different and then they think it's theirs . . . you know, like original?' She was looking down to where she was smoothing the sand with a stick.

'Anyway,' she continued. 'Then people began to smuggle the finch back to Australia. People think it's the real thing.'

I heard the plane coming about two minutes before it swooped over the beach. We were already in the foliage. The boat was a dead giveaway, but the tide was in and the sand would be too soft to land on.

We moved further into the green shadows.

'They'll always be looking for us,' Verve said. She didn't elaborate, but I knew what she meant. We faced an uncertain future.

I touched her arm with my hand. She looked at me, her eyes as straight as anybody's had a right to be. 'I want to tell you one thing: If they catch me it won't be a matter of my being able to get away by giving information. Do you understand that?'

I nodded. She simply wanted to know that I understood the stakes we were playing for. I nearly laughed.

'Let's bring all this to a head,' I said, 'and at the same time buy a little time.'

'How?' She leaned against the trunk of the palm tree with the casualness of a long-legged athlete.

'Ring Angela and arrange to meet on the island out there,' I nodded towards Fitzroy Island. 'She'll tell Robe, and while they're thinking they don't have to try and track us down anymore, we'll be on the way to wherever the birds are.'

'Well,' she said. 'At least we'll know they're on the island.'

She went to her bag, took out the mobile phone and dialled.

'Angela,' she said, walking up and down in the sand as if she were in an office. I didn't want to cramp her style by listening so I moved away. She finally gave me a nod, and held up thumb and forefinger in a circle.

'How far is it to the birds?' I asked, coming over to her.

'We wouldn't make it in that boat,' she said. 'Have to be by four-wheel drive.'

'No thanks,' I said. 'It's too dangerous in town. We'll take Truman's yacht.'

Verve backed away from me as if I were mad. There was incomprehension in her eyes. 'On the island again. I don't want to be out there. The first chance they . . . we'll be killed.'

'We can do it,' I said.

She shook her head, stunned.

'Listen,' I said. 'We've got no choice. We can't go back to Cairns, and they know where we are. If we don't leave soon they'll have us. We don't have the stuff to last in the bush. We have to keep moving. We have to keep going with this.' If you backed down on things you would be hurt by them later. Somehow I had to convince Verve of this. I didn't know how. I had never convinced anyone who didn't really know already.

'It only looks dangerous,' I said. 'They won't have us killed on a tourist resort while they're there. That would be madness.'

'They're all mad,' she said.

'We front confidently. We really rub their faces in it. They would have to assume we have support. People don't act that way if they haven't got support . . . You see what I'm talking about?'

I saw understanding arrive and her eyes lost their frantic look. 'You're like Charlie,' she said.

'I'm better, because I can always let go. Charlie was the monkey with his hand in the jar, refusing to let go the sweets so he could get his hand out. I take it right up to that point and still drop them.'

We returned to the trees skirting the beach. We could rest here and watch for anything that approached over the sea. Coming from behind us by road and bush track would take a day or two from Cairns.

The water was tantalising. It glimmered, glistened and threw us reflected sheets of sunlight. 'Why don't we swim?' I said, knowing it was not a good idea. The nasties of the shallows hug the coastline in the clear water. The islands are free of them, so tourists either swim there or use the motel pools.

'It's dangerous,' she said, grinning.

'It's not even summer,' I said. 'Why are you laughing?'

'I just happen to have panty hose in my bag. They don't sting through panty hose.'

'Nothing can,' I said.

She opened her bag and tossed me the panty hose. I began threading them on over my legs.

'Hey, come on,' she said. 'Shorts off.'

'I dunno about this,' I said, stripping naked.

She giggled. 'Now do you know how a women feels?'

She cut the crutch of one pair of hers and drew her arms through the legs. She thrust her head through the cut.

'Are you sure they don't sting through these things?' I asked, following her example.

'I'm sure,' she said. 'The lifesavers in Darwin all wear panty hose.'

She took off to the water. I followed. 'Just keep your head out,' she called back.

We circled each other in the water. My mind was divided between the dangers of the deep and my curiosity on how nylon would slide against nylon. It was a weird sensation on the skin. I rejected the feeling I should feel like a dork. I swam casually towards her. She grinned at me. 'Wow,' she said. 'What's this going to feel like?' Initially it was interesting and erotic, but I soon wanted to shed the nylon cladding for more intimate textures.

We were in a transported state, and so the plane was undetected until the roar rolled over the forest, its shadow flicking across the beach, the machine riding a wave of sound.

'Keep still,' I said. 'Don't move.' There was a chance they mightn't see us. But she was past any control and took me with her. We were convulsively clutching at each other, fair targets.

Finally, as the plane was on a turn back over us, we could run. Verve was laughing as we dashed into the foliage. The plane roared over us and inland over the forest. 'Oh Christ,' she said, dropping with laughter. 'I don't believe this.' We dressed hurriedly and I checked the hand gun for sand. I wasn't sure whether my hands were shaking from laughter or fear. I had wrapped the gun in my shirt, and there was no grit visible on the breech block where the film of oil would first pick it up.

The sound of the plane disappeared. We looked at each other. We were both still weak from exertions and fright. 'We're safe here,' I said. 'They can't get to us.'

'Helicopter,' she said.

'You're right. We'll move.'

The day lightened with our speed. The island was two hours off.

Even though the outer reef protected these waters from the huge ocean swells, a considerable chop was rising once we left the protection of the coastline. The boat stopped planing and began bashing a bit. We were glad of the padded seat and spray screen.

As we moved into the lee of the island we phoned ahead and rented the same bungalow I'd had before. There was no-one on the beach. I wondered if the trees hid a welcoming party.

Then I saw a kid playing near my bungalow and I knew it was clear.

I anchored the boat only metres off the beach in front of my rented bungalow and waded ashore, through the clear, safe water. A few couples were sprawled in the patchy shade of the casuarinas, but there was no real air of expectancy. No helicopter had landed city thugs here, yet. We would have to take the yacht at night. We had hours to fill in.

I left Verve in the bungalow and went for a swim. I was suspended in liquid glass, and I could see 10 or 12 metres to the edge of the reef. I moved out over it.

The water spread away from me as a flat, stretching membrane glistening in the afternoon light. I duck-dived, pushing myself down a couple of metres. A bevy of small fish striped with various blues and yellows patrolled the reef in front of me. I peered beneath an overhang of rock carrying pink knobbled coral and beyond that a white filigree, and a large fish projected itself neatly into my path. Red with blue polka dots, the clown colours didn't hide his predator's skull and large thick-lipped mouth. The detail of him seemed to come clearer as I watched. And then I realised he was brightening his colours, in some deep, dark rage. He hated me for disturbing his fishing. He also realised I was larger than he was, and he gave ground easily, drifting over a panorama of red-leaved sponges. I had out-presenced him. I turned and gently moved back to the beach, following the beauties under water with a marvelling eye.

In the bungalow Verve was sleeping. I looked down at her, her hair lightly tossed across her face. Her limbs flung away from the torso for coolness. I lay down beside her, not touching, and slept.

She woke me late afternoon. She handed me a cup of coffee. She was dressed in loose white shorts with a white T-shirt and a dark blazer. The white socks and sneakers emphasised her tan legs.

'You seem a bit overdressed,' I said.

'I feel like I should be,' she said.

'Don't know the perfume,' I said.

'It's to stop sun spots,' she said. 'Wild apple and teatree oil. The Aborigines around here told Charlie about it. They said he needed it.'

'So, he got close to them?'

'Yes,' she said. 'He loved them. He said they'll never be stomped out. They have the knowledge that persistence—just existing in a balanced state—means identity.'

'Very profound bloke. Did Truman use the Murrays to find the paradise parrots?'

'Of course.'

She flicked on the TV. 'Hey, do we have to have it?' I knew watching a news service would bring on the thought of consequences.

'Why? Don't you watch the news?'

'Not the news according to the networks.'

'I want to see if we're on the news.'

'How could we be?'

'Back home, there's a program for video buffs, where they send in their news items for the day.'

'They were Japanese tourists. They wouldn't even think about it.'

The room was split with light and thunder and I threw myself at Verve to hide her. The window had split and there was a bullet hole dead centre, a crack radiating from it to the frame. It had missed me by about half a metre. The shooter had misjudged the distortions of the cheap glass.

I reached for the hand gun beneath the pillow and then threw a shoe to smash the light next to the television.

'Oh Christ,' I heard Verve say.

'Are you all right?' I asked.

'God, yes.'

I eased my way to the door. I opened it and sprang to the sand, rolling. Nothing. I ran about 20 metres, and saw a figure run into the foliage that hid the pool from the nearest units. It was as slight as a woman. The speed had been extraordinary. People who ran like that left themselves vulnerable to sudden disaster—an overhanging branch, a loose rock, the corner too close. I waited a few more seconds and then ran to the bungalow.

I knocked on the door. 'It's me,' I whispered.

'Come in,' she called.

'We leave now,' I said. 'Before they can work out what's going on.'

'Oh shit, I leave my stuff? Leave, again, with nothing?'

'I mean leave with everything. Our lives and the birds.'

'Sure.'

'We'll have to swim out to the yacht. I think it was a woman,' I said, considering.

'You don't think it was Angela?'

'No, but she'd hire a woman. Robe wouldn't.'

I was excited by her look. I had experienced pleasure there, and my body was assuring me everything was fine and I should enjoy it all again as soon as possible. This was not good for survival. Enjoy, it said. Forget about tomorrow.

'We'll take them by surprise,' I reasoned.

Verve moved to the window. 'The yacht has been moored further out,' she said. 'I hate thinking about what's in deep water.'

'So does everybody else,' I said. But I knew it wouldn't be a deterrent. Just about everybody in Sydney could swim and surf with sharks close by, even the local hoods. It was the Sydney pastime.

The plane sounded like a fast boat at first. Then it came on with more authority. It made me nervous. We went outside to watch it. The seaplane approached in a slow sweep. The spray spun out high behind it as it sliced the surface, and then settled, lower and lower on its floats, until it was chugging towards the beach with the speed of a fishing boat.

The prop stuttered to a stop and the pilot stepped onto the float and tossed out an anchor. Another figure stepped out after him. Marshall. For some illogical reason I felt safer. Verve touched my arm. 'We don't trust him, right?' she said.

We stood watching Marshall and his aides as if we were unconnected to their visit. Obviously they wanted a boat to collect them. They were going to have to wait. We sat down to observe the US ambassador's visit to an island where they had neglected to organise the protocol. Marshall waved and pointed to our boat. A little giveaway which meant he had complete knowledge of the day's activities. I walked down the beach, pulled the boat in and pushed it out with my leg as I stepped into it. It didn't quite make it to the float of the plane so I tossed them the rope to pull it alongside. The exhaust slowly dissipating over the sea irritated my eyes.

Marshall smiled in a perfunctory manner. 'Can we talk in your bungalow?' he asked.

'Sure,' I said. He stepped into the boat but his aides didn't follow him. One of them manoeuvred the bow towards shore, placed his feet on the stern and pushed it to the beach.

The boat bumped against the coral. 'He's a strong guy,' Marshall said. He turned. 'Do you like the plane? It was this or a chopper. I like the old machines. They use seaplanes right through Canada. All those fucking lakes.'

As we walked up to the beach where Verve was sitting, Marshall said, 'You're both holding all the cards.'

'In what game?' I asked.

'Yeah,' he said. 'There are a couple of games being played.'

Marshall showed his Vietnam training by sitting down on the front step. He could toss away ceremony for hands-on involvement. 'It's time to level with you,' he said. 'My country's interest in the smuggling is very straightforward. We want to save the endangered species of the world.' He smiled at us in turn, his hands out in a small gesture of beseechment.

I laughed. 'What are you talking about? Are you talking about Ark America?'

'That's not bad,' he said. 'We've never named it. But yes, that is exactly what I'm talking about. Europe wiped out most of its species, and they're gone forever. Now it's the turn of the Third World to destroy its creatures. They think catching up with the West is progress.'

'I don't believe a fucking word of it,' I said. I wasn't going to be bargained down on price because of misplaced charity.

'One of the unbelievers,' he said.

'Fucking right,' I said.

'How much do you want for the parrots?' he said.

I lay down on the coral. With my weight it felt like a bed of nails. I closed my eyes. I was letting him know it could be a long process. 'The usual thing,' I said, 'when a purchaser approaches someone who hasn't put their goods on the market, is for them to make an offer.'

'We're not going to offer a lot. We don't have a lot.'

'You've got a lot if you're talking about saving species about to become extinct,' I said.

'There's many ways of saving things. I'm not talking zoos and hothouses and huge environmental structures for delicate insects, I'm talking about the frozen zoo we have in San Diego. We freeze semen and ova. It's there to draw on to replenish dwindling stocks of endangered creatures. That way there are no ongoing costs. They keep blood samples, skin samples. No feeding, health problems. Don't even have to build zoos anymore. It's a big save.'

'So you've given up trying to save the newborn of the human species?' I asked. 'It only takes food.'

He looked at me with a smile. 'I didn't expect that from you, ma' man. From what I've heard the human race is the least of your concerns.'

'And the parrots, do they get cut up and stored? Or do they get to live?'

'They're supposed to be extinct. This is the first anyone has heard of them for about seventy years. We sell them on.'

'I'm impressed,' Verve said.

'Yeah, we're impressed,' I said. 'But that means you want what Verve has for nothing. That's not on.'

He stood up. 'We pay,' he said. 'But we've got to know who we can deal with. We just keep in touch with all the parties.'

'What worries me,' I said, 'is the killing. 'First Charlie, then Truman. And who killed the four blokes out at the Klima property?'

He sniggered. I sat up and looked at him. He stared at me with malevolence. 'Hell, we could fit you up with that. Course there's a fresh one out there.' He looked at Verve. 'The knife was left behind,' he said. Verve drew a quick breath.

There is a certain personality that thrives on having information and using it to make people do what they ask. You know the type would torture if they had a free hand. Marshall was close to that.

'You killed them,' I said.

He just smiled. 'I tell you, there's a lot happened out there before you came running along.'

'And Charlie?'

'We missed Charlie at the time,' he said. 'He was taking over: thought he was. And we were doing things slowly, you know, bureaucrats.'

He nodded his head. He had me summed up, he thought.

'So why have you been doing business with Robe?'

'You see, we make money on the side. We need people like him. We can't be seen to be involved. They just make a money drop for us. And we point them in the right direction. Now, if we got too close to the deal someone would get onto it. They'd find paperwork. One of us signed for something, or a dopey bastard filed for expenses. Look what happened to little Ollie North.' He stood up. I wanted to, but I wanted to be cool. I forced myself to stay down. Verve stood up, brushing her shorts. He looked down at me. 'Now Robe won't pay you anything, but probably tell us he did, so we wouldn't get our full share from him.'

'What have you planned for us?'

'I'll tell you. Give us the birds and we let you go.'

'Bullshit,' I said. 'The moment you know where the birds are we're shark bait.' I nodded out over the reef water. 'And someone on the island is already taking shots at us.'

'Just at you,' Marshall said. 'We don't need you.' He crunched down the beach in his leather shoes.

'Like you didn't need Truman?'

'We were dealing with Truman,' he said. 'We didn't do him.'

I had no reason to believe him.

'Verve knows where they are,' I said. 'That has to be a plus for her.'

'Not the only one who knows. There are the people looking after them. We'll find them eventually. We just want to buy a package deal, not a lot of trouble.'

'And what about Angela? Where's she in this?'

'Just more competition for you, boy.' He stepped into the bow of the boat and pushed it off with his foot, keeping it raised. The seaplane's motor spluttered as the boat touched the float. He was anxious to get away. He closed the hatch and the plane's engine roared. It didn't take off as I expected, but surged around the island out of sight. I thought I heard the note of the engine change.

'He's the one who set everyone up,' I said. 'Only the survivors get to deal.' I wasn't sure Verve would get to live. I was sure I wouldn't.

Despite the heat we walked the trail behind the resort to the peak that towered over the island. I had the misguided idea that if we knew the geography, saw it laid out in front of us, we would be safer.

All we saw from the peak was the inviting translucent blue water surrounding the island. No sign of Marshall or anyone else. We came down the trail feeling less secure than we had before the walk. Marshall, Klima, Angela, all could have people on the mainland who could paddle over during the night.

We walked to the restaurant and bought food. We took clothes and guns and walked straight into the few hectares of rainforest. The plan was to take the yacht, slip away without anyone seeing us. Stupid. But all we could do.

The hydrofoil bumped the small wharf and people were chatting excitedly as they disembarked. I could also hear a live band. A new wrinkle, or was it to mask our yells as we were turned into fish bait? I couldn't discount anything. By Christ, I'd take a few with me. That was the extent of my vision just then. My nervous system was flashing alert.

I watched Angela meeting two men who were the last off. They walked along the narrow wharf to the coral beach. Watching them from the high deck was a thickset athlete. He might have a 6-centimetre covering of fat, but that was there to absorb the punches. Beneath that was muscle tissue. He had the solidity of a wild pig. He certainly looked out of place on this holiday island.

For some reason I wanted to put my arm around Verve. I guessed it was me wanting to protect her, but for a moment I thought crazily that touching her would give me some protection.

In the dark we moved through the trees to the water's edge. We were lucky here. Smooth red boulders were perfect cover and they went into the night like steps into the forest.

They'll be onto us the moment we start the motors.' I knew nothing about sails. They were obviously ready to go. The mainsail was wrapped in a blue cover around the boom. The jib was furled as if all that was needed was a sharp tug on some ropes and the night breeze would hit it.

'We do it now,' Verve said. 'Take the boat. Let it drift. Hit the motors when we're in the dark water.'

My whole nervous system was informing me that we shouldn't be here. My mind had become blank. We were rabbits waiting to hear the hunters walking by. One more unfamiliar sound and we'd be up and running.

Slipping into the water a softness touched my leg. I thought it was kelp and prepared to walk through it. The touch had an insistent pressure to it. I looked down. I saw a white shadow where it shouldn't have been. It was a body. I grabbed the shirt and pulled it up. It was Klima. His throat fell open revealing much of its former workings. I dropped him, his head slipping beneath the surface silently. I had expected him to scream or struggle. Verve was transfixed in horror. I knew what she was thinking, we had to swim through this water, through whatever creatures were moving in to make Klima their own. I took Verve's hand and walked deeper.

'No talking once we're out there,' I said needlessly, Verve was trembling with fright.

'Voices travel for kilometres over water. The smallest whisper.'

We submerged gently and stroked slowly down the length of the beach. Verve shivered beside me. I thought for a moment she was going to turn back. The ghastly shadow of the hydrofoil on the water threatened to unnerve me. It seemed to stretch out its vast shape towards us. The lights on the bridge were dim but I could see the crew playing cards. In the passenger hold there was some cleaning up under way, and bar restocking.

We cleared the huge craft and were about a hundred metres off the yacht when two fins cleaved the water between us and the shore. I nearly pissed with fright. They were dolphins. Something you have trouble identifying after a decade of horror movies about killer sharks with genius IQs. I knew we were relatively safe. Rarely do sharks and dolphins move together.

At the schooner Verve moved up onto the deck using the several steps affixed to the stern. I followed. She lay on the deck in a pool of water. I glanced back at the surface, flat and dark. Verve opened the sliding door in the cockpit and we moved into the cabin. 'I've got clothes,' she whispered. 'You can use Truman's stuff. Charlie's will be too big for you.' She had obviously been on most of the trips with them.

I looked at the gun cabinet. Several hundred rounds for the Weatherby. There was a

Japanese semi-automatic shotgun called a Shadow, identical to the Browning 12-gauge. I taped it beneath the lower bunk. No telling who we would have aboard.

The problem of sailing the yacht I left to Verve.

'They'll know we're taking this thing away as soon as they hear the motor,' Verve spread out a navigation map of the coastline and turned on a small bench light. Droplets from her wet hair spattered the map. 'It's going to take us time to get the mooring loose, and they'll hear the anchor the moment I start the winch.'

She looked at me for a moment, but it wasn't me she was seeing. 'We start the motor the same time as the winch.'

Her eyes had an exhaustion and she was struggling with these details.

'They'll launch those aluminium boats and be here in about two minutes,' I said. 'Why don't we wait until the hydrofoil starts its motors. It'll cover our sound.'

'That's another two hours. They'll find we're gone.'

'Still take the same time to get out here. And we'll see them.'

Verve looked at me doubtfully. She could see my nerves were wearing thin. I saw why Charlie appealed to her. No matter how mad his schemes he didn't ever lose his calm and considered demeanour. He would have been a protector, to the last.

Chapter 14

The shoreline gave us echoes of inconsequential conversations as the diners left the restaurant to walk off their meal along the beach. The voices were suddenly in the cockpit with us it seemed, and the next moment they would be far away and indecipherable. No-one on shore had shown their hand. They were cagey. Perhaps they thought they'd be off the island before anyone found Klima's body.

We had set up watch from the cockpit, our knees resting on pillows, our arms on the moulded seats, and our heads only just peeping over the gunwales. The moon gave us the light of a false dawn. Visibility out over the water went for kilometres.

It was another hour before the hydrofoil started its engines. I smiled at Verve as I shifted position, and looked over the dark water crossed with candle flame shadows reaching out from the shore. I saw something that traced dread across the surface of my face, neck, back. One wet footprint glistened on the polished timber deck. It wasn't a damp smudge. It had small puddles spreading from it. I held a finger to my lips and motioned with my eyes for Verve to follow my glance. I had no way of knowing whether we were being watched or not. It was a large footprint. Neither of us had approached the cockpit from that direction. We had come from the stern. I slipped the hand gun unobtrusively from my belt and held it by the barrel beneath my body with my left hand, making a rough holster.

There was no way I could check the deck without giving us away. If the bastard thought we hadn't seen him we had some control of the situation. I could feel the stress building. I tried to reason. If he had a firearm it didn't mean he would use it. Definitely not if it were one of Marshall's men. They took pride in their close work.

I imagined the fast disciplined movement, the bastard bounding towards us to slither a knife in our soft stomachs. If I turned and he was behind the mast, and odds on he was, I would precipitate the action. I pointed to the doorway to the cabin. If we were below we could prepare a welcome for him, although if he didn't take the bait and follow us in, he would have the upper hand on the deck.

I motioned to Verve and we moved down into the cabin.

I squatted down behind the stove. We were in the dark but any figure descending into the cabin would be silhouetted against the night sky.

Suddenly, the silhouette was there, blotting out the night sky. I said, 'Come in.'

The figure ran backwards. The balanced speed of the movement was shocking. No-one could do that stuff, and yet there it was. This had to be one of Marshall's people, recruited from one of the frigates.

I bolted the batwing doors and turned on the light. The curtains were drawn over the small windows. Verve's eyes were wide with a curious wonder.

'How do you stop that?' she asked.

'With something like that,' I said, pointing to the Weatherby. 'I need to get away from the boat though, about a hundred metres, so I can see him move anywhere on the deck. The moon will be up soon. I'll do it from the water. Verve went to a compartment hidden behind the gun case. She slid the surface and revealed the hand guns. She took a colt automatic and .357 Magnum and began loading them. She looked up at me. 'There could be more than one.'

'Could be.'

She tossed the Magnum to me. 'Why can't you use that?'

'Hand guns are for blasting away at 15 metres. You just hope you hit something. I can't chance it with someone who moves like that.'

I removed the Weatherby from the glass case. I took the shells out of the drawer. The problem with wildcat bullets is that with more power and velocity you often get a marked inaccuracy. I was going to need to rely on this rifle giving me an accuracy without deviation. I might only have a hand, a kneecap as a target. The scope was German and gave a variety of powers. The Zeiss lenses meant a depth of vision that would enable a powerful magnification close to the target. It would also mean shooting with both eyes open. While one kept track of a moving target, the other aligned the target meticulously.

I loaded the magazine and oiled the bolt before gently pushing it home. I slipped a condom over the barrel end but the sight edge ripped it. 'They're so weak,' Verve said.

I placed another one over it and fixed it with a twisted rubber band. I slid the rifle into a plastic garbage bag and tied the plastic in a knot. Verve took me to the forward bulkhead and pointed upwards at the hatch. 'He's going to expect you through this or the one in the stern,' she said. 'You've got two seconds to get over the side.'

I slipped out of my clothes, donned a pair of Truman's togs, and slipped flippers on my feet.

'You'll have to go over a rail about a metre high,' Verve said.

'Look,' I said, whispering close to her ear, 'you go to the stern hatch and knock against it. I'll give you five seconds and then I'll reef this one open.' Verve left.

I shoved the hatch back quickly, took the rifle, slipped it over, and hauled myself into the night. I went forward on my stomach, lifting the flippers out. He was certainly not in front of me. The deck, the top of the cabin, was empty right to the stern. I whirled quickly, forgetting the Weatherby.

The bastard had been hanging off the bowsprit by his knees. In one flourish, he flipped his trunk upwards and dove towards me. With a clutch at the Weatherby I rolled into the water under the rails. The hatch was already slammed shut. I surfaced with my finger on the trigger—it was covered with plastic but I could still fire it. He had already disappeared.

I let myself sink, pointing the flippers directly down. A metre below the surface I turned and began kicking towards the stern. I'd make 30 metres before I had to surface. I angled away from the boat. The surface above me was a pewter sheet.

Finally I moved upwards, my instinct to breathe very close. I gasped the air and sank again immediately. I had no idea whether I would be seen or not. Up again for another lungful in exactly the same position. And then down again, moving towards the stern.

I needed more air before I got there. I had totally miscalculated my underwater capacity. It had left me.

Minutes later I drew a slow, quiet, but desperate breath.

Then with my breathing under control, I began kicking quickly beneath the water, using the flippers to get my shoulders above the water. I gauged a double curve of each flipper so that I could slow my kicking. I was easily supported.

I ripped the garbage bag so the telescopic sight was exposed. Sighting the rifle I discovered I would need to be at least 50 metres from the yacht to cover its deck. The stern seemed to be about 4 metres high from the angle I had.

I listened. I could only hear the gentle dribbling of small wavelets against the hull. Then I heard the bastard coming. There was a quick scuffle on the deck and a splash. He was in the water with me.

This approaching man turned up the fear far more than any approaching ocean predator. I had to use my sphincter muscles savagely to stop myself fouling the water.

I was loathe to drop the Weatherby. I moved silently to the yacht's stern ladder and balanced the rifle on the second rung above the water. It was hooked there by the trigger guard and the telescopic sight. I ducked beneath the water, dove down several metres and watched the surface for a moving silhouette. Surfacing occasionally for air, I spent about five minutes on these futile exercises. For too long I stared against the shore lights, thinking that strategically it would be the best direction for him to come. I retrieved the rifle. What would happen to Verve if they moved against the boat while I was still in the water?

He came for me from the shadow of the hull. He'd been waiting for me to exhaust myself, floating there close in on the steel, his head and body camouflaged by the weed growth.

When I saw the movement I thought it was a toss of a curious dolphin. Then I saw him coming for me, a quick shadow. I did the most sensible thing when you're caught off balance like that. I panicked and took off. I let go of the rifle and swam. I had settled into a fast rhythm and I was out-distancing him easily. The problem was my direction. I was heading north away from the island. Five minutes later I saw he had stopped. He was 30 metres behind me.

The shore lights were dipping as the deeper water contained a hint of the swell over the outer reef. I let myself become part of the water, letting it flow in and out of my mouth, almost as if I was gaining sustenance from it. I swam at him and he turned instantly, moving away. It was too glib. He was trying to sucker me in. I let him swim. He stopped when he couldn't see me following, then came forward slowly. Only my eyes were out of the water. The only reason I could see him at all was because he was occasionally silhouetted against the shore lights. His head was turning too rapidly. He had lost me.

I began moving west, circling him, keeping my eyes on him. I wanted to be closer to shore than he. When I was a hundred metres away I slipped beneath the surface and swam for the shore. Once I heard a sound, a slight ding of a bell, and it echoed, and I thought it could be an anchor chain moving or the hydrofoil straining at the wharf.

Thirty metres in I surfaced for air, forcing myself to exhale slowly. The swimmer was almost half out of the water, working furiously on his fins to get height. After half-a-dozen breaths I submerged again. This time my heart had slowed and I felt more at home. I made even more distance. I was off the westerly point of the island when I surfaced, and wasn't sure of the current that flowed there. The mainland wasn't too far off.

I looked at the yacht. It was dark and still. Verve was still safe. How long would it be before they decided something had gone wrong?

Closer to the shore I decided to wait for him. He would expect me to have swum back to the yacht. As I was calculating odds on the various pieces of action whirling through my mind the moon went dead. Deep cloud took away its light. With the lack of vision came a severe dread. It would be hard to tell if I began drifting, and if I saw my hunter again it would be by mistake not design. I began breast-stroking to the shore, carefully, not making a sound.

It only took me minutes, which was a surprise, but I came up in junior mangroves, the mud so soft I had to slide through it. I didn't mind. The islands of the reef were without the severe nasties of the mainland, and the mud gave me camouflage. The stink from the mud gave me a good feeling. I smelt like something dead. I stashed the flippers and headed to the boulder beach.

I liked the red boulders. They were smooth and they had long folds in them that easily accommodated the human body. I took a shot at lying on top of the second highest. He would expect me to take the highest. I was about 4 metres up and concealed from anyone approaching. Even 50 metres out my skull would only look like an outcrop.

I watched the yacht. If they had me Verve would only know when they came for her.

He almost took me by surprise. His body slithered up with the small waves and he just kept oiling up over the smaller boulders. Christ, he could have been a large centipede. And then he stopped. I wondered why. He had smelt me. There was a mangrove stink where there shouldn't have been. Fuck. I went for him, landing on his back with my knees. He was so fast he was turning as I landed. He didn't take the full brunt. His back was hard, my knees slid off, hitting the rocks. I grabbed a small rock as he came for me. I whacked him. His knife struck my shoulder and sliced there. The rock hit his nose, not stopping him, and I struck again. It was like a kid bouncing a ball. He kept rising and I kept striking, no time to aim, an element of nightmare: stuck there, repeating my actions with no result.

Finally he fell. I followed him down, needing to hear bone give before I left him.

I was shivering as I staggered away. I felt like the victim.

Focus, focus, my mind whispered, but I didn't, and I was caught again by the mangrove mud. My feet refused to lift and I fell forward on my face, my arms too weak to respond to the brain.

I remembered the flippers as I lay there. The mud made soft sucking sounds. I couldn't have cared if it was quicksand. Flippers wouldn't have helped anyway if I was sinking. I put my arm down straight away from chest. Stupid if it was quicksand, but I wanted to get to my worst possible moment without hesitation. My fist struck solid matter so I began the slow process of sitting back. My mind must have wandered because I was suddenly aware of sitting in the mud like a baby breathing through my mouth. Blood was oozing from the flap he'd made of my shoulder but the mud had blocked most of the bleeding. The pain in my knees became a severe throb. I leaned back, pushing down with my legs, and squirmed backwards over the mud. Standing on solid ground I leant against a tree trunk for a time, wandered unbalanced over to the flippers, and then down to the water west of the boulders.

In the water I ran my fingers over my knees. They were more painful than my shoulder, and when the flippers around my wrist dinged one knee I nearly screamed.

I was in that state where you imagine that whatever has been threatening you would be a welcome relief compared with the torture of existing.

Luckily the stern ladder descended deep into the water. Most boats only have them to the waterline. Truman had thought of everything.

I lay on the deck for a moment, and then I shuffled into the cockpit and put my head against the cabin doors. 'Verve, it's me. Open up.' The door swung open with my weight. The lock had been smashed. She'd gone. There was enough blood to slip on the steps down. I began sobbing.

I woke to the sound of the hydrofoil taking off. One a.m. They're coming to get me, I thought. They have the island to themselves. I wondered if it was Verve's blood I was sitting in. Deep down I felt the smallest kindling of rage. I let it build. I fed it. Verve was gone. I allowed myself to see her generosity, her cunning, her body. I loved her. I stood up and walked to a porthole to look at the water. It was placid. The moon was on the water. A warm tropical night. A night crawling with the deadliest species on earth. People trained to kill.

I felt the pain then.

I looked down. My knees looked like swollen footballs. There were welts lined with mud. Left they would turn the wounds into raised tribal scars or festering legs. I went to the galley and ransacked the cupboards looking for medical gear. Truman wouldn't have neglected anything. The only thing that had stopped him was an expanding splinter of metal to the brain. They had known nothing else would. I found the cabinet. Everything I needed. Iodine. I laughed when I saw it. Illogical joy. It was the only thing that could kill coral so the bugs in the mud would also be knocked out. Needles and thread. I could mend myself. How long did I have?

With the .22 lying beside me and an extra clip, I began the restructuring process. I probed the slices in my knees with iodine soaked cotton wool, pushing it into the wounds with a fork from the galley. They had to be clean. And they weren't so deep. The swelling was from the damaged sheaths of sinews and tendons. After that I poured in more iodine. I melted magnoplasm until it was like cooling wax and poured it over the cuts. Overnight it would drag out any beginnings of infection. I hoped. I bound the knees then. I thought I would have to sew the flesh there, but I decided against it. The shoulder would really need the pain threshold I had and I didn't want to wear myself down.

The only knot I knew beyond the old granny, which tended to give readily, and would be totally disastrous in stitches that were meant to hold flesh against flesh, was the knot for a fish hook. The problem with that was it needed the metal of the hook for leverage. That meant each stitch would need a double bind so that there was leverage for the knot to be pulled against. The needle had to be pushed twice through the same hole, or close to it. My only luck with this wound was that the cut went upwards. This meant it would drain freely.

I was worried about the time factor. I went to the mirror on the inside of the cupboard near the head. I pulled the curtains over the portholes and switched on the lights. The shoulder was seeping blood but no major vessels had been sliced. I wondered if I should probe up there. The thought of the fork made me ill. I gauged I would need at least eight stiches. They'd be pretty far apart, because I certainly wasn't going for the cosmetic effect.

I cut 2 metres of thread. I was going to need plenty to pull the knots tight. With only one hand I would need to use my teeth. With my shoulder to the mirror I began.

I had overestimated my pain threshold. With the first I went too high up on the flap and nearly passed out. I discarded that hole. I went to the edge of the flap and was quick pushing through. Second time through it appeared to be numb.

I lasted for six stitches and couldn't begin another. I took four Panadol, discarding the aspirin because it promoted bleeding.

After the nausea had gone I managed to examine the smashed doors. There was a bullet hole high to the left. Verve would have been facing the door, so it was she who had been doing the shooting. I remembered that strange underwater sound. It may have been a shot hitting steel. She had wounded someone. At least shot at them. Somehow they had grabbed her. They had obviously taken her because they wanted to know what she knew.

A grunt of bitter laughter burst from my chest. I lay on the floor of the cabin, rolling, hurting with laughter. I was alive. Gradually the laughter subsided and I began to breathe regularly. Where the hell had they gone?

I switched on all the lights in the cabin and went to the navigation desk and snapped on the light there. Verve had left a message. She had ringed in red a small portion of coast. When she had gone to the map when we had first come aboard, the map had been unmarked. Checking on the scale of measurement it seemed to be about a hundred nautical miles to the north, give or take a few miles. It was close to where Charlie had been found.

I had to get the yacht started. It was the only way I could get there quickly. They didn't have a great start unless they had a fast boat or a seaplane. They had both.

The diesel motor wasn't a problem. Fuel to be switched on, a warm-up ignition of about thirty seconds and a starter button response.

Leaving the motor idling, I examined our moorings.

The winch operated on the same principle as those on the front of four-wheel drives so cranking the stern anchor up was no problem. The mooring on the bow was a heavy chain attached to a buoy now on the deck. I released the buoy over the side and I was free.

I eased the motor into forward and felt the prop take hold, in a fashion. There was barely any headway at all. We were moving, but about 2 miles an hour. This was a big boat. I couldn't believe it.

The weed was the answer. It was preventing water flow, or stopping the prop biting the water, or both. I headed off anyway. No sailor, I had no idea of sail riggings at all, or how to operate them. At this rate it was going to take me a hundred hours to make the destination.

Chapter 15

I loved a woman once who masturbated whenever she was tense. I actually forgot to ask her if it relieved her tensions, although from my own experience it would just suspend it for an hour or so. Unfortunately it wasn't available to me at this time.

I needed to clear the hull of weed. I left the motor on idle. In the forward locker there was a light chain which I looped down into the water and over the bow. I began sawing and tearing at the weed with the chain. Dark dobs sprang up around me.

To get the prop clear I turned it over very slowly and edged the chain down the hull. There was a frightful noise as it struck, clanging thuds, the chain reefing in my hands. I pulled it back immediately. But it had down the job, cleaning the prop of mussels, barnacles and weed. Now the yacht began moving along at around 8 knots.

After securing the wheel I went down to the galley. The only food aboard was tinned. I lit the stove and heated baked beans. I opened cans of fruit and ate from them.

I found I was catnapping, eyes closing unbidden, and by the time dawn lit the coast in marvellous colours I was feeling ill. I had never been seasick and so it was the injuries that made me vulnerable. I straightened my knees as much as possible every few minutes, wanting them to heal while maintaining elasticity.

Mid-morning I walked cautiously up to examine the jib arrangement. The sails might give me a few more knots. The jib was up in a second. It was merely a matter of unrolling the damn thing. It pulled away from a steel retainer that was spring loaded. I tried the mainsail. I stripped away its blue cover, worked out which rope to haul on and up it went. I had heard of sailors starting out to sail around the world with only a few weeks' experience but this was ridiculous. The offshore breeze was easy. The yacht ducked a rail close to the water and the speed picked up. I knew changing direction would be a problem, but so far I didn't need to. I scanned the horizon for floating objects but only saw some very low islands seaward. I went below.

First I scrubbed the blood away with cold water, and mopped. Flies were already wandering around the cabin. Old blood leaves a bad stench. I wasn't going to make it down on my knees for the final clean so that funky blood smell would be accompanying me.

I broke open locked drawers beneath the navigation maps. Empty. I smashed the wood at the bottom of the drawer. It gave away, although I realised I could have slid it back.

I was rewarded with the yacht's log and a notebook. The notebook was beautifully illustrated. It was Truman noting birds and their behaviour and characteristics. The treasure was on a double page in the centre of the book. It was a map of the beach I was heading for. He supplied all the details except the scale of distance, although he had sounded depths. Upriver was an abandoned abattoir and south of that was the camp. Presumably where they were holding the birds.

I sat back, gingerly, and looked around me. This was a craft with secrets. The wood panelling was so oppressive in its unbroken denseness—it ran the length of the yacht—I began to sound the panels; they had to be hiding something. This searching gave edge to my thoughts of Verve. It was her I wanted to see again. An endangered species herself, she had to be alive. She was the reason I was living now. A woman of her style should not be lost to the earth.

I sat on one of the bunks and tried to work out from memory how much the cabin space was short of the deck space. It seemed about a metre in all directions. I took the butt of the .22 rifle. Two blows to the panelling, revealing nothing, and the stock broke at the pistol grip. I used it as a hammer them, smashing the centres of the panels, and then levering the wood away. Behind one panel I found a huge single-shot rifle. It was a Barrett .50, some thought the best sniper's rifle. The bolt action was way back in the stock, behind your ear when you sighted. This gave it about an extra 30 centimetres of barrel. It was silenced with a drum about 45 centimetres long. A flash disseminator appeared to be built in. The shells were about 15 centimetres long, armour piercing. Truman would have been safe even if chased by pirates in the China Sea. The scope had beautiful optics. I was several miles out from the coast but putting it up to a clear porthole I was suddenly in the foliage—close anyway—ashore.

Behind the radios there were panels that slid open to show cages structured with complicated perches, water reservoirs designed to be operated by the birds. The cages stretched over some 3 square metres and were half a metre deep. There was also an incubation unit with deep scalloped rests for the eggs. The yacht would have to turn over to destroy that cargo. None of this would have escaped a thorough search by customs so I reckoned the yacht must sail under different names in different ports, pretending it had only been out for a day's sailing. More likely it met fishing contacts off the coast and transferred the cargo to vessels that weren't regularly searched by customs.

I was tiring again. I crawled onto a bunk. My knees throbbed and my shoulder was in agony. I wasn't moving enough to keep everything loose. Through a porthole I watched the passing sea, occasionally we dipped so that I could see under the dark silver surface. I didn't want to think about Verve. Didn't want to know what she was going through. I just willed her to stay alive. The worst scenario was that they were already at the bird camp. My rest was fitful. Images of Verve finally drove me from the bunk.

At the navigation table I began planning an approach. It would be in the evening. I knew I could find the bay because I had Cape Tribulation as a marker. It would stop me going too far north.

I read Truman's chatty notebook, focusing through the pain, finally allowing it to keep me awake: 'The roos are just processed here. They're brought in warm. And they're substituted for beef and exported. They avoid the blue dye that brands them dogs meat. They're substituted for beef after the health inspectors have been through.'

'The bad part of all this,' he wrote of my destination, 'is that all the offal goes into the river. This makes it dangerous water. There are crocs and sharks in the river and the sea. The good part is when they're full they come into the sandy shallows and just loll around. It's marvellous to sit above them, suspended in water as clear as air. The bad part is that the abattoir doesn't operate all the time and they get hungry, demanding and aggressive.' The only boat I could use in close was rubber.

The notebook had more than just information on coastlines. As I flicked through it I wondered if Robe knew about this compulsive scribbler, building evidence against everyone. Throughout the entries there were character notes on Charlie and Robe. He liked Charlie: 'He is generous despite the streak of vanity that gives him too much confidence. He is too lazy to plan properly, relying on his intelligence and speed to carry him through all difficulties. Knowing he relies on these things, he is too anxious. His nervous system kicks in with terrible cost . . .' Too much like me, I thought.

Robe 'is a creature without redeeming qualities. Psychopath. He is truly the killer ape of our African genesis, smart, unscrupulous, and always the first with a weapon in his hands. Angela picked up on him immediately. He would kill his friends if he suspected them of encroaching in any field he sees as his own. He had no hesitation in having Charlie's people killed. Charlie thinks he can deal with him now. I suspect he has liaisons with people larger than Charlie suspects. Charlie won't have this.' Angela had met Robe previously, so she must have come from the States before to check out exactly what Truman was dabbling in.

I read on. Truman had been perceptive: 'The problem with dealing with these people is that they don't know a solid deal when it's put in front of them. They're always looking for the deal behind the deal, and that's dangerous. Soon they'll begin to think they can make their own deals. I'll have to be alert to any changes of relationships.' I laughed when I read that for I saw my own madness. For a split second I saw myself as an assassin fly, the big one who eats from the smaller ones. How many of us in this little happening were as demented?

I flicked through the pages, looking for Angela's name. It came up several times, but without the longing of a spouse separated from a lover. Close to the end of the journal he commented, 'Angela is becoming more demanding of results. It's not as if it's her money. Until now she has processed my demands without comment or censure. Why is she becoming more interested?' Obviously she had been brooding on the earning potential of Truman's interest. And he didn't see that?

As the sun rose to full morning strength a north-westerly truly filled the sails and I took a slight tack away from the coast to use it. The diesel still thumped away.

When I tacked west for the final time it was close to evening. I looked at my wounds. My knee swellings had subsided. I dressed the knees lightly, piling on the iodine. I poured iodine over the shoulder dressing.

I leaned over the bow as we moved quietly over the reef, only a jib moving us through the final half mile of shallowing translucent water. I ran the huge anchor down about 400 metres from shore. Truman's notebooks made it clear that if I went closer in I would beach the yacht at low tide. I doubted even Angela would recognise the yacht in this light. If I hadn't finished my work by morning the yacht would give me away.

I walked onto the top of the cabin, untied the folded rubber dinghy and pulled the plug on the compressed air. The dingy sprang into shape. It was large. But it didn't look big enough to frighten larger predators. I tossed it into the water.

It seemed strange to leave the boat. Already I had become used to it. Learning to sail it had made it mine somehow. It might be a small floating object in an ocean, but it was a far better proposition than whatever waited on the shore. I was calm though. The Barrett was rocking on the rubber floor, its barrel almost as long as the space it rested in, and I had the Smith and Wesson. Hardly jungle gear, but I could kill people from 800 metres away. That would frighten them. The tiny outboard motor ticked away on low revs. I hadn't attached it to the stern board. I held it over the side myself. If the creatures below decided to taste rubber I could whack a speeding prop down their gullets. I was ready for anything.

On the steepest part of the beach there was a run-out slide, the sand cut like a channel through to mangrove mud. Crocodile.

There were more run-outs further along the sand. These were the reptiles' escape paths.

They didn't want to be caught up on the bank without the fastest possible route to the water.

In the shallows I stepped from the rubber dinghy and hauled it up the beach. In the morning my footprints and drag mark would be clearly visible in the sand. My knees had only twinges of pain now I was warming up. I pulled the dinghy into the undergrowth.

I was in the stillness of the rainforest then, with the 8-odd kilometres to walk in the dark to the camp marked on Truman's map. The bird calls that travelled the forest floor emphasised the still quiet. The moon began to sail above the treetops. Underfoot the ground was easy going. The moss beneath the ground cover had some give in it. The trees towered, and when you saw the tops of them you wondered how such huge leaves could be held against the sky with such wispy stems. Other trunks were huge and mottled, bulbous and tubular with age, running straight to the heavens. I was worried about the stinging tree. Its leaves injected you with hollow darts, tiny, and they stayed in your skin for months. Apart from the initial crippling pain, any environment you walked through was let, via their hollowness, directly into your flesh. But deeper into the forest the floor became readily negotiable; I only had to step over snaking trunks and soft ground. It was slow, but I knew I was making progress.

I became confident. With that expansion of spirit I began to think the night walk would be a breeze. Three hours later I began to hear voices to the south-west. Changing direction I saw light ahead. It was hard light. There was a hum of a generator.

Closer in I saw the Aborigines I had seen on the beach with Updine. They were standing around a large stump embedded with a metal spike. They were getting through the thick skin of the coconut to the shell, cleaving the matted material away with strong whacks down on the spike. They were in khaki shorts and T-shirts or shearer's singlets. I didn't see Mick. And there were no white skins.

There were small huts around the large clearing, they were roofed with palm fronds. As my eyes adjusted to the light I saw they were cages.

The voice from behind me was calm and reasonable. It was Mick. He spoke his inconsequential propaganda as he assessed the circumstances. 'You like the forest, brother?' he asked casually, knowing the fright he had caused. 'All our medicines come from the forest,' he said. 'Only about thirty per cent of whiteman's medicine comes from it. We've had about fifty thousand years to find them, man. You'll cut all the fuckers down before you do. Fuckin' progress, hey?'

'It's not medicine going to come out of the forest, mate,' I said. 'It's going to be blokes with guns.'

'You know, mate, you look like a kadaicha man, sent out to do tribal killings. Do you see yourself that way? I mean look at the weaponry man. I saw one once, slinking through the bush, covered in mud and paint. He was going to scare the shit out of someone before he killed them.'

'I'm looking for a friend,' I said. My hand was close to the Smith and Wesson. I had no idea whose side this mob were on.

Mick's voice had reached them in the clearing and they were walking over.

'You're not looking for the birds?' He gestured with a big smile across the clearing to the cages.

'Verve was grabbed on Fitzroy Island,' I said. 'Eventually they'll force her to bring them here.'

'Shit,' he said. 'Some real bad blokes on their way, brothers,' he added loudly. They scattered, picking up firearms, mostly .303s with cut-down barrels, and hot cartridges necked down for .22 or .270 slugs. A couple of 44-40s for pigs, and a 30-06 with a Mauser military action to bring crocs to a stop.

'Take it easy,' I said. 'They're city blokes. They mightn't even get here.'

'Listen, they can shoot can't they, otherwise they wouldn't be here?'

'Yeah, but they're not hunters.'

'They don't have to be, the bloody birds are in a cage.'

'Yeah, but they're not going to get you. I mean you'd have the drop on them.'

He grinned at me as if I were a dope. 'We'll have the drop on them. I'll tell you what mate, we don't shoot anyone here. Not for quids, right. We're not crazy bastards.'

I hefted the Barrett onto my shoulder. 'Is there any high ground here?' I asked.

'See that tree, mate,' he said. 'That is a Moreton Bay fig. That is the highest ground around here. We're all gone now, brother. When they've finished with you we'll come back and bury you.'

Mick disappeared across the clearing, following his mates. He knew the score. There was no higher authority for any of us to appeal to. We had to survive in our own ways.

I walked to the tree. It was huge. It was responsible for this clearing. Its spread had pushed back the forest, stopping the light with its foliage, and preventing anything else taking its nutrients from the soil. Its own great sucking roots made a meal of any plants that had the temerity to grow close. I looked up at the tree. Its branches stretched 20 metres horizontally out from the trunk.

I slung the rifle over my back and began climbing. The trunk was gnarled; very easy going even having to avoid bumping my knees. About 12 metres up I found a fault in the trunk, as if it had been badly injured at one point and had turned in on itself, leaving a recess of the style you might find in Gothic architecture. I backed into it. From the ground I was completely concealed. I could only watch the cages by leaning out a little. But through the leaves I doubted if any of these city slickers would see me. I slid down to sit, my legs out before me, a knot of wood supporting them behind the knees. The pain was lighter. There was no growing infection there. The rifle was between my knees. I slept for hours, deeply, unaware of unfamiliar sounds around me.

Morning broke over the jungle with a blast of bright bird songs. The sun was emerging out of the sea, golden light shot through a darker sky. I didn't move. For a moment I thought the birds had been disturbed by intruders. But the clashing sounds were more argumentative than calls of fright. I stayed where I was, quietly testing and stretching my body for over an hour, while keeping watch on the surrounding forest.

I left the Barrett and descended to the clearing.

The parrots were gorgeous, different from anything I'd seen before. The pale blue and green of the sea slashed with red and black. Cheeks were pale blue with a black cap on the head balanced by a slash of red above the beak. The effect was not gaudy but hypnotic. The colours were seamless, the feathers looked soft, barely any sharp lines; the birds' presence was welcoming. There was a feeling I've had when watching dolphins surface near the beach, surprising you, and yet making you realise there is a total rightness to their existence.

The voices had a sweet tone, like the turning of the coral on the beaches of the island. An incredible lustre to the notes, unlike the sounds of most parrots I had heard. And they were gymnasts. They didn't have that larrikin attitude of some parrot types. I remembered seeing corellas in the Mallee. They flew upside down, fought with each other, fell upside down, and I saw one flying backwards for a moment. In the trees they were monkeys, hanging upside down by one claw. By comparison the paradise were Olympic gymnasts.

These were civilised birds. One of them looked at me, head on one side, the eyes dark liquid. It seemed to be asking questions. An incredible sadness hit me. That was how I felt it, a profound grieving. The look was as wise as any owl. It knew what was happening, and it was living with it. There is no way a scientist could tell me that people were the only creatures that understood the concept of death or loss. But this bird was accepting it, no self-pity at all. Simply asking, with its presence, the most important question of them all. To each person that was a different question.

I remembered the paragraphs I had read in Truman's notebooks. He and Charlie had almost lost them. They had little bugs that were eating into their lungs, and Charlie diluted some cattle lice chemical and experimented on some other birds. Just a drop on their beaks gave off enough whiff to kill the little suckers. Truman had written about the parrots with real affection. He had also liked the way Charlie could focus on a problem and solve it. Charlie had speculated that it may have been these bugs that destroyed the birds in other areas.

I looked across the clearing, and moved around a cage, careful to watch the forest fringe for anyone approaching. A moment later I heard noises in the forest and a panicked flock of birds. At the back of the cage was a termite mound, transported here, I saw, because it was damaged, showing signs of travelling. I left it before I had a chance to examine it.

They came in a large chopper. Hearing the whine way off I had climbed the tree again and saw it come in from the south-east, low, over the sea of eucalypts. I realised now why there had been a wait. They couldn't use just any chopper pilot for the work to be done. They would have needed to fly one up from Sydney. Those things took time.

I wasn't quite prepared for the chopper to fly directly to the clearing. As hectares of foliage began to heave on its slow approach I climbed part of the way down the tree and ran back along the branch to the fold of trunk, crouching there, hoping that the visitors wouldn't catch a glimpse of me. I needn't have worried. The dry mulch that flew high in the air was good enough camouflage.

It was a huge metal creature. A big Sikorsky. In the air it didn't seem as if the clearing would hold it, but there was plenty of room in front of the cages. It settled in the clearing like some rocking mammoth. Five armed men sprang from its opening doors and took control of the clearing as if it were a military exercise. They were in jeans though and T-shirts. This was Robe's little army. My luck was out. I might get two or three of them before I was located but there were still more to descend from the aircraft. A nightmare.

I found I was holding my breath as the others descended.

They were all young men until Esben Robe stepped down. There was no doubt who was in control. In the clearing he was tall and broad, with the hard look of getting down to business. I was waiting for Verve though, staring into the shadowed cabin, waiting for the fall of her hair as she stopped to descend. Angela was next. Her suit was rumpled, soiled, her shirt torn. She'd been beaten. Her life expectancy was pretty much nil. She was Robe's partner no longer.

My heart was pounding. If Verve wasn't safe I would begin shooting. One shot for Robe, one into the engine cowling, and then I'd wait.

Verve's condition shocked me. She descended with a short coat around her, only her underclothes beneath that. They had spent the night entertaining themselves. I put the scope on low power and looked at her face. Her eyes were focused. Her face swollen and bruised. The ordeal hadn't dulled her. She was full of rage. She must have known there was hope for her. They would need someone who knew about these birds. A heavy-shouldered man was behind her. When they reached the ground he held her arm in a rough proprietorial way.

Robe looked in the bird cage first.

'Beautiful birds,' he said.

A fat T-shirted bloke giggled. 'Let 'em out. Hate to see birds in a cage.' He slapped his leg in appreciation of his own wit. His automatic weapon was light, or he was strong, because it easily slipped under his arm and hung halfway round his back on its sling. He retrieved it quickly.

I moved out on the massive branch in front of me. It was like moving on a wide bush path after walking through the rainforest. The mobility gave me about as much scope as a dog with a running leash on a clothesline.

I gauged that if I began shooting them now the best they'd be able to do would be to monkey up one of the neighbouring timbers and try and find me in the foliage. But too many coming at once would mean I would be exposed.

As the swinging blades of the chopper slowed to a stop the copper from Cairns, Albert March, jumped down. Now I knew whatever was going to happen here would be subject to an official cover-up. Things were beginning to look desperate.

Verve spoke up. 'We'll have to feed the birds,' she said. 'Nobody's been here for a while.' Robe walked to her across the clearing. His reply didn't have her stridency so I didn't hear its tone. He slapped her to the ground though, a nasty backhanded blow. I covered him—the cross hairs wandering over his dome—in case he stepped in to inflict serious damage, but his gesture had only been to let her know she was nothing, and she better act like it. He would have let the birds die if it meant he would remain boss here in this clearing. A dangerous man. A psychopath. Even Marshall wouldn't let him live once he had what he wanted.

My finger had tightened on the trigger, and when I didn't pull it, only taking up the first pressure, there had been a flush of sweat. I longed to be able to whack the bastard down, drill him to the earth.

Robe walked to the bird cage. I could hear him talking as he moved around it. 'So these are the little bastards causing so much trouble.'

'It's no trouble.' It must have been March. I didn't recognise his voice, but I remembered he had a sort of nonentity mildness when he had first spoken to me. Hell, how long ago was that? Only a matter of days, and I had forgotten his existence.

Robe must have stood looking at March, speculating, because after a minute or so he said, 'You must be fucking joking. I'm here, aren't I? I hate this shit hole of a place. I had to come up here to look after what you dickheads couldn't.'

'Hey,' March said. 'The birds are here. We get them out. Where's the trouble?' He had the optimism of someone who could walk away from responsibility. Optimists without craft or experience are stupid. Robe began explaining to him as if he were a kid.

'The trouble is,' Robe began, 'we have people around who know too much.'

'She can't do anything, she's up to her neck in this. She puts us in and she puts herself in. Never known that not to quieten a criminal.'

'Do you think she reckons she's a criminal? Is that what you think?' His voice took on a deeper timbre—angry disbelief. I wondered if he was talking about Verve or Angela.

'And am I a criminal? Are you a fucking criminal?' The questions didn't require answers, he was just forcing crime down March's gullet.

March was suitably chastened. 'I know, Esben,' he tried to reason, 'but we can fix that here.'

I watched Verve regain consciousness. She wasn't certain she should open her eyes. I saw her face pull together, her lips regain their place, a tongue flicked out to taste the blood. Something of a relief.

March was trying to get hold of the circumstances by restating what he thought were facts. 'So, what's the problem? They're here now, aren't they?' He looked down at the ground, kicked some dirt.

'And where's the Yank?' Robe said. 'That's heavy stuff. If we don't deal with him we're in for trouble forever. God, the bastards that try and do you for money.'

High up some birds fluttered through the dappling sunlight, almost like fish in the green translucence. Fish of the air, just swimming in another chemical soup. There was a flick of a large shadow across the bough in front of me. The birds suddenly startled, flew from the space, out through the greenery to the sky. Something had frightened them. The shadow had been large enough for a person. I didn't like it at all.

Verve was talking again. 'The birds eat those,' she said.

'What?' Robe demanded.

'The seeds you're kicking. The grass seeds.'

'Shut up,' Robe said. He looked at Angela. She stared at him from a submissive brow, her head down.

My skull prickled and I felt someone behind me. I wondered if I would feel a rifle being pointed at me. That shadow was no mango bat or whatever they called them here, flying foxes. They were no bigger than a fox. That had been a large shadow, broken up by the spaces between the leaves.

The rifle was beside me, the butt of the stock at knee level, the barrel above my eyes. If I moved to sight up through the leaves close to the crown, whoever it was would know I had seen them, and I was a better target than they. The hopeful sign was that they hadn't dispensed with me yet. Had to be one of Mick's tribe. How had he got past me?

Verve was sitting on the ground, her arms on her knees. She had a twig in her hand which she was breaking into small pieces. She had decided to be patient. Sitting like that she was no threat at all. Very clever. There would come a point though when she would have to rise to her feet. A delicate operation, requiring considerable timing. Too early and they just might shoot her. Too late and they would have grown used to her being no trouble at all, and shoot her. She knew Robe; knew she would have to tell him that he needed her to save the parrots anyway. If she could convince him of that her life would last a little longer.

I waited for that moment on which I could act.

Above me I heard a weird whistling sound. I looked up to see the bird behind the noise, but there was nothing. I thought it was quite close.

Below me Robe said, 'Okay, get the cages out, load them up.'

Two of the T-shirted kids boarded the chopper and tossed the cages out.

'They're hard to catch,' Verve said to Robe. 'You might lose a few. I can do it.'

Robe smiled at her. 'You can't even fuck right, bitch.' He grabbed her, ripped the coat off her, ripped the bra straps down and paraded her in front of him. He put his arms over her shoulders and pulled at her breasts with his large hands in a mock milking. His employees whistled and called out Yeah, and Wow, and Give it to her. I brought up the Barrett. He was about to die when he pushed her to the ground and turned to Angela. Verve slowly slipped her arms through the straps. She was slow because she was sobbing and couldn't see clearly.

'You,' Robe said to Angela. 'You get them.'

Angela was eager. She took a portable cage and opened the door. She placed two birds in it and handed it out, taking a second cage back in.

Chapter 16

I lay on my back on the branch looking up, my rage barely controllable. I was panting heavily and felt light-headed. I could do anything. I wanted to swing the Barrett down on Robe and dismember him. At this range I could cut him in half. Although I knew I was hyperventilating, I turned to do just that. Verve was seated in the shade with her back to the cage. The others of the party were confident now, all sprawled around the clearing. Robe walked to the chopper, thumbed to the pilot to get down and sat in the driving seat, a small fan blowing at his face. March was leaning against a tree, almost lost in its shadow.

I put the scope on Robe's face. He was edgy. Right now he was as vulnerable as he had ever been. He was in a negotiating position, but that was all. He would have very little to offer if Marshall came pounding through the forest now. Marshall wouldn't need him at all. And if Robe did what he usually did to win, the most powerful government in history would fall on him. No-one killed an American ambassador with impunity.

Robe waved over the fat T-shirted man. He whispered a few words and the fat man's face lit up. He walked over to Verve. 'Get up, baby,' he said. 'We've got business.'

Verve was slow and he kicked her thigh, hard. A cry escaped her. He pulled her to her feet and pushed her towards the jungle to the west of the clearing. From where I lay she would be lost in the foliage if I couldn't follow them. I needed to be in the westerly quarter of the tree. To get there quickly I risked being exposed. I needed to lower myself 6 metres down the trunk and run out on a long branch that disappeared into a mass of *Pisonia* trees. I used my knees, feeling them break open against rough bark.

The Barrett was heavy and had so far proved useless. If the gun wasn't truly silenced I was dead. When I took the Barrett into my shoulder, my legs wide and bent to balance the weight, I saw the fat boy raise his hand gun to the back of Verve's head. The shell took his head and part of his off-side shoulder. The blood sprayed upwards from his arteries like a gaily performing fountain. The sound from the Barrett had been a small grunt, not unlike that of a pig. The shell continued on in the undergrowth like a boar through thick lignum. The headless fat man pulled a shot off as his torso hit the ground.

I turned with the Barrett, working the bolt in the butt behind my ear, and slipped in another round. I put that through the engine cowling. Nobody was going anywhere. The exploding metal in the chopper came so close to the echo of the gun that they'd be connected. Robe threw himself from the chopper. Glancing around I saw Verve running deeper into the jungle. She knew someone was on her side for a change.

Confusion reigned in the clearing. Robe yelled, 'Get that fat bastard back here.'

Two guys ran out of the clearing after their fat mate, their guns up. They were heading away from me. I couldn't resist it. I blew a hole in the leader's back and he twisted forward, hit the ground flat and skidded whack into the trunk of a tree. The second man turned, his eye catching me in the branches. He was amazed. I worked the bolt again as he raised his M-16. The shell took a part of his weapon into his body. Turning back to the clearing I found it empty. I was in deepest shit. I lay down on the branch. I couldn't hear or see a movement.

Out of the silence the heat had brought down, came a very cheeky voice.

The voice came down from the treetops to the south of the clearing. 'Are you white blokes gunna continue to fight amongst yourselves?' Mick's tone was amused. His casual question was a flash of genius. As Robe had seen nothing but his own people, the sound for him could only be his men fighting.

'There are a couple of dozen of us here,' Mick continued, exaggerating. 'We can see most of you, right now. If you run we can track you down. I suggest you step into the clearing. The live ones only.'

One of the young city blokes stepped back into the clearing. He had a light machine .223 with a skeleton stock, and pointed it to just about all points of the perimeter, trying to locate the sound of the voice from the memory of it.

Mick issued a warning. 'We can bargain, you know. Everyone of us has guns. We could drop you like emus drinking. That means you're sitting emu, right.' No matter he was talking about life and death, he was cool.

'Now, this is how I see it. You all want our birds, okay? And we want to be paid for them, right. In cash.'

Robe was back in the clearing, looking up at the greenery. His tone was indignant. 'Now what the fuck . . . ?' A ludicrous sound against the deep, oppressive weight of the jungle. He felt that too, for he lowered his voice. 'I've spent thousands on these bloody birds already. Are you telling me there's nothing in it for me unless I talk to you?' I could see he saw things differently from most. His money and his words were more important than anyone else's. He'd had his own way for several decades.

'Fucking right, boss,' Mick answered. 'We've made two deals on these birds already but they fell through 'cause the other parties carked it.'

'Now wait a minute,' Robe said. 'I made one deal. With the Yank. He said it was tied up. He didn't say you were in.'

'Are you sayin' we shouldn't be in? Is that what you're sayin'? We catch the birds on our land and we get nothin' for 'em?'

Robe couldn't bring himself to consider a deal without the required research. He needed one of these black blokes with his hands behind his back and a knife at his throat. 'This is the way it is,' Robe said. 'Capital gets the biggest slice of any venture. That's a known, right?'

'That's a known,' Mick repeated, chuckling. 'That's a known. I'm gunna use that. I like it.' Robe didn't understand that he had to be friendly with Mick just to survive here. He was without transport, food and water probably.

'There's been a change in our position, boss,' Mick began again with some sarcasm. He giggled. 'We've got a claim in the courts for all this land. It's one big sacred site, man. And those birds, we own 'em. We decide what's done with them, because they're one of our sacred parrots.

'See, we're not stealing them, like you were gunna, we're selling them to the people we want to sell them to, and you know what boss, we don't want to sell them to you.' Mick finished with a breathless laugh.

Another voice yelled out, 'Yeah, why don't you bugger off?'

It was so outrageous I laughed.

I felt bullets thudding into the timber beneath me and watched the trails of others through the foliage to the open sky. I heard the loud *whomp* of a 30-06 and turned and looked down to see the gunman with half his skull missing. After a few bewildered steps, like a beheaded chook, he dropped to the ground, blood spilling from his brain container to the dirt, as if someone had knocked over a cup of coffee.

Silence.

Mick was equal to the occasion, although his voice had a stridency, close to hysteria. 'Okay, you bastards,' he called. 'These forests are full of bodies, brothers. Most of 'em put here by whiteman. A few more ain't goin' to make no difference.'

Silence.

Those below me were motionless. No-one bothered about the dead gunman whose legs jumped in occasional slow spasms.

Mick again. 'Everyone in the clearing, right out in the middle.' I hoped he wasn't going to get carried away here.

'You in the tree,' Mick called as the others moved to the centre. I left the Barrett on the branch and walked to the trunk. I took my time going down, keeping my knees away from the bark. But being in such a fury I was too impatient and hurt myself again.

I heard Mick again. 'The copper too.' How did he know March was a copper? Not that he mightn't have seen him in the general course of events, but it seemed strange.

A few metres to the ground and I sprang down. I looked towards Mick, coming over. 'How did you know he was a copper?'

'We know him for . . . for a long time,' Mick said. 'He's a good mate of the copper who got stabbed by a mate of mine. That Updine raped me mate's sister and killed her. Me mate's dead now. They caught him in a pub, cut his knackers off, and dropped him into a mangrove for the salties to feed on. Lot of boongs disappear like that.'

Mick didn't speak again until they were all standing in the centre of the clearing. 'Guns down,' he said, 'and two steps back.' Everyone did as they were told.

I walked over to Robe. He watched me coming. 'You'll be fuckin' dogs meat,' he said. I kicked him in the nuts. He didn't squeal, just subsided to his knees, growling. I drove my fist into the side of his neck. I felt the toughness there go slack. He went down then and I was disappointed. I kicked him high in the stomach and listened to the collapsing lungs discard air. Slowly he began to suck it in, reinflate.

'Who are you working with?'

'Fuck you,' he said. I kicked him in the ribs and took out the Smith and Wesson. 'If you don't fucking know who you're working with you're no fucking use to me,' I said.

'I work for myself,' he said.

'What about that sea serpent who came after me? He wasn't yours?'

'The ambassador arranged that.' He said ambassador as if the word would save him.

'Why did he kill Klima?'

'Too many,' he groaned, 'wanted the birds.'

March was doing his best to look like a frightened numbat, nostrils wide and working hard. But I knew he only had to reach the trees and he'd be dangerous again. If he had a sense of direction he would make it to a tourist area in a day or two.

'Okay,' Robe said, hoping that turning on his back would ease his breathing. I kicked him over again. I admired his tenacity. He'd talk from the grave to keep power. He pointed to March. 'We're not with him. The bastard's been fucking up.'

'He come with ya,' Mick said.

'He said he knew the area.'

'Reckoned that, did he?'

'Yeah,' Robe said. 'The lying bastard. I paid him good money too.'

March turned on Robe. 'We're in this together.'

'You fuck-up,' Robe breathed into the dirt.

March began to sound desperate. 'We never raided your clubs, or closed the whorehouses. Jesus Christ, that's something. You've been making real money for bloody years.' He was still fucking up. He should have been down on the ground helping Robe to survive.

Robe was recovering quickly. With his resources, his cold hard personality, he would begin to be a force again. I didn't want that. I broke his nose with the barrel of the Smith and Wesson.

'Listen Robe,' I said. I didn't go on because I didn't appear to have his attention. Then he looked at me. His eyes were hot slits. The cold blue was lost forever. 'Listen shithead,' he whispered through the blood, 'when I want to hear from you I'll be in hell.'

'Shouldn't be too long then, Esben. This is for Verve.' I shot him in the throat. The blood splashed my eyes. 'And probably for Charlie,' I murmured. His whole body tensed for a moment as if it were going to make a last desperate argument and then it relaxed, giving it all away. I went to the bird cages and washed out my eyes with water. And then my face. He didn't look like a carrier. He looked healthy. But he was the sort of bastard that could kill while dying.

Angela was watching this as she stood with a bird cage in her hand. She was looking in horror at Robe's body. She looked at me. The power fluctuations were confusing her.

'Tie them up,' I said to Mick, nodding at the small group left. 'I'm going for Verve.'

'Yeah, well there's an old codger lookin' for you,' Mick said. 'That bloke you left with a cut throat. He knew you'd find your way back. He's been waitin'. His neck healed funny. He whistles out of it like a bird. It hasn't healed right, got a' infection, somethin' like that. His burns is okay. We smear 'im with warrkarr and piss and clear up easy. He took off when the shootin' started.'

My blood chilled a little. The whistle in the tree. The bastard had been close. Why hadn't he shot me then?

I looked over at the Moreton Bay fig. The trunk was 4 or 5 metres across. Half-a-dozen people could have slipped down on the other side without discovery. I had to take it Stevo was already in the jungle, watching.

I started off, but Mick called me back. ''Nother thing, mate.' He held a finger up to hold me there. 'If you're goin' back to the yacht, those crocs down a' beach are trained see. We feed 'em up in the forest when the abattoir's not workin'. They got no fear, man.'

'Train 'em, what the hell for?'

'Charlie's idea. Keep away the coppers, anybody.'

I saw the smallest movement from March. He balanced himself, putting a hand on the trunk of a tree, glancing over his shoulder into the rainforest. He knew he had to run for it.

I didn't do anything. I knew Mick wanted him. But he came for me from 20 metres away. I put my hand up as if I was stopping traffic. 'I'm a cop,' he yelled, and kept coming, dragging a gun from the back of his belt. 'You're not,' I said. The Magnum bucked in my hand, uncontrolled. I hadn't aimed. I missed him. His gun was cleared of his clothing when I caught him in the chest with a second shot. He stopped instantly, tossed backwards.

I walked into the jungle and one of Mick's mates pointed the way. Several hundred metres out Verve was sitting with her back to a tree trunk. She had been given a shirt, jeans and boots. She had pulled her hair back from her face. When she saw me she started crying, her body rocking with emotion. 'Robe's dead,' I explained. 'Oh Christ,' she groaned, still for a moment, 'it's not over yet.'

I heard the step behind me and threw myself away from Verve, dragging at the hand gun. It was Angela. Her face was sharp. She was already weighing exactly how it would turn out. 'The Aborigines think they can split the assets,' she said. 'They think they have control here; that they own the birds.'

'They're part of it,' I said. 'They have a right.' I was bewildered I would have to explain this to her.

'Truman paid them for everything,' Angela said, 'catching them, the nets, the rockets to take them over the trees, looking after them. They're mine. Truman's estate is now mine. I own it all.'

'You bitch,' Verve said. The tone was hard, but ready to break. 'You gave me to them,' she yelled at Angela. She snatched the Smith and Wesson I had lowered.

Angela backed away, her hand out as if to catch the bullet.

'I had to stay, right,' she said. 'I had to know what I was doing, or neither of us would have got out of it alive.'

'Neither of us were going to,' Verve said. 'You just threw me to them.'

Angela was trying to creep away. 'They wanted you. They would have had you anyway. We might have pulled a deal, negotiated. It delayed things.'

'For you,' Verve breathed. 'They hurt me. They didn't stop. You didn't try to stop them. You laughed when Robe suggested it. You just said, "The little bitch will like it". This is how much I liked it.' The shot tugged at Angela's shoulder, splashing off a piece of flesh and cloth. The second shot caught her in the side, and she fell with her hands out, twisting to catch the speeding bullet. Verve kept firing, her movements manic.

Finally, after clicks on fired chambers, she stood with her hands by her side, the gun hanging down, staring towards the clearing. I took the gun from her, my fingers scorched for a moment by the hot barrel. I reloaded it quickly.

'There's nowhere to go,' Verve said. 'It'll end here.'

'I've got the yacht.'

'No,' she said. 'We can't get away. Marshall's waiting for Robe to come out. I heard it all coming here.'

Where's he waiting?' I asked her, looking into her eyes, not finding recognition. She didn't answer. I touched her arm and smiled at her. I wanted her to hold together. 'We can beat them,' I said.

'They said you were dead. That you had been killed like . . . Klima . . .' She pulled back from me, drawing herself together. I felt it was a strange reaction but I didn't think it through. 'They're just going to sell the birds,' she said. 'It's got nothing to do with any zoo. They have collectors who will pay anything for the paradise.'

'Where did the chopper come from?' I asked.

'A beach,' she said, pointing south. 'We went in a boat. Spent the night there'—her voice broke at the memory—'and we came here. They had tents there. Food. The helicopter came in the morning. Most of the time I was blindfolded. God,' she yelled, and struck at a tree with the flat of her palms.

I didn't want her to disappear, withdraw into the blackness of trauma. She had to keep talking. 'Tell me what happened.'

'I don't want to,' she screamed, bending down, her hands clasped flat between her knees. 'I don't want to say, anything. Damn you!'

I leaned towards her. 'Say it now, get it all out.'

She slapped me hard, catching me across the temple. It was hard enough to unbalance me.

'For Christsake,' I said. 'Don't hide what you know.' I grabbed her hands. 'Keep it down and it'll explode.' I was desperate, chasing around through the trunks of the trees, getting in front of her, demanding. It was a weird dance around Angela's body.

She stopped, her face in turmoil. 'What do you want to know?' she screamed. 'They fucked me.'

'Yeah?' I said.

'They beat me. They made me suck.' She pulled her lips to one side, teeth were missing. 'They laughed. They all did it to me. It was like I was nothing, hurting, tossed around.' Her voice was rising. 'They made me come.'

'Hey, Jesus,' I said, putting my hands out to quieten her. 'That's mechanical. It doesn't mean anything.'

'It does, it does,' she said. 'They beat me, and they laughed at what happened.' I held her. Slowly the crying stopped. 'It was Marshall's people who took me off the yacht,' she said. 'They ran me across the island and Marshall called them and told them I was to go with Robe. Angela thought Robe would go along with her deal. She didn't know the bastard. And I didn't know her.'

Mick came up, hesitantly. He would have heard the furore. He wasn't too impressed. His people had been victims for centuries. He looked down at Angela. 'A big waste that one. If anyone is going to come looking for her . . .

' He shook his head. 'Too much payback going on,' he said. He looked at me, and gestured at Verve. 'She knows the huts, she can rest up there.'

'Marshall will be coming here, Mick.'

'He won't find anything.'

'He'll find us,' I said. 'We can't run from this one.'

'I always run when it gets too big. That's why I'm still around, brother.'

'Listen mate, if anyone hears about what's happened here . . .' I knew it had all caught up with me. There were very nasty decisions to be made. There were Robe's gunmen. I felt light-headed. No matter what they had done to Verve. I had a glimpse of what I might have to do. An executioner walking behind them, pulling the trigger. 'We've got to go to the end,' I said.

'We let that mob go,' Mick said, pointing back over his shoulder. 'I'm not killing them.'

'They came to kill you,' I said.

'I'm not them,' Mick said. Two weeks ago that was an answer I would have given.

The only way out of continued slaughter on both sides was to appear to Marshall a larger force than we were. He had to imagine that taking us on now would be a major war he should avoid. He had to be forced to deal with us.

For a moment I wished I could just take Verve and run. We could survive for weeks in the rainforest. But I knew sometime in the future they would track us down. It was best to get it over with now. I was surprised by the solution my mind threw up. We should kill them all. The bastards deserved it. Marshall had had people killed all his life. Had certainly tried for me. I could live with it. I saw there was no chance of beating Marshall. We would be followed for the rest of our lives anyway. They simply didn't let people like us get away.

We followed Verve, walking through the timber to a small hut that had been fashioned around a tree trunk. Its walls were cut saplings, and blocks of wood. Around the entrance were tools and plastic water containers. The roof was thatched leaves from the pandanus palm.

'If you and your mob stay,' I said to Mick when Verve went into the darkness, 'we can bluff him. All this shit about the US navy is not believable. He's just got a friend doing him a favour. Christ, it couldn't be official policy. We just have some opportunists after some big money.' I watched the doorway for Verve to emerge. She was totally unpredictable, soaring between personalities that she had used to survive.

'Couldn't it?' Mick said, breaking through my thought. 'You naive, man.'

'Mick, we can do this. We could kill them. Take it all.'

'We don't know what he's got, brother.'

'What can he have?'

'Plenty. He hit Charlie's boat with a rocket from a seaplane. One of those things that follow the heat. He was trying to get away, man, swervin' around, the exhaust smoke on the rocket was like a snake movin'.'

'Okay, let's leave it till we know whether we can do it.'

I couldn't help the feeling of rage. The casual dropping of the details of the information I had wanted since I spoke to Mick all those days ago was a shock. Marshall's image shimmered with my emotion. A huge strength was given to me to bring this one off. In my mind Marshall shattered and dissolved.

I searched through Robe's pockets. He was one of those old-time boasters who carry wads of cash; just rolls of bills clipped with a rubber band. He did carry a small computer organiser though. Easier to destroy than a note book. Just a step, or a clap of the hands, and all the data, all the contacts disappeared. He hadn't had a chance to do that. I flicked it open, went for the phone numbers and ran through them in search of Marshall's number. It was there. Even his mobile. We had a way to bring him in.

Chapter 17

As night fell Mick and I discussed how Marshall would come. I thought by seaplane which meant on a calm day. There had been plenty of those and the bay was protected from afternoon winds. Mick guessed he would come through the jungle because Charlie had once told him of soldiers scouring the jungle to the south.

We had decided not to contact him immediately; it would alert him to our new status. Let him think we were dead or running. He would come in without back-up or too much caution. Once we spotted him on the move we could announce ourselves. We planned to keep him off balance with the mobile phone.

Mick's men had automatic weapons but nothing that would give any authority with a group more than 300 metres away. I had the Barrett .50. I wanted them to come by way of the sea. I could do half of them before they came into range with their own weapons. Classic sniper tactics. If they came in their rubber duckies, they'd never make it to the beach. They'd either drown or have to discard their own equipment.

Mick liked that. His grin was wide now he thought we could win this thing. He also thought he could assemble some prehistoric help. The crocs were hungry. Their presence would unsettle anyone bent on running through the shallows with violence on their mind. He just needed some bait to bring them around. I didn't have the stomach to dig up Robe, March and Angela an hour after burying them, and neither did Mick.

We didn't have to search for bait.

Screams of rage and fear burst around the evening clearing, hundreds of birds rising with a clatter of wings from the treetops. Shots followed. We ran to the front of the hut where our prisoners had been bound and gagged. We were in time to see a horrific scene, one shape, bound hand and foot, desperately jumping away as Verve swung the gun on him. She didn't bother to aim.

'Jesus,' Mick said, truly worried. 'I hope she's on our side.'

'She is,' I said, not wanting to see Verve tied down. I wasn't going to be the one to do it. There was doubt in my mind though. It registered that I shouldn't leave her alone. She could no longer be relied on. That flickering line that exists between sane and insane had been crossed. Once crossed it can lose significance. For the rest of her life she might be bright with contrasts.

'You know,' Mick said, as we put the bodies on timber bearers. 'We gut roos to take back to camp. They're much lighter.'

I didn't answer him. I wasn't sure whether or not his suggestion was a joke.

Setting the baits on the beach was a messy business. We had to have them in the second bank of trees so they couldn't be spotted by anyone approaching. We had no canvas so we had to suspend them with ropes. We also had to keep the predators in the water, so the odd shot had to be blasted across the beach. When a projectile furrowed the sand their numb brains registered the speed as too fast and heaved themselves away. A marvellous sight. They were hungry though and they learned quickly. The sight and sound display hadn't hurt them, so they knew they could hang about. They had been fed on and off over the years the abattoir had been in operation. They didn't have a great deal of inhibition around humans.

When we settled down in the evening, back from the bait, and high in the trees, with a clear view of anything coming across water, Verve and I found ourselves talking again.

I tried a jokey approach. 'How are you feeling?' I asked, 'after your . . . aar, therapy session?' I saw the victim flop forward again and Verve panting, firing more shots into the brain. How did you make that vision light?

'Terrible,' she said. She looked at me and I caught her eyes. They avoided mine like an animal that didn't want to be offensive. Not because it was frightened but because it had no real need to consider me at all.

She was silent for a while. 'Men have to pay,' she said.

'Yeah,' I said. 'They do.'

Out through the trees the sea fired when the moonlight rose. I didn't think there was any way I was going to sleep. My knees were dressed from the chopper's first-aid kit and my shoulder was stiff but not painful.

The early part of the night was uneventful, apart from scufflings from the huge lizards, and their peculiar barks of disappointment. We left the lookout to Mick's blokes. They could stay immobile watching kangaroos for a day before striking. These men were natural hunters. Their genes spoke to them of stealth and concealment.

In the very early morning I became restless. Our bargaining chips were the parrots and we'd left only one man with them. I knew it was unlikely, but if Marshall did have access straight to the top of American security, they had probably marked the chopper by now. Perhaps a radio had been left on in the chopper, or the spy satellites could pick up cooling metal, even at night. He had the technology to check that. I knew it was bullshit they could read the paper over a Muscovite's shoulder, as the propaganda had claimed, because weather conditions would have to be perfect, and they never were with pollution as severe as it is over the cities of the world. But a cooling heap of metal in virgin rainforest was another thing. It was a case of early morning panic. But I gauged I could get there and back before the light.

I saw that Verve had tied herself firmly to the tree, so I crept down and made my way over to where Mick was standing with a mate. 'I'm going to check the camp,' I told him.

'Shit,' he exclaimed. 'I don't believe this.'

'It's only that they're good in the forests at night with that equipment they're testing.'

'That's all bullshit,' Mick said.

'I dunno, Mick. I just want to hear what's going on.'

'You won't hear nothin'.'

'Okay, I'm restless. I need to move.'

'We need all of us here,' Mick said, anxious.

'I'll be back,' I said.

'Fuck off, then,' he said. 'If you're not back on daylight, we're gone.'

I'm claiming the night, I told myself. The forest floor was soft and friendly, and the dark forest seemed to speed past me. I was following a swiftly flowing creek that was heading in the direction of the camp for a distance. The going was easier there.

I felt the blow as if a large weight had slowly descended on my head, and as I fell I marvelled that there was no pain. I had many troubled dreams. A nightmare that I was being chased in a forest and my pursuers were desperate to kill me. The horror of it arrived in the dream in an incredible totality. When I gained consciousness, thinking great, that's over, now I can go about my business, the full impact of my nightmare descended on me. I was lying on the forest floor and someone was watching me, someone very still.

I vomited, and had to move my head away from the mess, reluctantly. With movement the pain descended mercilessly. When I stopped the movement—of only centimetres—there was a tremendous relief.

'Chuckin' your guts, mate,' the figure said, a strange whistle to his buried words. Fuck, I thought, I'm about to be dead.

He was a disgusting sight. Mucus dripped from his inflamed neck, and the scarring had twisted his face. He smelled fetid. His eyes were gazing rather than seeing. His clothes were filthy rags and the areas you could see of his pallid face through the patchy beard were gleaming with sweat.

I didn't care if I lived or died as long as the pain stayed away. I was willing to become a puddle and melt away in the dirt. I felt the tears from the pain chill as they rolled down my cheek and across my nose.

Stevo prodded me with his toe. 'By Jesus, you're going to pay for this mess.' He kicked my stomach.

'I know,' I said.

'You and your piss poor pack of boongs. They're not gunna help you.'

'No,' I said. I had to focus to get the next few words out. 'I left you alive.'

'Yeah,' he said. 'So fuckin' what?'

'Yeah,' I managed, signifying nothing.

'I'm gunna knacker you first, mate.' He chuckled, the sound, a horrible gurgle. Queenslanders love references to the male nuts. 'And the knife's blunt. Ya know how the weaners jump round.'

Occasionally there are moments in life that make your whole life worthwhile. You can die happy just witnessing the right events. When it all began to happen I was stunned. Didn't have time to be frightened.

The old croc had eased himself out of the creek. He paused, silhouetted against the water; the original dog from hell. And then he came. He seemed to move the forest floor to meet Stevo. Small bushes were tossed aside. Stevo heard him and turned. There was nothing that could have beaten the beast as he headed the last few metres, his jaws steady and open, despite his speed. Stevo was a sick man and carried the smell of that with him. The great jaws turned towards horizontal as they grasped him. I heard one of Stevo's legs snap, and he began screaming. He was hurried to the water.

I was so relieved it wasn't me, I started laughing. The pain bottomed then, and I knew I could bear it. I watched the demolition of Stevo with pleased amazement. Carried into the creek that way, I could only guess at the contortions of his infected vocal cords trying for a solid sound to mark his passing. The old beast began spinning in the water to disorient his victim. He needn't have bothered. Each time Stevo surfaced in a turn he was whacked down on the other side like a rag doll.

I knew I had to move. Old crocs keep a larder, stuff their meat under ledges and tree roots below the water line and wait for it to rot. I didn't want to join Stevo. I stumbled away from the creek and lay in some natural mulch of rotting vegetation.

During the early morning a cooling rain misted through the forest. I lay in it, postponing pain by not moving. As my skull cooled I located a centre to the pain at the back of my head. I felt the raised ridge there. Slight pressure didn't hurt it. Nothing much was wrong with me except I didn't want to move. It was as if the blow had struck to the very heart of my existence and, not having been killed, I was finally without anxiety. My life was suspended for a time. Wet earth beneath my head was cold and soft. I placed the raised ridge of my head in the coldness and shivered with the deliciousness of it, as if I had a slight fever.

Dropping in and out of sleep over the next few hours finally gave me the energy to move. When I woke I found I had been lying in chick weed. I began eating it raw. Good bush tucker, it was high in nutrients.

Mick was perfunctory when I staggered into the camp. 'You look like shit,' he said. 'Now take a look at what we're up against.'

It was one of those grey pilot vessels with storm windows battened down and it was low in the water. It looked about 15 metres long. It was about 600 metres off the beach, and about 800 metres from the yacht. 'Just what the hell is that?' he asked.

I knew negotiations always worked out better if you felt mean and nasty about having to part with what you had. And you had to let the purchaser know how you felt. I took the Barrett and lay amongst the roots of a pandanus palm. I worked away at it until it felt really comfortable. The wet I ignored. None of the rifle range bullshit of lying on the ground with your legs spread in a balanced way and your elbows forming a tripod. I lay the wood forestock of the rifle on one of the roots. The Barrett had a suspended barrel, which meant the steel didn't touch the solid structure you handled, and floated free so the wave that travelled through the steel when the bullet was fired didn't stop or bump, and destroy accuracy. I allowed the scope to travel the deck of the craft.

I dialled Marshall as I watched through the scope. There was movement through an aft cabin window, but I couldn't identify him. He answered the phone.

'Just wondered what you're doing off our beach?' I said.

'Who are you?' he asked.

'Speerman. Do you want to deal?'

'No deals,' he said.

I put the scope on the roof line of the cabin, and held the phone between the bandage of my shoulder and my ear. I squeezed off a shot. The pain started hard but it bottomed well within my limits. Out over the water a great piece of timber flew in the air. The boat had only been painted to look like steel. I could hole it seriously any time I liked. Something was wrong though. On the mobile Marshall said, quite calmly, 'Are you still there?'

'Yes,' I said. He wasn't on board the boat. That frightened me. I turned and looked over my shoulder. Nothing appeared to be approaching. Mick walked over to listen in. Verve descended a tree and picked her way through the slush.

Out in front of me the grey vessel was getting under way.

'You want the parrots?' I asked Marshall.

He was slow answering.

The boat was moving off at speed. It was well out of my range now. I hung up.

'I don't feel right about this,' I said to Verve. Her face was yellowing around the bruises. Her eyes were still swollen. She looked terrible. I touched her hair but she shrugged my hand away. I glanced at Mick. Nothing.

'He has to be out here somewhere,' I said.

Mick looked at me and I felt its significance. 'Ask her to ring him,' he said. 'She's working for him.'

My rage surged but the pain showed me it was unnecessary.

'I was,' she said, confessing defiantly. 'I'm not now. He had Truman killed . . . and Charlie . . . he gave me up to Robe.'

Verve had never pretended anything with me. She had enjoyed fucking. But that act didn't naturally bring loyalty with it. A wave of disappointment moved through me, but I stopped it before debilitating self-pity took hold.

'Take it easy,' I said to her, because I could see she expected to be hit. 'We've got to get out of this.'

'Fuck you,' she said. She had wanted instant confrontation.

I handed her the phone. 'Talk to him,' I said.

I fed her the numbers and she pressed them and then looked out over the water, hanging the phone loosely from her hand.

'What do I say to him?'

'Just say you told me everything and that if he wants to buy, you'll negotiate.'

'I will?' she questioned.

'They're your birds, aren't they?'

She heard Marshall answer the phone and said, 'Wait,' without lifting it to her ear, but she covered the mouthpiece with her hand. She wanted to know how I had come to regard the parrots as hers. So did Mick.

'Now wait a minute,' Mick began.

'Don't feed me any bullshit about sacred fucking parrots, Mick. You've got land rights and that's it. You took payment to look after them.'

'You want us to fight them, and we don't get anything?'

'Ask her,' I said.

'Half,' Verve said. She didn't look at me.

Verve lifted the phone. 'How much are you offering?' Verve asked.

She listened and then flicked off the phone. 'He said fuck all,' she said.

We heard the plane minutes before we saw it. It came into the bay low over the jungle. It was a beautiful sight as it touched down, a fine arc of spray behind it lit to gold by the sun.

Within two minutes of it sputtering to a stop a flat rubber boat was heading to the beach with eight men. I walked to the palm where the rifle was propped and looked them over through the scope. They were armed with high velocity weapons. Closer, I saw they had visors down in the style of motor cyclists. This was the latest gear they had been testing on jungle landings, laser technology to detect heat and interpret it. A variation on virtual reality—reality. It would need a lot of testing before I'd feel confident of it in daylight.

'Those blokes think it's night time,' Mick said. 'Their screens are all black with lights every fuckin' where.' Mick knew about the infotech soldier. His mates had read the local papers and watched the same television program I had.

If Marshall's people didn't leave the beach Mick had the upper hand. They could be shot down in the open, on the sand. No laser targeting equipment could help them cross it quickly.

'Okay, Verve,' I said. 'You go down and talk.'

'Yeah,' Mick said. 'Tell them to stuff off back to their boat or they're dead meat.' He needed to say something.

Verve was halfway down the sand by the time they landed. I took my stance behind a solid trunk, squatting. It occurred to me that they could probably sense heat radiating from the side of any cover we took. I could probably get one shot off before their automatic weapons pinned me down. But they seemed easy targets as they knelt on the beach levelling their weapons up at the forest. I hoped Mick's people were out on our flanks beyond the reach of their limited laser field.

Verve approached the covert killers as if she were expecting a social introduction. She was slapped to the ground, out of their line of fire. On reflex I dropped that bastard with a shot through his reality mask. He exploded, what was left of him flopped back in the shallows. Something landed with a splash moments after his torso disappeared. His blood had already attracted nature's disposal experts. I moved back behind the trunk.

Their automatic weapons opened up to cut a swathe through the jungle. Mick and I looked across at each other. They were way off target. Perhaps in daylight their laser vision was distorted. They knew they wouldn't reach the trees at a run, because their fire petered out. Perhaps Marshall had ordered a cease-fire.

'If Marshall wants to talk,' I yelled. 'Get him here on the sand.'

Their weapons were lowered.

One of the automatons pulled Verve to her feet and pointed towards the plane. Marshall had obviously asked for her.

'Verve,' I called, 'you're not going anywhere. Stay on the beach.' She crouched down.

Mick whispered across to me. 'Have them stay here. We go out in the boat.' Mick's mind was still on the money. Mine was on killing Marshall when he was out in the open.

'Okay,' I called, 'everyone drops their weapons on the sand.' There was a hesitation. They were relaying that message. Down went their arms. This was too easy. I didn't like it at all.

'You walk down,' Mick said. 'I'll cover you.' I looked across at him. The bastard was grinning at me. 'You're the boss,' he said.

I yelled, 'Helmets off. Now!' We waited for the message to be relayed again and slowly the helmets came off.

The faces were young and tough. They didn't look any less dangerous without their equipment. They were a hand-picked team obviously. They'd probably seen some nasty action in the Gulf, Panama, Haiti. Most of them were black.

'Have your blokes grab the weapons,' I said.

Mick put his fingers to his mouth and let go a piercing whistle. About ten blokes emerged from the jungle and wandered over to us, their rifles over their shoulders and held by the barrel, or low and balanced beside them.

They swarmed down to the beach, made the mercenaries kneel, relieved them of their side arms. One of Mick's mates whacked a helmet on his head and moved forwards like a blind man, his arms reaching. There was a ripple of laughter.

After gathering up the automatic weapons, the side-arms and the knives, Mick's men backed off about 20 metres.

It was then we heard the choppers. Two of them seemed to rise out of the jungle onto the beach, close to 800 metres away. I raised the Barrett and put a shell into the cockpit of the seaplane. A dry explosion and then a small lick of flame. I turned, working the bolt, slipped in another shell and hit one of the choppers disgorging armed men. The second was getting away but I caught it in midair. A fire ball filled their section of the beach. When I lowered the rifle I was hot with excitement. No-one was going anywhere. It was marvellous to have your enemies underestimate your fire power.

Along the beach the last of the survivors disappeared into the rainforest. We were being hunted.

'We're taking hostages,' I said to Mick.

'Hard to keep them when you're running,' Mick said.

'We're not running, Mick.'

We retreated back up the beach, the soldiers had their arms bound back at the elbows, the seven then bound together with webbing from their packs, only their feet free. 'Anyone tries to kick gets their feet blown off,' I said.

'Fuck that, man,' one soldier said. 'This was supposed to be an easy training exercise.'

'Training exercise?' I said, for a moment thinking of the wooden boat off the beach, looking at Mick.

'Yeah,' he said, 'capture some parrots and shit.' I relaxed.

'But this is some private stuff, right? We're being used?'

'Yeah,' I said. I ran forward to Verve and grabbed her arm.

'Now we can get out of this, without sweat, if we use our heads. I've just got to know you're not pissing around with us. That you're not still with Marshall.'

'If I were you'd kill me?'

'No,' I said. 'I'd just leave you here.'

I called Marshall, the phone slippery in my hands. 'We do a deal,' I told him. 'Or I ring the media. I tell them we're bird smugglers and we're being attacked by Americans, who must have lost half-a-dozen men by now. Our countries have treaties, we're supposed to be friends, and there's a US force landing on our beach trying to steal our birds. How does that sound, you know, for starters?'

'You're in real shit. Shit you'll never get out of. How do you explain the killings?'

I tried to laugh, realised it wasn't going to work, and changed it to a growl. 'You'll do the explaining,' I said. 'Some helicopters crashed while training. You can have it looking right by the time the press get here. Do we have a deal?'

'Sure thing,' he said. His voice was too easy.

'We'll be listening to the news tonight,' I said. 'We hear it, we give you half the birds and their eggs. We go our own way then. Now I want to see all your boys out of the bush and on the beach. Have them picked up.' I left the line open.

We watched the grey launch round the southern point and speed back into the bay. They launched a rubber ducky with a V keel and a powerful outboard. Through the scope I watched them loading a large angular box. Christ, I thought, it had to be more weapons. Did Marshall think we were stupid?

The craft was 300 metres away from where I squatted beside the palm. The wood stock came up to my cheek and I rested my head against it. I placed the cross hairs just below the tip of the bow. I gently squeezed off the shot.

The rubber duckie behaved like a horse falling at a jump. The occupants were catapulted high in the air.

'You bastard,' Marshall yelled at me, as I put the phone to my ear. I laughed. Marshall had seen that happen which meant he was somewhere in the trees along the bay. He was no longer a remote figure calling the shots. He was on the ground with us.

'Marshall,' I said. 'I want your blokes on the beach now. 'If I don't get that I blow your grey slug out there to buggery.'

'Okay,' Marshall answered.

Another boat came towards the beach. It was aluminium and it was fast. It broached sideways as it came to the beach and two blokes ran from the jungle to hold it. The others followed, boarding it quickly. And then a fast figure hit the sand. It was Marshall, and he could move. He dived into the boat as the motor screamed, the boat turning dangerously, and it was away.

I lifted the Barrett.

Somebody hit me softly on the side of the head and I blacked out. When I woke it was dark and the moon was out. My head was dangerously pumping. Concussion, I thought. Nobody had hit me, but they had left me. I was propped over the roots of a pandanus palm above the tide mark.

Something touched my outstretched hand. It was just the gentlest of nudges. I looked over to my hand, a slow process. A severed leg touched me as if it were a kitten wanting a home. I gagged, tried to push it away with flicking fingers. My fingers could barely move. I looked along the water line. I couldn't lift my head. Along the moonlit beach I saw the rubber duckie, a crumpled black mass.

I saw the croc watching me. He was about 30 metres away. My sphincter muscle threatened to open, and I had to clamp down hard, gasping at the effort. Anything like that would only bring him in quicker. I wanted to scream but I felt that might trigger him as well.

He moved forward without swimming motions. His mouth was open about 30 centimetres. He hadn't decided to snap. He just left it open like a sheep dog threatening to bite as he growled his way out of trouble. I wanted to believe in God and anything else that was on offer. I know there is a powerful force in the universe, I told myself, that's got be God. I began to will my body to react. When it didn't I decided it was all a dream. Then it occurred to me that I didn't want to experience a croc attack even in a dream. It was a stupid thought, but it made me cry.

As he came his mouth opened further. I was sorry for what I had done to Updine. In the soft light I saw down his throat. It was like a plastic moulding. No tongue, no horrible redness that you might see in a snarling dog. The teeth were big but they didn't look sharp. His gullet was closed off by a moulded flap. Nothing sinister there at all. It was an innocuous sight, compared to what I had expected. Two metres away I screamed and yelled. '*Yaaaaaaahaaaa*,' the sound hit his open mouth, and like a naughty creature he made a grab at the floating leg, catching it in the corner of his mouth, and made off.

It disappeared below the surface. I continued yelling. I couldn't stop. I knew there would be others, probably right now approaching me from behind and I wouldn't even see them. God, I said, I believe. I promise. I'm a good person, you know that. I have never killed anyone that didn't deserve it. 'Oh shit,' I yelled. 'Fuck it.' I began to feel the pain of the blood re-entering my arms. I forced a numb hand into my pocket for the Gerber. 'I've got it,' I yelled. I thumbed the blade open, turning to meet any attack from there, knowing the best I could do was cut out the throat flap as my arm was seized. I scrambled up onto the leaning part of the palm. 'I believe in the force,' I said. Somehow I evaded more thoughts of God.

I made my way across the beach. There were soldier's bodies there. I didn't ask myself who killed them. I knew. I found a Glock tucked in a shoulder holster. It felt beautiful in my damaged and swollen hand. So light and yet the balance seemed to steady the shaking.

Chapter 18

The clearing was empty of people and parrots. The big chopper looked sad with its drooping blades. The door of the cage that had contained the birds was ajar. The other cages had always been empty, but I checked them anyway. In one of the huts was a wooden table and chairs. I sat down and rested my head. I could smell food. Honey. I went to the bench and opened a saucepan. Wild honey. Honey comb was submerged in it in great chunks, and bits of bark and leaves. Mick and his mates were still living with some of the old ways. The native bee was little and stingless. Gradually he was being driven out by the aggressive European bee. Pursuers of honey caught these small bees when they went for water, tied a thread to the body, not too tight, and followed them on their flight back to the hive in some high tree trunk.

In another corner of the hut was a day-old damper, the bread cooked in the oven of hot ashes. I devoured great dollops of it after dunking it in honey.

Outside I felt the warmth of the sun. I walked around the perimeter of the clearing and found what I was looking for. Tyre marks. They had headed out in a four-wheel drive. Shit. Well, at least I was eating. The problem was that I had no transport. And also, it seemed, no friends.

I walked into the other hut. This was larger, and Mick's mob used blankets, not skins. There were a few clothes there. None that I needed. Over the doorway were two spears and a woomera. I took them down. They were stamped GREETINGS FROM ALICE SPRINGS.

From my own experience I knew that the drive would be slow and tortuous. In ordinary circumstances I had a lope of about 12 kilometres an hour, plenty of speed to catch them, assuming they had left at first light. I wasn't capable though. My head was gingery, a gnawing feeling that I could black out if I didn't treat it with some caution.

I walked into the cage and went to the termite mound. They were rare enough these days. The smooth surface coated with the spit of insects had half-a-dozen holes and lying in them in the dim light, warmed by the honeycombed insulation, were the eggs of the paradise parrot. In each nest were four or five white eggs. Unbelievable. How had they managed to leave them behind? Each of those fertilised eggs would be worth tens of thousands of dollars. What the hell was happening? I looked at the base of the termite mound because this was red earth I was looking at. It was a renovation. Mick had found the mound, delicately sawed through and transported it. I saw that it had been repaired in places, the breaks and cracks obviously smoothed and healed with water.

How long could they be left before they chilled? The parent birds' body warmth had to replenish the heat the mound slowly lost.

I heard the vehicle about fifteen minutes before it came into the clearing. Again I used the huge Moreton Bay fig as a retreat.

They were hurrying. Without even a cursory look around they went to the eggs. Verve was carrying a specially padded jacket, which she swung onto Mick's shoulders as they entered the cage. She needed the jacket to be worn as she carefully slipped the eggs into their places. I looked over at the other parrots in the cages in the back of the vehicle. With the rocking of the four-wheel drive I'd have said they were in a considerable state of fright.

When the two emerged from the cage a few minutes later I saw Verve attempt to swing the coat off Mick's shoulders. Naturally, with the eggs in residence, she wanted to wear the jacket. Mick swung away as if she had made an impolite grab. He placed his arms into the sleeves. They must have gone to the old abattoir for the jacket.

A second later two of Mick's mates approached Verve. They did it very well. I hardly noticed their slow encroachment of her territory. One of them went to cross her path, hesitated to let her go by, and the other stood up from where he had been lounging against the vehicle. They seized her arms at the same time and twisted them up behind her in two half-nelsons. Then they bound her wrists, one on top of the other. They took a knife from inside her shirt and the automatic from her belt. Mick accepted these weapons and smiled at her. She stood looking at him.

'Hey Mick,' I said. 'I'll kill you now, if you don't tell me why you've been a bad bastard.'

'We're all sitting emus here, brother,' he called. 'For anyone.'

'It seems to me no-one got away to come back.'

'What are you talking about? What about Marshall?'

'Untie Verve.'

He made no move. 'Just one of you, mate,' he said. 'Wacha gunna do?'

I jumped down from the tree and told Verve to walk towards me, keeping the Glock on Mick. 'How did I get left behind?' I said.

'Mick forced me to leave you,' she said.

'Really.' I looked at her face, trying to find some deep mark left by her deceit.

'So we left you on high ground,' she said.

Mick laughed at me. 'I bet your dick has a brain all its own, brother. How many millions of dollars here, you reckon? I reckon an operation like this is worth a hundred million. What's your fucking life worth?'

'The birds are worthless,' I said, 'if you have no-one to sell them to.'

He looked at me closely. 'I don't want you to stuff it up. They either deal with us, or we slip back into the forest. That's what we want.'

'We kill Marshall,' I said.

'You're bloody mad. What about the others?'

'Listen, Mick, they know they're being used. With him gone the whole thing folds. If the story gets out there'll be a cover-up.'

'No,' Mick said. 'They look after their own.'

'What alternative have we got? They're out to kill us.'

Mick was very agitated. He strode around the clearing, trying to avoid my logic.

'We tell him we want to talk, will give him half the eggs, and then we kill him. It's him or us, mate.'

'So, how do we do it?'

'We make him feel safe, go out to the boat with the birds. He'll think we're desperate.'

Mick didn't like it. 'We're shot easy out there,' Mick said. 'Like Charlie.'

I looked around at his crew. They seemed to have no interest. This was all Mick's play. I caught sight of the Barrett leaning against a tree trunk and picked it up.

Mick walked around for a few minutes kicking dirt. I looked at Verve. She was with me. 'Okay,' he said at last. 'We try it your way.'

We packed half the birds into one cage and Mick still wore the jacket with the eggs.

The walk back to the beach was slow. I didn't mind. There was to be the final confrontation and I wasn't eager for it.

Seeing the grey launch anchored out on the bay, Verve called Marshall. I listened to his voice. Despite the loss of his men he was still laid back, laconic. Yes he could accommodate us, but just for the one batch of birds. There were to be no repeats. 'Come out and we'll talk a price,' he said.

Mick's mates kept back from the beach. They could give Mick, Verve and me some cover as we motored out to the launch about 400 metres out. Verve was on the outboard. I could see the coral deep down in the water with graphic clarity.

Marshall watched us approach. We had a cage covered with canvas propped between the centre seat and the bow. Marshall was turning back and forth in a fishing seat. I pulled the canvas back to show some birds. Verve cut back the throttle and we drifted about 10 metres off the launch. I couldn't see anyone but Marshall but I knew there would be plenty of armed people below.

'You're in a power of trouble, boy,' he said.

'How many birds you want?' Mick asked. 'That's what we're talking about here?'

Marshall was still swinging in his seat.

'Why did you want me dead?' Verve asked, as if she might be wanting to do something about that. Hell, I thought, a wild card to consider, and she's armed.

'I didn't,' he said.

'You didn't look after me,' she said.

'Can't look after everyone.'

'Angela wanted me dead.'

'Maybe she wanted to deal herself,' he said. 'We could have accommodated that.'

I broke in. 'And now you have to accommodate us.'

'I don't have to do a goddam thing I don't want,' he said. He stood up and looked down into the clear water. Mick had one of the automatic weapons and I had the Glock. 'There's some nasty critters down there,' Marshall said.

'We're talking about birds,' I said. I couldn't understand the delay. I knew delays meant trouble because they stretched people to snapping point. Marshall laughed. 'Is that what we're talking about?' he said, taunting. 'We're talking about money, you little cocksucker.'

He looked over our heads to the beach. His faced tightened. I was tempted to look. Behind me was a crackle of fire on the beach. He must have landed men there earlier. Mick's mates were attacking or being attacked.

I turned quickly, stupidly. Verve didn't. She grabbed the Barrett and fired at Marshall. The *whomp* cracked my ears. There was a numbness. I fell away from her, the world around taking on softer edges. Marshall was hanging over the stern, blood pumping into the water. A Glock was in his hand, pointing towards the water. He was trying to get a better hold of it. He was going fast. Verve and Mick were waiting for other heads to emerge from the cabin or the hatches, their weapons swinging back and forth.

'The motor,' Verve screamed at me from a long, long, way away. 'Start the fucking thing.' I could barely hear her.

I attended to the task. I had to be slow and methodical. I had to recall that she hadn't shot me but Marshall. The rifle had been fired from behind my ear, and the ringing now was painful. I had to fight blacking out. The motor caught at the first wrench and, turning up the power, the boat scudded away too fast for my reflexes. Verve sat beside me, taking the outboard. 'Lie down in the bottom,' she said, because I was swaying dangerously.

I vomited over the side of the boat watching the flash of dark shapes spearing towards Marshall's boat. Sharks close to the bottom, trailing the scent of blood.

Hammerheads are peculiar predators, their eyes are on the end of fleshy stalks like real heads of hammers, sometimes as far as a metre apart. If you catch one and haul it aboard, it turns its head so that one of the eyes at the extremity of the hammer can see you, decide what to do. In a way it's much like the human gesture of turning your head to see what is behind you. The great head came out and delicately took Marshall's arm in its maw, partially severing it. Then it took a stronger chomp on the shoulder, and with its descending weight flipped him over the stern of the boat.

I was still feeling remote when we reached the sand. Two of Mick's men were dead at the edge of the sea, and along further there were three jungle fighters, dead inside their hi-tech rigs. The rest of Mick's men called to us from the forest. We had won another round for no gain.

I lay in the dappled shade on the edge of the sand while they buried their people. Verve gave me water. It had a sweetness I hadn't expected. But then the heavy pain arrived. I couldn't have cared whether I died or not.

Night came down fast. Mick fed me some bitter herbs and Verve held cold wraps to my head. Mick said they should get me to the yacht and Verve said the rocking would kill me. I agreed with her but couldn't tell her. I knew what I wanted to say but it came out as incoherent mumble.

I drifted in and out of consciousness. Sometimes it was daylight and sometimes it was night. And then one cool morning I woke, the light brilliant, the pain gone. I could hear birds using their clear calls high in the forest. I left the camp stretcher and walked out in the clearing. There was no-one about. The cage was in the early morning sun. The parrots were brisk, ruffling their feathers, calling, flipping about the foliage. I heard the prolonged bawling squawks of the young. The eggs had hatched.

I found I was smiling and turned that way when Verve said behind me, 'Thought you were gone for a while.'

'So, what's happened?' I asked.

She went into a hut and came out with a newspaper. She held it up in front of me. SHARK KILLS US DIPLOMAT, the headlines ran. She turned the paper over and began to read. 'The American ambassador and three of his aides were killed by sharks while diving off the Great Barrier Reef, north of Cairns, yesterday.' She looked up. 'That was five days ago. Very tidy, I'd say.'

'Yeah,' I said. 'An official cover-up.'

I sat in the shade watching the birds as if they were fish in a bowl. 'Why am I alive?' I asked.

She didn't bullshit me. 'They'll be chasing us,' she said. 'We need each other,' she added.

'They'll be out there now,' I said.

'Not while all the press boats are looking for the grisly remains and taking shots of sharks and crocodiles. She smiled at me. 'We'll be gone in a day or two.'

Her smile was a mask. I saw that now. She could hide anything behind it. I wondered if I should walk off into the bush and hitchhike to Cairns.

I walked over to the cages. The parrots were solemn, looking out with hurt faces. They fidgeted under my gaze as though they knew they were in for a grilling. They weren't feeling they were with friends. I turned back to her. 'We let half of them go,' I said. 'The breeders. We take them out of the forest into their country.'

'How do you know where they come from?'

'I can feel it,' I said. I could smell their air was dry. Could see and hear them amongst small leaf foliage over red dirt. The thought of Marshall's frozen zoo and international collectors was depressing. It meant no-one would bother saving wilderness for the wild things because a genetic laboratory could always re-create them.

Verve came up behind me and put her hands in my pockets. She lay her head on the back of my shoulder. The simple gesture released a flood of affection. This woman could kill me, I thought, and I'd probably enjoy it.